The Haunted Screen: Ghosts in Literature and Film

To
Philip, Susan, and Chloé

The Haunted Screen
Ghosts in Literature and Film

by
LEE KOVACS

McFarland & Company, Inc., Publishers
Jefferson, North Carolina, and London

The poem quoted in Chapter 9 is "The Dead Woman" by Pablo Neruda, from *The Captain's Verses*. Copyright ©1972 by Pablo Neruda and Donald D. Walsh. Reprinted by permission of New Directions Publishing Corp.

Acknowledgments: I am deeply indebted to Geraldine Duclow of the Free Library of Philadelphia for her unflagging patience and advice in helping identify some of the stills used in this book. Many thanks as well to Mary Corliss and Terry Geeksen of the Museum of Modern Art in New York, the staff at the Bibliothèque du Film in Paris, and Claudine Lesage for locating some of the *Liliom* stills.

I thank Melissa Goldstein, who read portions of this study with unflagging devotion and great care.

This book exists because of the interest and support of Nina Auerbach whose enthusiasm for the subject matched my own.

I could not have completed this project without the ongoing support of my son Philip, who generously and wholeheartedly supplied technical assistance. My greatest debt, however, is to my daughter Susan, who read ongoing drafts of the manuscript and offered advice and encouragement when it was sorely needed. Her intellectual and emotional support mattered most.

And to David Tanenbaum, who would have been so pleased.

The present work is a reprint of the library bound edition of The Haunted Screen: Ghosts in Literature and Film, *first published in 1999 by McFarland.*

Library of Congress Cataloguing-in-Publication Data

Kovacs, Lee.
    The haunted screen : ghosts in literature and film / by Lee Kovacs.
        p.   cm.
    Includes bibliographical references and index.
    ISBN 0-7864-2605-5 (softcover : 50# alkaline paper) ∞
    1. Ghosts in motion pictures.   2. Ghosts in literature.
I. Title.
PN1995.9.S8K68   2006
791.43'675—dc21   99-38703

British Library Cataloguing-in-Publication data are available

©1999 Lee Kovacs. All rights reserved

No part of this book may be reproduced or transmitted in any form or by any means, electronic or mechanical, including photocopying or recording, or by any information storage and retrieval system, without permission in writing from the publisher.

Cover images ©2005 PhotoAlto

Manufactured in the United States of America

McFarland & Company, Inc., Publishers
    Box 611, Jefferson, North Carolina 28640
         www.mcfarlandpub.com

Contents

Introduction	1
I. The Gothic Ghost	7
1. *Wuthering Heights*	9
II. The Romantic Ghost	29
2. *The Ghost and Mrs. Muir*	31
3. *Portrait of Jennie*	50
4. *Letter from an Unknown Woman*	68
5. *The Uninvited*	87
III. The Theater Ghost	105
6. *Liliom*	107
7. *Our Town*	126
IV. Contemporary Ghosts	145
8. *Ghost*	147
9. *Truly, Madly, Deeply*	160
Bibliography	177
Index	181

O that 'twere possible
After long grief and pain
To find the arms of my true love
Round me once again!
   —Alfred Lord Tennyson
    Maud, 1855

I cannot live with You—
It would be Life—
And Life is over there—
Behind the shelf
        —Emily Dickinson

They say the movies should be more
like life. I think life should be
more like the movies.
        —*To Mary with Love* (1936)

Introduction

In the late 1930s and 1940s, Hollywood produced a small cluster of romantic ghost stories. These films had astonishing casts, celebrated directors, and unique musical scores. All these films were adaptations of well-known novels. The late 1930s and 1940s was a strategic time for the production of the fantasy film; World War II was raging in Europe, and in 1941, with the bombing of Pearl Harbor, the United States entered the war. Sandwiched between films like *Dangerously We Live*, *To the Shores of Tripoli*, and a plethora of wartime documentaries, a small slice of diversion, a bit of romantic illusion, quietly made its way into the movie theater. The romantic ghost film falls into a genre that has been called, rather pejoratively I think, a "woman's film." But Donald Cook explains, a little more satisfactorily, that these films derived this appellation because "they were melodramas ... constructed around a popular female star" (p.401n). Cook cites a few examples: *Leave Her to Heaven* (1945), with Gene Tierney, *Humoresque* (1947), with Joan Crawford, and *The Razor's Edge* (1946), again with Gene Tierney. Included in the "woman's film" genre are three of the films that are part of this study: *Portrait of Jennie*, *Letter from an Unknown Woman*, and *The Ghost and Mrs. Muir*. These films were produced at the same time as the *film noir* genre, and the fantasy films served to contrast the bleak view of man and his environment that characterized the *noir* genre. The romantic ghost film enjoyed only a fair amount of success, and after their theater runs, they disappeared for a time, later to have a short but happy revival on television in the early 1950s. Today, most of these small quiet gems have faded into obscurity—except of course, for those who remember the times and the films, or those who saw their revivals in the early days of television, or more recently, those occasions when a dedicated cinephile (usually European) attends a theater revival of one of these films and then writes ecstatically about its merits. Indeed, these films deserve attention because their marriage of the supernatural and the melancholic, of the beyond and the here-and-now, creates an unforgettable atmosphere of suspense and despair. The ghost film delves into the recesses of human consciousness and uses the world of the beyond as a mirror of the heart.

The ghost story is an old but still potent genre. In his introduction to *The Oxford Book of Twentieth-Century Ghost Stories*, Michael Cox explains the resiliency of the literary ghost story:

> Though ghost stories, as a literary genre, are deeply imbued with their own past, and though innovation has come more through ingenious reinterpretation than radical reinvention, they have always maintained an adaptable relationship with the contemporary world [xi].

The ghost story genre, therefore, has a long literary history. And Cox's assertion that the ghost story, in one form or another, moves easily from past to present indicates that the genre conveys much more than just its shock value—it can and does metaphorically act as a reflection of the times.

Today, the ghost story's resilience is manifested in the success of recent films such as *Michael* (1996), *Ghost* (1990), *Truly, Madly, Deeply* (1992), *Casper* (1995), and more recently, *City of Angels* (1998)—all of which attest to the genre's successful transition into the present. In a recent article in the *New York Times* (4 April 1998), Gustav Niebuhr writes that "fascination with angels has run at high tide in recent years, and there's little sign that it's letting up. In part, this is a sign of the time, a feature of renewed interest in spiritual matters, an end-of-century trend."

Many of today's ghost films are remakes of older films; *The Preacher's Wife* (1996), for example, is a remake of *The Bishop's Wife*, which was produced in 1947. So in a sense, it is the 1940s ghost films; the antecedents of the present-day films, that have spawned this renewed interest in things spiritual and things supernatural.

The small group of 1940s romantic ghost films; is the focus of this study, and my approach to this discussion of the ghost genre and its filmic adaptation is to bring together the literary source and the film. Contrary to the perception that these films are merely slices of illusion produced to give a war-weary nation a bit of diversion, this study will demonstrate that within the relatively short span of time in which they were produced, each film presented a different and compelling view of society. And this chain of haunting, from past to present, signifies that the ghost story is not merely a window into the beyond, but actually a reflection of human nature, a pathway into the mind.

Emily Brontë's novel *Wuthering Heights*, a Gothic example of the genre, and William Wyler's 1939 adaptation of Brontë's work seem to be the best way to begin because this film presents a shift toward a more serious treatment of the genre. Brontë's novel is in the tradition of the Gothic, a wildly exaggerated, pessimistic, and terror-ridden genre that exults in its depiction of the tormented ghost and its equally tormented human counterpart. The ghosts of the literary Gothic are fearsome creatures. They weep and wail, they hover about castles and moors, they are unrelenting in their passion, and they are deprived of their once-human form. Haunter and haunted live in different spheres; they cannot relate, they cannot connect. Only death brings them together, and the death scene is always a terrifying depiction of their union.

The novels and films that follow *Wuthering Heights* are the "romantic" films: *The Ghost and Mrs. Muir*, *Portrait of Jennie*, *Letter from an Unknown Woman*, and *The Uninvited*. All these films are, in a sense, a prolongation of the Gothic, but they have a contemporary (at least 1940s contemporary) look. Haunting and haunter both have human form, and what is more astonishing, they manage to fall in love (in one instance, they live together); and in their literary form they depict the socially, culturally, and emotionally conflicted man or woman. Each film is distinctive; they all bear the unique characteristics of their equally unique directors: William Wyler, Joseph Mankiewicz, Fritz Lang, and William Dieterle. These are not cookie-cutter films; the director's style and point of view make each film a separate and remarkable experience.

Liliom and *Our Town* are theater ghosts, and they comprise the next section of this study. The succession of theatrical and filmic adaptations of *Liliom* are a perfect illustration of how the genre constantly reinvents itself. The play was produced in Hungary in 1909, and it was brought to the American stage in 1921. Frank Borzage directed the first film adaptation of the play in 1930, and in 1935 Fritz Lang remade the film. In 1945, Rodgers and Hammerstein produced *Carousel*, a loose adaptation of the original, and in the 1950s, *Carousel* was made into a film.

I have chosen to discuss these plays and their filmic adaptations because they depict still another version of the ghost genre. *Liliom* introduces the "ghost for a day" apparition, a spectre that returns to earth to do a good deed so that he may leave the fires of hell to which he has been temporarily assigned. And *Our Town* introduces still another component to this dynamic genre, a community of ghosts. Both *Liliom* and *Our Town* are dark plays that encode social, cultural, and political commentary into the fantasy genre. *Our Town* anticipates the last section of this study because both *Ghost* and *Truly, Madly, Deeply* continue the theme of the community of ghosts.

From Novel to Film

The relationship between reader and novel is an intimate one; it is a contemplative relationship in which text supplies content and reader interpretation. Film shatters this intimacy, first by placing both text and viewer in a public forum, and then by subordinating text to accommodate the actor (especially if the actor is a star and has great audience appeal) and the particular artistic style of the director. Although I appear to suggest a certain incompatibility between film and novel, I propose that this union is essential in preserving the continuity of the literary form, and film is the next logical sequence in the evolution of genres.

Georg Lukács argues that the novel, like a ghost, is essentially homeless; that because it is an act of artistic creation that is born in a specific time, its form is a subjective rendering of that time frame, and it is doomed to be reinterpreted, redefined, and re-created when its relevance, its meaning, no longer reflects, or is alien to, current social and cultural changes. That is why, Lukács claims, "the epic had to disappear and yield its place to an entirely new form, the novel" (p. 41). But though the form undergoes a transformation, a cultural adaptation, it does not entirely disappear; its essence survives. Therefore, in Lukács's view, although the epic has disappeared, the ghostly essence of the epic, the heroic figure, the hero, lives on.

Lukács's discussion of the changing form of the novel provides a compelling argument for the marriage of novel and film. The novel provides the source for the film, and in turn, the film preserves the essence, the spirit, of the novel. The adaptation redefines the novel's parameters so that it becomes part of the present. But although the film hollows out the text until what remains is its contours, its ghostly residue, the text still remains the absent body that we need to understand in order to interpret its adaptation. And this absent body contains critical elements that the film adaptation cannot preserve, the novel's complete and sometimes complex narrative structure that is its very heart. This book gives you both to consider: the novel, the homeless textual ghost of the past, and its filmic adaptation.

Music comments on text; therefore, it is an essential component in providing the adaptation with some of the missing narrative, the "heart" of the text that has been lost in its filmic translation. Classical music (Bach, Beethoven, Mozart) and the musical scores of contemporary film composers like Bernard Herrmann (*The Ghost and Mrs. Muir*) and Alfred Newman (*Wuthering Heights*) link with plot and character to provide mood and commentary to the hollowed-out, ghostlike adaptation.

The 1990s films *Ghost* and *Truly, Madly, Deeply* have no corresponding text. And because they are free from any textual source, they are relatively free from the past. In these films, the ghosts themselves are the metaphor for the absent literary source.

The 1990s ghost story, like its predecessors, is a mirror into the heart. But unlike their predecessors, these modern ghosts are presented as reflections of our own faithlessness, petty sins, and weaknesses. In the 1990s, the ghost doubles the penetrating power of the camera lens, transporting the viewer into a universe that is both unknown and uncomfortably familiar.

I.

THE GOTHIC GHOST

CHAPTER ONE

Wuthering Heights

a novel by EMILY BRONTË
a film by WILLIAM WYLER

The Novel

Any discussion of Emily Brontë's novel *Wuthering Heights* should, I think, begin with some definition of the literary Gothic. In *The Literature of Terror: A History of Gothic Fiction from 1765 to the Present Day*, David Punter offers this explanation of the Gothic novel of the 18th century:

> the classical was well-ordered, gothic was ornate and convoluted ... gothic represented excess and exaggeration ... the product of the wild and the uncivilized ... gothic fiction is the fiction of the haunted castle, the blackly lowering villain ... ghosts, vampires [pp. 1, 6].

Wuthering Heights, like its predecessor, Mary Shelley's *Frankenstein*, is a classic example of the literary Gothic. Although in plot the two novels are separate and distinct, they both supply their characters with an astonishing array of physical and psychological deformities that ensure their alienation from the real and the rational.

Emily Brontë's novel spins with its complex assortment of narratives and multigenerational characters. Reason and order confront unbridled passion and excess. In *Wuthering Heights* Brontë creates a whirlwind of obsession and misery, and hovering above, around, and through this circle of torment are Catherine Earnshaw and Heathcliff, whose limitless passion embodies the very notion of Gothic. All these elements—love, terror, haunting, and two supremely attractive and powerful protagonists—are the ingredients of a remarkable novel and an equally remarkable film.

In the novel, the narrators, each with his or her own vision and version of the tragedy of the house called Wuthering Heights, resurrect the tale of Catherine Earnshaw and Heathcliff. Each narrator has a particular story of his or her own that weaves in and through the narrative and conveys to the reader that the tale of Catherine and Heathcliff is an ironic commentary on his or her own capacity or incapacity for love. The narrators are ordinary—ordinary in appearance and ordinary in their lives and their duties. In relating the story of Cathy and Heathcliff, these narrators set aside the limitations of their lives and live vicariously in the passion, violence, and excess that personify Cathy and Heathcliff.

In the novel, Catherine and Heathcliff set the uneasy and exaggerated standard by which love is weighed and measured. Their passion exists on such a grand scale that it is able to defy temporal and spatial boundaries. Catherine tries to convey the scope of her obsession to Nelly Dean:

> my great miseries in this world have been Heathcliff's miseries ... my great thought in living is himself. If all perished, and he remained, I should still continue to be; and all else remained and he were annihilated, the universe would turn to a mighty stranger; I should not seem a part of it. My love for Linton is like the foliage in the woods; time will change it ... my love for Heathcliff resembles the eternal rocks beneath; a source of little visible delight, but necessary. Nelly, I *am* Heathcliff. He's always, always on my mind, not as a pleasure, but as my own being [p. 109].

Balance Catherine's declaration of despair against the response given by Nelly Dean.

> If I can make any sense of your nonsense, Miss ... it only goes to convince me ... that you are a wicked, unprincipled girl [p. 109].

Nelly has cared for and reared, almost from birth, several generations of the Earnshaw/Linton children. Her devotion is class-determined—she is a servant, pressed into service at a young age. And when she is urged to leave Hareton Earnshaw, her current charge, to live in the rarefied halls of Thrushcross Grange with the newly married Cathy, she describes their parting summarily:

> Little Hareton was nearly five years old ... we made a sad parting ... I kissed Hareton goodbye; and since then he has been a stranger [p. 116].

The emotion and passion that define Catherine do not exist for Nelly. She is a simple soul; she lives in an orderly world, one in which life and death are dealt with and accepted as part of a time-defined universe. The qualified love she has for her charge reflects this attitude, and her words indicate the constriction and the set boundaries of her sense of time and order.

The other characters in the novel, Hindley, Isabella, Linton, and Lockwood, all have Nelly's limitations. They are tragic in the agonies they experience; their miseries seemingly are without end, but their characters (as Brontë paints them) do not excite the imagination. They are characters who appear weak and insignificant when compared with the fiery and passionate Cathy and Heathcliff—the reader tolerates their pain but is infinitely moved and awed by the larger tragedy of the two protagonists. However, Cathy's brother Hindley exhibits a malevolence, rancor, and dissipation that also clearly embodies the Gothic notion of excess. Hindley's personal tragedy is born when Heathcliff is brought to Wuthering Heights. His unbridled jealousy of the newcomer, his fear of being disinherited by this nameless homeless interloper, creates the atmosphere and another tension on which the story turns.

Heathcliff's passion for Catherine has its contrasting double in Mr. Lockwood, Heathcliff's unfortunate tenant. Mr. Lockwood has just had a "disastrous" experience in love:

> I was thrown into the company of a most fascinating creature; a real goddess in my eyes, as long as she took no notice of me. I never told my love "vocally," still, if looks have language, the merest idiot might have guessed I was head over ears; she understood me at last ... and what did I do? I confess it with shame—shrunk icily into myself ... at every glance retired colder and farther and, overcome with confusion ... she persuaded her mamma to decamp [p. 39].

The feebleness and sterility of Lockwood's "passion" is challenged and diminished by the depth and vehemence of Heathcliff's emotion for Cathy which is personified in his reaction to her death:

> Catherine Earnshaw, may you not rest as long as I am living!... Be with me always—take any form—drive me mad! Only *do* not leave me in the abyss, where I cannot find you! I *cannot* live without my life! I *cannot* live without my soul! [p. 197].

Who Is the Haunted?

But who is the haunted in *Wuthering Heights*? Is it indeed Cathy who, through her own volition and sheer strength of will, is the tormentor rather than the tormented? An answer may lie in another question: Who is Heathcliff? Who and what defines him? He is introduced as a homeless waif, a foundling, discovered by Mr. Earnshaw and brought to

Wuthering Heights. Nelly calls the foundling "it." "It" has no name; "it" is at the mercy of the people and the house that have suddenly encircled him (it is at this moment that Hindley Earnshaw's hatred of Heathcliff is born). It is Cathy's father who names him, but it is Cathy who creates him. The strength of will that forms Heathcliff and then damns him is Cathy's will. The passion that drives Heathcliff is the fear of being left alone without his creator's prodding, relentless energy.

Who rules Heathcliff? The women who inhabit his prison, Cathy, Nelly, and finally Isabella. They each give Heathcliff his place in their society, and from their individual viewpoints they define him. Heathcliff is a magnificent example of nature gone awry. His pain and his anguish drive all the narratives, and Brontë utilizes her literary genius to make his anguish almost palpable. His captors, his women, both love him and despise him—as a force of nature, he compels those around him to act, to feel, and to experience. Heathcliff exists as a contradiction of society, and he exists because he has been created as an extension of the will and force of several indomitable wills. Much like Shelley's *Frankenstein*, a dependent monster is born who cannot exist outside the confines of the creator's world.

But Cathy has the strongest will of all. She is Heathcliff's champion, his fondest companion, his childhood. The chains that Cathy creates to bind Heathcliff to her are many and complex—she is a friend, a mother, and a lover. Her multidimensional roles are at the very heart of Heathcliff's existence, and I would argue that Cathy is more mother than lover. In a novel where marriages are short-lived (Mrs. Earnshaw died scarcely two years after Heathcliff's arrival, and Hindley's wife after giving birth to the "last of the ancient Earnshaw stock"), women appear destined never to rear their children (Nelly Dean is surrogate mother to most of the motherless brood). Cathy's function in her relationship with Heathcliff expands to include the role of child mother, "Cathy taught him what she learnt, and worked or played with him in the fields" (p. 71). Cathy is mother to Heathcliff because she evinces a constancy and intensity of love and attention that give Heathcliff the security that becomes the touchstone of his existence. And when Cathy is dying, Heathcliff's pleading words, "do not leave me in the abyss where I cannot find you," are a cry of dread that brands Heathcliff as a child forever lost. And the mother/creator taunts him with her last words:

> I wish I could hold you ... 'til we were both dead ... I shouldn't care how you suffered ... why shouldn't you suffer? ... how many years do you mean to live after I am gone? [p. 188].

More victim than villain, Heathcliff is the product of woman's will. And when Cathy returns to haunt Heathcliff, she returns as a child ghost with all the vestiges of her sexuality left in the world she departed. This final separation again mocks Heathcliff. Mother, lover, and companion have reverted into childhood—the tiny ghost who begs to come home will never again see her child counterpart—only the adult Heathcliff remains. The man child is again caught between two disparate worlds, the one he inhabits and the one where Cathy lives. In death, as in life, Cathy and Heathcliff exist in spaces that defy closure.

Houses and Spaces

The house, Wuthering Heights, is an isolated, wild, and unformed place. It is a house, as Susan Wolstenholme suggests in *Gothic (Re)Visions*, that is "an uncanny disjunction between what is ordinary and familiar and what is strange and terrible" (p. 7). The "disjunction" that Wolstenholme describes, this distinction between ordinary and terrible, mirrors the unbridled emotions that drive Heathcliff and Cathy.

Where Wuthering Heights metaphorically stands as a testament to the destructive forces of nature, its neighbor Thrushcross Grange evokes the concept of a civilized and cultured world. And as such, it defines the trajectory between the untamed world of childhood and the finished world of the adult. The two houses are the foundations upon which the novel turns, and the many characters flit, like so many displaced apparitions, between the "before" and the "after" that these houses metaphorically represent. Judith Wilt in *Ghosts of the Gothic: Austen, Eliot, & Lawrence* explains why the aspect of space contributes to the mood and setting of *Wuthering Heights*:

> No single aspect of plot, image or mood says "Gothic" to us so clearly as the aspect of place. The castle, the tower, the graveyard ... and sea—all those settings scaled to purposes other than an individual normal man's ... Power, the Gothic says, resides in place [p. 276].

That Heathcliff and Cathy cannot place themselves in one world or another, or that the choices are so dramatically disparate, is the tragedy of *Wuthering Heights*. The characters are faced with two choices only— childhood or adulthood, the wildness of nature and youth or the confines of the trappings of culture—there is no in-between, no alternative.

Heathcliff is bound to Wuthering Heights, and like Peter Pan, he is unable to cross the boundaries from the child world into the adult world—

he can only watch and brood as Cathy/Wendy "grows" into adulthood. Wuthering Heights is Heathcliff's "Neverland"; it is the creator's world. But circumstances force Cathy reluctantly to cross the line from one house to another. One evening, Edgar Linton asks Cathy to marry him and, unaware that Heathcliff is listening, Cathy confides the news to Nelly Dean. Nelly asks Cathy whether she loves Edgar and Cathy playfully answers yes. And then Nelly asks about Heathcliff. Cathy gives her reply, "it would degrade me to marry Heathcliff" (p. 107). In his misery at hearing these words, Heathcliff runs away from Wuthering Heights. Unfortunately, he does not hear the rest of Cathy's sentence, "so he shall never know how I love him" (p. 107).

After three anguished years of waiting and searching for the missing Heathcliff, Cathy accepts Edgar's proposal and becomes the reluctant mistress of Thrushcross Grange. For a time, Cathy allows herself the luxury of her new position, but then Heathcliff returns, an outwardly changed man—a gentleman, the new owner of Wuthering Heights. In his new role as master of a great house, and dressed in the attire of a gentleman, Heathcliff satirizes Cathy's role as mistress of the Grange. Heathcliff's new persona and Cathy's joy at seeing him again reluctantly persuade Edgar that he can tolerate Heathcliff's occasional presence at the Grange. But inevitably, Cathy's obvious affection for Heathcliff and Edgar's growing jealousy of this affection culminate in a quarrel between the two men. They come to blows, and Heathcliff is ordered from the house. In a fit of despair, Cathy falls desperately and fatally ill. For six long weeks, she lingers between life and death, and then one day a maid brings the unhappy news that Heathcliff and Isabella (Edgar's sister) have married. Again, emulating what Heathcliff perceives to be Cathy's unforgivable infidelity, he enters into a disastrous marriage. Heathcliff despises Isabella with the same fervor and passion with which he loves Cathy: "And I like her too ill ... except in a very ghoulish fashion. You'd hear of odd things if I lived alone with that mawkish, waxen face" (p. 134). The "odd things" that Heathcliff foretells are depicted in a letter that Isabella writes to Nelly Dean: "Is Mr. Heathcliff a man? If so, is he mad? And if not, is he a devil?" (p. 165).

When Heathcliff learns of Cathy's illness, he rushes to her side, and in an exquisitely wrought scene, Nelly Dean describes their final meeting:

> In her eagerness, she rose and supported herself on the arm of the chair ... an instant they held asunder, and then how they met I hardly saw, but Catherine made a spring, and he caught her, and they were locked in an embrace from which I thought my mistress would never be released alive [p. 190].

That night, after prematurely giving birth to Edgar's daughter, Catherine dies.

Having crossed the boundaries between child and adult though still an unrepentant child, Cathy is buried in the churchyard that lies between the two houses. As testament to her ambivalent passions, she is buried in neutral ground away from both houses on "a green slope in the corner of the kirkyard." True to the Gothic ghost story, the unhappy Cathy returns to haunt the house and the man she cannot bear to leave.

The Film

Adapting a story of this complexity is a formidable task. The key to the filmic adaptation lies in novel's structure. This novel, with its multinarrative, multigenerational, and loose structure, can be "broken" or splintered into many stories, each powerful enough to exist on its own. Thus, a workable, even notable filmic translation is possible merely by focusing on the compelling history of Catherine and Heathcliff.

William Wyler's perception of the film is one that is almost faithful to the novel's Gothic mood of "excess and exaggeration." Catherine and Heathcliff are portrayed as lovers precariously balanced between sanity and insanity and life and death, and the advent of Mr. Lockwood is the catalyst by which their story is told.

The filmic translation loses the multigenerational, multinarrative structure of the novel and focuses on the tumultuous love story of Catherine and Heathcliff as it is retold by Nelly Dean (Ellen in the film). Cathy is a ghost and she haunts Heathcliff, and through the unwitting intervention of Mr. Lockwood, whose unannounced arrival at Wuthering Heights triggers Ellen's narrative, we find out why.

The film is brilliantly constructed so that specific incidents that appear in the two opening scenes of the film foreshadow the story that is yet to unfold. The story of Cathy and Heathcliff comingle with Lockwood's own nightmarish experience at Wuthering Heights and is interwoven in the ensuing narrative. Ellen and Lockwood, the narrator and the distraught dreamer/listener, both participate in the retelling of the story of Heathcliff and Cathy.

Several key incidents that Lockwood experiences in the early scenes resurface in Ellen's narrative — the violent storm that drives him blindly into Wuthering Heights; the attack by the dogs; the broken windowpanes through which Lockwood thrusts his hands in order to reach a broken shutter, the insult that Heathcliff shouts at Lockwood, and the small group of people who turn and silently stare at the stranger who has entered their house.

The opening scene introduces Mr. Lockwood, the new tenant of the Grange. He is lost and wandering in a fierce and unrelenting snowstorm. Falling, stumbling, and half conscious, Lockwood reaches the gates of Wuthering Heights, he struggles to push them aside, and then, exhausted by his efforts, he enters the house. As he closes the door behind him, he is suddenly attacked by a large dog—he calls to a tall, dark man standing before the hearth to "call off your dog," and then, and only then, does Heathcliff shout at the animal to stop its attack. A small group of people is silently seated and surround the tall dark standing figure, and at Lockwood's shout for help, they turn and silently gaze at the intruder. No word is spoken until Lockwood, half-frozen and almost incoherent, introduces himself as the new tenant of Thrushcross Grange. He explains his unfortunate dilemma, that the storm has driven him off course, and he asks for someone to help guide him home. Heathcliff curtly refuses his request and Lockwood is forced to remain for the night. As Heathcliff, accompanied by his dogs, abruptly strides from the room, he further humiliates Lockwood by telling him that he will have to sleep with one of the servants. Lockwood, appalled at this discourtesy, angrily retorts that he prefers to sleep in a chair. Like the novel, Heathcliff impatiently explains that he and the members of his house are unaccustomed to receiving guests, and orders his servant Joseph to prepare a room for his unwanted and unwelcome visitor.

The scene that follows is taken almost intact from the novel. It is the scene that introduces Cathy, the child ghost, and it begins Nelly Dean's narrative.

Lockwood is given the "bridal chamber" in which to sleep. The room has been locked and sealed for many years. It is dirty, dusty, and cold. A windowpane is broken and the wind and snow blow through the small pane. There is no fire nor can one be lit. As Joseph explains, "The chimney's been block up for years." Lockwood stuffs his scarf into the broken window to stop the draft, throws the dust-filled bed comforter onto the floor, climbs into the bed, and falls into a restless sleep. The sound of a broken outside shutter crashing against the window awakens him, and Lockwood, more asleep than awake, staggers to the window to close the shutter. The window will not open. Lockwood then removes the scarf he stuffed in the window earlier and thrusts his hands through the broken glass in order to grasp the broken shutter. It is at this precise moment that

Wuthering Heights: Heathcliff (Laurence Olivier) and Cathy (Merle Oberon) enjoy a glimpse of heaven. (Film Stills Archive, The Museum of Modern Art, New York)

Lockwood hears a small pitiable voice crying in the storm and then feels a small cold hand touch his own. Hysterical with fear, Lockwood shouts for Heathcliff. Heathcliff appears and Lockwood repeats what he has seen and what he has heard. He is sure, he claims, that the voice was a woman's and that she called herself Cathy. Heathcliff shouts at the frightened man to "get out, get out of the room." Heathcliff then runs to the window, flings it open, and in a voice filled with grief and despair, begs the tiny ghost, his "heart's darling," to come in, to stay with him once more. And then, as Lockwood (who has run downstairs) and Ellen watch in horror, Heathcliff runs down the stairs, opens the front door, and flings himself out into the raging storm. Lockwood, frightened and bewildered by the events he has both experienced and witnessed that evening, asks Ellen for an explanation of Heathcliff's mad and erratic behavior, and Ellen answers quietly that "she calls him; Cathy calls him." Lockwood, now completely distraught, feebly mutters that he does not believe in ghosts, that it is impossible for the dead to return to earth. Ellen offers to tell him the story of Cathy and Heathcliff so that he can judge for himself whether the dead can haunt the living. Lockwood seats himself in a chair by the blazing fire and murmurs in an exhausted childlike manner, "Yes, tell me a story."

The Dogs

Ellen's narrative includes an early scene in which Heathcliff and Cathy are depicted peering through the brightly lit windows of the Grange. They have come, at Cathy's request, to watch the people inside the house dancing. The Lintons' guard dogs watch the interlopers as they gaze in the window, and as the two try to climb back over the wall, the dogs attack them. Heathcliff tries to help Cathy but one dog clamps his teeth on Heathcliff's arm. As the two try to escape, another dog fastens his jaws around Cathy's foot. She screams in pain, and when Heathcliff shouts for help, the Lintons and their guests leave their festivities and come outside. Edgar Linton calls off the dogs and carries the bleeding and fainting Cathy into the house. Heathcliff rushes after Cathy but because he is merely the "Earnshaws' stable boy," he is driven from the house. Cathy is forced to remain behind.

This scene duplicates Lockwood's arrival and introduction to Wuthering Heights. His unannounced presence and the ensuing attack by Heathcliff's dog doubles as Cathy's introduction to Thrushcross Grange. The wound Cathy receives compels her to remain at the Grange just as Heathcliff's refusal to supply Lockwood with a guide forces him to stay the night at Wuthering Heights. In a brilliant inversion of Heathcliff's humiliation at the Grange in which he is ordered away because he is a stable boy, Heathcliff humiliates Lockwood, who now lives in the Grange, by suggesting that he sleep with the servants. Lockwood may be forced to remain at Wuthering Heights, but he cannot, like Heathcliff, be driven away—the storm forbids his leaving.

Windows

The sequence in which Lockwood thrusts his hands through a broken window in a barren dirty room is replayed by Heathcliff in a later scene. As Ellen recalls, after Cathy is bitten by the Lintons' dogs and carried into the Grange, she remains there for an unspecified time. Cathy entered the Grange as a beautiful, disheveled, wild girl, a female counterpart of the equally unkempt, unruly Heathcliff. She later emerges from the Grange as a mirror image of the beautifully dressed, perfectly composed women she and Heathcliff had so enviously watched from the outside window. Young Edgar Linton is now obviously in love with the girl who has been recreated, in manner and dress, by her stay in his home. But when Cathy returns home and sees Heathcliff, her passion overrides her newfound propriety, and in a momentary renunciation of the new life she has experienced, she rips her newly acquired finery into shreds and runs to the moors, where Heathcliff is waiting. But later, in a strange reversal of attitude, Cathy accepts Linton's visits and his courtship.

One evening while Cathy is awaiting Linton's arrival, Heathcliff enters her room unannounced. Cathy again is magnificently dressed and she stands in stark contrast to the shabby, unkempt Heathcliff. Cathy assumes a superior attitude toward Heathcliff, and in an act of supreme cruelty, she addresses him as a servant and orders him to wash his dirty hands. In a sudden burst of frustrated rage, Heathcliff slaps the astonished Cathy. In horror at what he has done, Heathcliff rushes to the stable, which is an inversion of the vile and dirty chamber Lockwood is given, and stares out the window next to his bed. In an agony of remorse, he thrusts his hands through the window. As Ellen tells it, it is she who washed and bandaged Heathcliff's torn and bleeding hands. This sequence, as Nelly Dean describes it, parallels Lockwood's own experience with the broken window. The broken window, for both Heathcliff and Lockwood, becomes a metaphor for pain and horror.

Storms

Mr. Lockwood arrives at Wuthering Heights in a blinding snowstorm. That same night, after Lockwood tells Heathcliff that he has seen and heard Cathy's ghost, Heathcliff rushes madly into the storm and to his death. In the film adaptation, it is Lockwood who initially experiences the unrelenting forces of nature that later in the narrative metaphorically depict the ferocity of passion that consumes Heathcliff and Cathy. Storm sequences, rain and snow, lightning and thunder are peppered throughout the film to visually reinforce an event or an emotion that is to change or alter the lives of the two protagonists. Ellen describes the blinding rainstorm that changed the lives of Cathy and Heathcliff. Edgar Linton had come to dinner and later had signaled the servants that he was ready to leave. Nelly had just washed and bandaged Heathcliff's "poor hands," and Heathcliff, hearing Cathy approach, hid in the doorway outside the kitchen. Cathy burst in to tell Ellen her great news: Edgar Linton had asked her to marry him. Ellen recalls that she asked Cathy several pointed questions. These questions are lifted intact from the novel: "Do you love him?" asks Ellen. "Yes," replies Cathy. "And how do you love him?" Ellen continues. Cathy flippantly answers, "I love the ground under his feet and the air over his head." Then Ellen asks, "What about Heathcliff?" and Cathy utters the unforgivable words, "It would degrade me to marry him." As Cathy prepares to finish her statement, Ellen notices the candles on the table flicker. Heathcliff has heard all that he can bear. He slips away unnoticed into the dark. But what Heathcliff does not hear is the conclusion of Cathy's impassioned speech in which she tells Ellen that she loves Heathcliff, that he is "more myself than I am. Whatever our souls are made of, his and mine are the same. Ellen, I am Heathcliff!" Ellen then tells Cathy that she is certain that Heathcliff overheard their conversation and as she speaks, Heathcliff is heard driving a horse forward in the pouring rain as Joseph shouts after him to come back. Hysterical with grief, and calling Heathcliff to come

Tableau vivant: Heathcliff (Laurence Olivier) plays the part of a gentleman in *Wuthering Heights*. (Theater Collection, The Free Library of Philadelphia)

back, Cathy runs wildly into the rain and the darkness. She runs to the moors and as the storm intensifies, she utters Heathcliff's name as she slips into unconsciousness.

Cathy is again rescued by Edgar Linton. He brings the seriously ill Cathy into his home, where she remains for many months. Still weak and frail, Cathy succumbs to the peace and security of the Grange and Edgar's unflagging devotion. This scene replicates Heathcliff's mad dash into the snowstorm that was depicted in the opening scene of the film when Lockwood tells him that he has seen and heard Cathy's ghost. Just as Heathcliff hides behind the kitchen wall so that Cathy will not see him, Cathy's ghost is visible only to Lockwood and it is Heathcliff who now calls for Cathy to return, to come back to him.

Groupings

The faces that turned and peered silently at Lockwood as he entered Wuthering Heights were positioned as a *tableau vivant*, a living but unmoving picture. The faces in this early scene belong to Ellen, Joseph, and Isabella, who is Heathcliff's wife and Edgar Linton's sister. Ellen and Joseph are depicted as elderly (when Ellen begins her narrative, she says that "it all started forty years ago. I was young then"), and Isabella's appearance is slovenly—her clothes are ragged and her hair uncombed. Indeed, at first glance, Isabella, not Ellen, has the appearance of a servant. Heathcliff stands by the hearth. He is tall, impressive, and brooding. He is positioned as an authority figure, one who dominates his household. Wuthering Heights and its inhabitants are seen through Lockwood's eyes. To Lockwood, the house is a living nightmare and the four people he sees and who see him are part of this nightmare.

The extension of this *tableau* takes place in the Grange. Ellen's version of this *tableau* focuses on a happier time. Cathy and Edgar are married; Isabella is young, lovely, and beautifully dressed, and the drawing room in the Lintons' house, where the scene takes place, is beautifully appointed. This is the place and the room that Heathcliff enters on his return home after several years' absence—his first appearance since the night he furiously rode away in the storm. The people present in the room are Cathy, who is seated at her needlepoint, Isabella, Edgar, and Ellen. Heathcliff strides into the room and the faces turn toward him. Heathcliff is now well dressed and well groomed; he, like Cathy, has for the moment assumed the outward trappings of gentility. Those seated stare silently as he enters, and it is Edgar, like Lockwood, who approaches

Wuthering Heights: Heathcliff (Laurence Olivier) and Cathy (Merle Oberon) on the moors. (Film Still Archive, The Museum of Modern Art, New York)

Heathcliff and welcomes him—the others remain silent and watchful. The seated motionless characters again are positioned to emphasize Heathcliff's dominant role. Like the raging storms that pummel the moors, Heathcliff's larger-than-life persona, his disturbing physicality/sexuality, serve to mock the almost lifeless doll-like figures seated before him.

Setting

According to J. Dudley Andrews in *Major Film Theories*, André Bazin, the critic and film theorist, greatly admired William Wyler's work in part because he "provided the spectator with a vast amount of information to see and he encouraged that spectator to choose to a large degree his own perspective on what he saw" (p. 162). In this context, the two houses, Wuthering Heights and Thrushcross Grange, are depicted as polar opposites whose doubling is further enhanced by the fragmentation of the narrative in which Lockwood sees Wuthering Heights in its death throes and Ellen tells a "story" that describes the house as it once was. Wyler adds his own perspective by inserting this prologue to the film:

> On the barren Yorkshire moors in England, a hundred years ago, stood a house as bleak and desolate as the wastes around it. Only a stranger lost in a storm would have dared to knock at the door of Wuthering Heights.

Wuthering Heights, as Lockwood experiences it, Ellen tells it, and Wyler describes it, is presented in three ways to the viewers. But the frames in which the house is depicted embody the Gothic model of hidden forces, exaggerated and frenetic behavior, and moral and social decay.

Ellen remembers a time, forty years ago, when Wuthering Heights was a "happy house." She describes the childhood house that formed the relationship between Cathy and Heathcliff. The house is situated on the edge of the moors, a vast open area of wild, uncultivated land that stretches to the horizon. Wuthering Heights' proximity to this wild and "uncivilized" landscape is a metaphoric extension of the disorder and chaos that, even in Ellen's softened recollection, is still the hallmark of Wuthering Heights. On one side of the moor stands a high rock surrounded by an endless sea of wild heather. Penistone Craig, as this windswept rock is called, is Cathy and Heathcliff's fantasy castle. The moors and Penistone Craig are self-contained universes where the rules of society do not exist. To convey this sense of freedom and unrestraint, Wyler photographs the early scenes between Cathy and Heathcliff out of doors on the Craig. The two striking figures photographed on the high, windswept rock with a sea of heather beneath them and the moving sky above indicate to the viewer the spiritual unity that exists between the two. This natural setting also serves as a contrast to the sealed, claustrophobic atmosphere of the Grange which ultimately entices and then traps the free-spirited Cathy.

The viewer must rely on Ellen's subjective narrative to see or envision

Thrushcross Grange. Ellen remembers the Grange as a great house that gleamed in its sumptuous wealth and culture. The beauty of the house suggests a fairy-tale castle inhabited by beautiful people, beautiful furnishings, music, and dancing. Thrushcross Grange may be compared to the fabled gingerbread house in "Hansel and Gretel" that stands as a temptation, a wonderful facade, which entices children to enter.

The vastness, the open space, that is represented in the moor scenes is never present in Wyler's depiction of the interiors of Thrushcross Grange and Wuthering Heights. All action takes place indoors in various settings that are created to demonstrate a claustrophobic atmosphere, a sense of entrapment. Indeed, the peripheral characters are almost never seen out of doors. Ellen tells her story by the fireside; the exquisitely dressed Cathy sits quietly in the drawing room with her needlepoint, Isabella moves from Thrushcross Grange to Wuthering Heights never again to be seen out of doors, and Linton, master of the Grange, is rarely depicted outside his domain.

Wuthering Heights' proximity to the moors and to the Grange signifies its ambivalent connection to the natural world and the world of convention. The two worlds are incompatible simply because they are, in the Gothic sense, exaggerated examples of life and living. In Wyler's visual depiction of Wuthering Heights (as Ellen remembers it), the house is dwarfed by the vastness of the moors beyond. Photographed from a high angle, the house is rendered small and insignificant by the wild countryside that surrounds it. Thrushcross Grange is never photographed in its surroundings or as an entire structure. It is a house of interiors, a seemingly balanced world untouched by the vagaries of the outside world. The two outcasts, Cathy and Heathcliff, first see the Grange by peering through a window. What they see is completely out of proportion to what they know—a world with no physical boundaries. As a true child of nature, Heathcliff is the lone skeptic; he is unimpressed with this "unnatural" world of manners; his ideal world is the castle that he and Cathy found high on Penistone Craig. Cathy, however, wants to enter this castle of pleasure and beauty and eventually does.

The incompatibility of the two worlds is personified by Cathy and Isabella. Cathy's entrance into and acceptance by this world of dreams turns her into an unhappy facsimile of the house and people she once saw through a window—glittering, beautiful, and devoid of the extremes of passion that once defined her. Isabella's move to Wuthering Heights turns the beautiful princess into a slovenly, miserable creature, a poor, almost comic, caricature of the once free, high-spirited Cathy.

Unlike Wuthering Heights, the Grange disappears from the film when Cathy dies. Isabella and Lockwood are the only poor reminders of its existence. Because the Grange embodies rationality and order, and Wuthering Heights the "wild and uncivilized," the two houses are eternally locked in battle. With Cathy's death and Isabella's fall from grace, the Grange has lost its feeble edge in the conflict.

In contrast to the other characters in the film (and novel), Heathcliff's character remains constant. True to the Gothic model of a figure who cannot be explained by rational societal or cultural norms, he remains untouched by the vagaries of time and the demands of society. But Cathy is an ambivalent creature—obsessed with Heathcliff but enchanted by the beauty and promise of the Grange, she betrays Heathcliff by choosing a life with Edgar Linton. The beauty she once coveted becomes a facade of manners, and the passion she shared with Heathcliff becomes an antiseptic colorless alliance with Edgar.

In a film where each past event has a current counterpart, Wyler depicts Cathy's longing to return to Wuthering Heights by referring to a past scene. On the fateful night in which Edgar had asked Cathy to marry him, Ellen said that she thought that perhaps Cathy should take her place among the "Linton angels." Cathy's prophetic response is lifted almost verbatim from the novel:

> I don't believe I belong in heaven. I dreamed once that I was there. Heaven didn't seem to be my home and I broke my heart with wanting to come back to earth and the angels were so angry, they flung me out on the middle of the heath, on top of Wuthering Heights, and I woke up sobbing with joy.

This earlier declaration foreshadows Cathy's death and her ghostly return to Heathcliff and Wuthering Heights. Wyler brilliantly and ironically intertwines Cathy's earlier prophetic disavowal of heaven by inserting a small scene at the Grange in which Cathy is seen concentrating on a needlepoint canvas that has as its "hero" a small smiling angel.

Another characteristic of the Gothic novel is its highly charged, highly stylized narrative. Catherine and Heathcliff's violent declarations of emotion and exaggerated passion run the gamut of human and almost inhuman feeling. Wyler's choice of Laurence Olivier and Merle Oberon to play these roles is a brilliant one. Olivier brings his brooding handsomeness and his vast theater experience to the part. His depiction of Heathcliff is as supremely theatricalized/exaggerated as the narrative itself. His meetings with Cathy are charged with emotion—violent, passionate, full of despair and anger. His presence dominates the screen and each agonized meeting with Cathy depicts his obsession and his separateness from the society in which she lives. Merle Oberon's depiction of Cathy, the unpredictable "wild heart" (as Ellen calls her), is quite remarkable. In contrast to Olivier's physicality, Oberon relies on nuances of expression to depict Cathy. She is playful, passionate, and willful. When she is the mistress of the Grange, she is a model of physical and emotional restraint. These are two characters who, despite the intensity of their passion, will never be together. And Wyler utilizes these two actors, with their unique acting skills, to depict the emotion and despair that ultimately merge their characters into a final unholy alliance. Cathy's death scene is a supreme visual example of the two contrasting acting styles.

Upon hearing of Cathy's illness, Heathcliff rushes to the Grange to see her. Cathy lies in the half-world between dreaming and waking, and in an extraordinary visual moment, Merle Oberon (Cathy) opens her eyes and sees Heathcliff. Thinking that she is dreaming, her eyes half close as if to keep the dream. But then, in the hope that Heathcliff's face and form might really exist, she opens her eyes again. The joy that transforms her face is a total and complete renunciation of Edgar and her life at the Grange. This entire scene is played without dialogue. Silently, passionately, without word or gesture, Cathy Linton reverts back to Catherine Earnshaw. The two hold onto one another and then, in contrast to Oberon's visual (and silent) depiction of her joy, and in keeping with his characterization of Heathcliff, Olivier violently breaks the silence:

> Oh, Cathy, why did you kill yourself?... I never broke your heart, you broke it! Cathy, you loved me! How could you throw that love away for a handful of worldliness?... Misery ... and death would never have parted us. You did that alone, like a greedy wanton child.

Cathy pleads for Heathcliff's forgiveness and asks him to carry her to the window so that she might see the moors once more. As Heathcliff pushes the windows aside with Cathy in his arms, Penistone Craig looms in the distance. Cathy's last words to Heathcliff are "Can you see the Craig? I'll wait for you there—until you come." The doctor, Edgar, and Ellen enter the room. They see Heathcliff holding the dead Cathy in his arms. As the doctor approaches, Heathcliff says, "Leave her alone, she's mine."

The assembled group begin their prayers over the dead, but Heathcliff's despair and his agony rise far above their words:

They're praying for you, Cathy. I'll pray one prayer with them. Catherine Earnshaw, may you not rest as long as I live on. I killed you, haunt your murderer then. I know that ghosts have wandered on the earth. Take any form, drive me mad, only do not leave me in this dark alone where I cannot find you.... I cannot live without my soul.

And thus Ellen's narrative ends. Cathy, as she foretold, was flung out of heaven onto the middle of the heath, and it is there, on the night that Lockwood arrived at Wuthering Heights, that Cathy and Heathcliff were reunited on Penistone Craig.

The film's ending departs from the Gothic model and turns to one of almost religious redemption. Wyler was forced to abandon the more literary ending in order to pander to Hollywood's need to give the viewing audience a "happy ending." The audience is given a final scene in which houses and hauntings fade into the past and the viewer sees Heathcliff and Cathy finally reunited. They ascend, hand in hand, upward and away from the viewer's field of vision.

* * *

No happy ending can disguise Cathy's powerful presence. She is the dominant force in both novel and film. Cathy is Heathcliff's obsession, and this obsession continues unabated until his death. Seductive, violent, and almost heroic in his unending dedication to Cathy, Heathcliff cannot master or redirect his vast reservoir of emotion beyond Catherine Earnshaw. The novel says it best:

> I cannot look down to the floor, but her features are shaped on the flags! In every cloud, in every tree—filling the air at night, and caught by glimpses in every object by day ... the entire world is a dreadful collection of memoranda that she did exist, and I have lost her! [pp. 356, 357].

Heathcliff speaks these words almost twenty years after Cathy's death and shortly before his own. Cathy's constant hold on Heathcliff extends, as the novel insists—and the film inadvertently (and sentimentally) depicts—into eternity.

The two other men in the film, Edgar Linton and Cathy's brother Hareton, each exhibit less than admirable traits, yet they symbolize the social markers that help exclude Heathcliff from society. Edgar Linton is weak, ineffectual, and docile. He is Heathcliff's opposing double—the controlled, well-mannered, well-bred scion of a great house. Cathy effectively destroys Edgar (in novel and film) in her death scene in which she and Heathcliff reaffirm their love. Cathy's dying declaration obscures Edgar's role in her life. And in the film, Edgar disappears after Cathy dies.

Hareton Earnshaw is cruel and heartless beyond measure, but he is the true heir to Wuthering Heights. From childhood on, his one obsession is his hatred, fear, and jealousy of Heathcliff. His obsession is more destructive than Heathcliff's, since it drives him to drunkenness and gambling, which ultimately deprive him of his family estate (Heathcliff buys the house and frees Hareton of his gambling debts). Hareton, in the film, becomes a drunken shadow who is forced to remain at Wuthering Heights as Heathcliff's "guest."

Wuthering Heights, both novel and film, takes up the issue of the flawed hero or antihero. The ghost genre, almost from its inception, appears to emphasize and draw on man's weakness. (Dickens's *A Christmas Carol* is one example of how the ghost story is utilized to depict man's fall from grace.) Beginning with *Wuthering Heights*, each successive novel and film under discussion will depict how the ghost genre emphasizes man's gradual and ignoble descent.

II

THE ROMANTIC GHOST

CHAPTER TWO

The Ghost and Mrs. Muir

a novel by R.A. DICK
a film by JOSEPH H. MANKIEWICZ

The Novel

The Ghost and Mrs. Muir represents still another shift in the Gothic ghost story, a shift that satirizes the manners, conventions, social attitudes, and scientific advances of late Victorian England. By setting her novel during turn-of-the-century England, R.A. Dick utilizes the ghost story to protest a social order that has become restrictive, exclusionary, and repressive. In the novel science, with all its various disciplines, is readily available to subdue the irrational, explain the illogical, and restore any "psychically" afflicted individual to his or her original "healthy" state. R.A. Dick argues against this collective conformity and uniform sanity and allows ghosts and hauntings to continue uninterrupted by the vagaries of time and change. The author has devised a counterworld, a small valiant society that consists of a young widow, her two small children, and the ghost of a retired sea captain. In defiance of the modern world, this unique "family" lives together in a strange and beautiful house by the sea for what constitutes an earthly lifetime.

Mrs. Muir is a widow with two children, a boy and a girl. After her husband's death, she and the children are forced to live with her husband's mother and two sisters. Mrs. Muir's financial circumstances force her into a social situation that she finds both repellent and frightening:

> she was forced to sell the pseudo-Elizabethan house ... in order to meet the very real debts which poured in on every side ... an opposing torrent of advice poured down on her from her husband's relatives ... flinging her

future this way and that, now into three-roomed flats, now into semi-detached villas, now into hat shops or tea shops, and now into housekeeping for single gentlemen, while the children were swept away from her into charity schools, institutions, and even adoption [p. 3].

While Mrs. Muir's future is being debated by family and friends, her social life is organized and orchestrated by her husband's family:

Edwin's younger sister had made her join all the clubs in town ... and it had been Eva Muir's life, with choral societies, dramatic societies, and literary societies [p. 5].

Mrs. Muir has no life of her own. The existence that has been portioned to her is dictated by her financial dependency on her in-laws and the specific social role relegated to a widow with small children. One morning, Lucy Muir decides that she has had enough: "This has got to stop. I must settle things for myself" (p. 4). She decides to strike out on her own, to live with her children in a house by the sea, and she chooses the remote seaside town of Whitecliff. She arrives in Whitecliff and walks into the rental offices of Itchen, Boles, and Coombe.

The scene between Lucy and the rental agent was lifted almost intact from the novel to the screen, and the exchange between the two has been a favorite subject among film critics and feminist writers who see this scene as Lucy's declaration of freedom—her break with Victorian repression. Jeanine Basinger declares this scene to be "Mrs. Muir's trial by combat," the defining moment that is "Mrs. Muir's first test as a woman alone, and she passes it" (p. 296). While this assessment of Lucy's determination to rent the house against Mr. Coombe's advice ("I think I should point out to you ... that for a single lady it is very isolated ... you will be living alone without a man's protection" [pp. 10, 11]) depicts Lucy as defiant and courageous. Basinger's view suggests a sense of modernity, of worldliness that clashes with Lucy's retreat from the world. Her immediate decision to rent and live in a haunted house is a renunciation of the present and one that thrusts her backward in time into the confines of a Gothic environment—a haunted house.

Lucy's present can be explained by her past. She was brought up in the country, in her father's house where "her absent-minded father ... lived mainly in the past among the Greek poets." Lucy had been reading a novel that ended with "a kiss in the rose garden, and they lived happily ever after," and so when Edwin Muir, who was rebuilding her father's library, "kissed her in the orchard, Lucy could see no other ending to her own romance" (p. 4). But when Lucy (a bride at seventeen) marries Edwin and moves to London, her romantic novel turns into a bad dream. Like Cinderella's in the fairy tale, Lucy's marriage includes the unhappy addition of "a widowed mother and two strong-minded sisters living almost on her doorstep" (p. 4).

Lucy's fantasylike early life in the country evokes an aura of predetermination in which her father's fascination with the past becomes Lucy's own inevitable destiny. Lucy is a by-product of the age of Romanticism. She has tasted the world of manners and convention and found it wanting. Gull Cottage, a throwback to the past, is her way back to a familiar and comfortable time.

In order to depict the concept of clashing ideologies and incompatible worlds, R.A. Dick places Lucy in a world of opposing forces where every character, every physical setting, and every situation has a corresponding and corrupted double. (Even the author, Josephine Aimée Campbell Leslie, uses an ambiguous pseudonym, R.A. Dick.) Lucy's perception of the real world is juxtaposed/doubled with her memories of her father's house. She perceives her early years as idyllic and her move to Gull Cottage is an attempt to relive those years. Cap'n Gregg and Edwin Muir are opposing doubles in that Edwin (as Lucy describes him) is weak, insensitive, and ineffectual while Cap'n Gregg is a colorful, passionate, sensitive phantom who symbolically embodies the romantic lover that Lucy read about long ago. The use of double imagery is peppered throughout the novel as Lucy's indictment of society.

Houses and Spaces

Edwin was a failed architect; he built "pseudo-Elizabethan" houses, and he had even "thought of turning an old windmill into a modern villa" (p. 9). Edwin is representative of the modern movement in which pure aestheticism is replaced by economic values based on middle-class utilitarian principles. As Lucy tells Captain Gregg:

> My husband studied architecture for years, but he never made such a satisfactory little house as this—though I believe he was very clever at prisons and post-offices [p. 36].

The destruction of an old windmill in order to build a "modern" villa is indicative of the small regard Edwin holds for the past. The theme of destruction of the past in order to create a more rational present recurs throughout the novel.

Built by a sea captain in an unspecified time, Gull Cottage stands in contrast to Edwin's type of architecture—a house not occupied for more than ten years, dusty, full of cobwebs and exotic relics of the past:

on the heavy black marble fireplace stood a clock to match, flanked by two exquisite Ming vases; a Persian carpet, perfect in design and coloring ... a red plush sofa ... a delicately embroidered Indian shawl ... and a red lacquer Chinese cabinet of a past century [p. 13].

Gull Cottage itself is depicted as

a small grey-stone house ... a grey stone wall curved out into a round bastion ... a large bow-window with faded blue shutters looked out from the upper floor over the sea, as if ... to catch the sun's rays from every angle of the day [p. 10].

Gull Cottage is totally out of synchronization with its "well kept neighbors." It represents a break in time and a break with convention. It is a small valiant monument to struggle against the outside world; it is a past that has kept its unflagging vigil against the intrusion of the present. And it is haunted. "I like it," said Lucy impulsively. "I like it very much indeed."

Lucy's withdrawal from the world is a metaphoric suicide suggested in part by the rental agent's description of Captain Gregg's death. When Mr. Coombe and Lucy inspect Gull Cottage, they are driven from the house by the sound of a "rich deep chuckle" (p. 16). The petrified rental agent and Lucy make a hasty retreat, whereupon Mr. Coombe admits that the house is haunted. "Why does he haunt?" Lucy asks. "Was he murdered?" "No, he committed suicide," answers Mr. Coombe. Lucy then asks if "he was unhappy." "Did that laugh sound unhappy?" the rental agent bitterly retorts. "No, it didn't," Lucy thoughtfully replies. "But if he wasn't miserable, why did he put an end to his life?" (p. 17). The words "miserable and unhappy," are manifestations of Lucy's own state of mind, and just as Captain Gregg supposedly ended his life in Gull Cottage, so too does Lucy use the house to close the door on her own.

When Lucy Muir occupies Gull Cottage, her relationship with the outside world ceases to exist. Connections with time, people, and places lose meaning and substance because she has severed her ties with society. Lucy's children are her only reminders of her past, and their connection to her and Gull Cottage is tenuous and time-defined. Lucy and Gull Cottage are their present; their future has yet to be determined.

In the novel, Lucy's meeting with Miles Fairley Blane is orchestrated by Captain Gregg. One evening, after a long and heated debate on the afterlife, the captain states that he continues his sojourn on earth because he fears that Lucy might marry again—that if she does indeed remarry, his plans for the house as a home for retired seamen will be in jeopardy. The debate ends in a wager. The captain states that "I lay you your rose trees to a new monkey puzzle tree that you'd fall for the first attractive man who showed he admired you" (p. 71). Lucy is furious at the captain's assertion that she would be so gullible and she ends the conversation by stating that "I am to be trusted—completely" (p. 71). The following day, as Lucy and her dog Tags walk along the deserted beach, Tags falls and disappears into a rabbit burrow. Frantically, Lucy runs for help and falls "into the arms of a man coming up the slope from the valley beyond" (p. 72). The man, or the stranger, as he is called for several pages of the narrative, tells Lucy that he imagined a man's voice urging him to "go back to the top of the cliff" (p. 72). The man obeyed this voice and subsequently discovered Lucy and her half-buried dog. After rescuing the animal, a sudden storm threatens—the skies darken and it begins to rain. The stranger urges Lucy to come to his nearby cottage where she will be safe and dry, and Lucy and her dog accompany the man to his home.

Like its owner at this point in the narrative, the cottage has no name. Nameless and precariously perched "half-way down a cliff," it seems, like Milton's Satan, to have sustained the fall from heaven only to have landed, for a brief moment, in Lucy Muir's newfound Eden. Temptation or Sexuality might be a good name for this odd little establishment, since it metaphorically represents Lucy's tentative move away from her antiseptic cohabitation with the ghost of Captain Gregg. The stranger's house, like Lucy's sexuality, is well hidden:

> he led her down the hill to a little stone cottage that perched on a grassy ledge, half-way down the face of the cliff. It was hidden by a huddle of ancient wind-bent trees, which stretched out their gnarled branches like witches' arms [p. 75].

Lucy remarks that she "never knew there was a cottage here," and the stranger (now identified as Miles Blane) replies, "it's well concealed." The house is small; it contains only the furnishings necessary for seduction: "The door opened into a living room, and an open door showed a bedroom beyond." Lucy is enchanted by this very attractive stranger. Like his filmic counterpart, Miles Fairley, Miles Blane is a man of many talents, I "paint a bit, and write a bit, and play golf and squash and ride, and play bridge and poker" (p. 79). Trained as a barrister, Miles asserts that the "law courts depress me." Blane's only true profession is to seduce women, and Lucy, just as the captain had predicted, falls victim to his charm.

Because the captain has orchestrated the meeting between Lucy and Miles Blane, their initial encounter and ensuing meetings are as fantastical and exaggerated as those that only a ghost could conjure up. Miles is depicted as more predator than lover and more satanic than human: "he lay in wait for her on her walks ... she could not avoid him" (p. 81). As a metaphoric transference of her own sleeping persona, Lucy perceives Miles as "some statue waiting to be brought to life." The words "magic and magical" that are spoken between kisses are the key to their improbable and contrived affair.

When Miles tries to convince Lucy to move into his little cottage, Lucy mistakenly believes that Miles means to marry her. She immediately brings up the subject of her children—that the tiny cottage would be too small for all of them. Miles explodes in anger, "I want you to forget the existence of everyone but me ... we ... can make our own world ... other people always butt in and spoil things" (p. 84). Miles's overblown reaction to Lucy's concern for her children parallels Lucy's own disenchantment with the outside world and her decision to leave that world behind. Miles, therefore, brings substance and a certain perverse reality to Lucy's innermost thoughts and feelings.

After Miles's preposterous proposal that Lucy leave her children and live with him, and Lucy's inability to refuse Miles's advances, Captain Gregg realizes that his "wager" has gone too far. He speaks to Lucy one night:

> "I must speak to you, Lucia.... Oh, Lucia, will you ever forgive me? It was all my fault, blind fool that I am—but there he was and he seemed ideal for my purposes.... I felt you needed a lesson, you were so complacent and cocksure, and, my God, you've got your lesson all right" [p. 86].

When Lucy asks for an explanation, the captain tells her that Miles is married, that he has a wife and three children, "the youngest only in his cradle." Lucy refuses to believe the captain. "I can't feel that Miles is evil. He makes me feel good and kinder than I have ever been" (p. 87). To which the captain mournfully replies, "The devil himself was in heaven before he fell, and his temptations may be full of beauty and great subtlety" (p. 88).

Lucy returns to Miles and confronts him with her new knowledge. Miles feebly offers to leave his wife so that he and Lucy can live together, but Lucy (with the captain's warnings resounding in her ears) knows that she cannot destroy one home, one woman's happiness, in order to build her own. Lucy's last visit to Miles's cottage is a confirmation of the captain's concerns. As Lucy approaches the cottage, she hears laughter—she peers in the window and sees Miles kissing another woman.

The imagery of a fall is peppered throughout the few pages in the novel devoted to Lucy's brief encounter with Miles Blane. The words *down*, *fallen*, and *hidden* that describe the house itself and the place where it is situated describe its function in Lucy's world. This house occupies no actual space; since it is "perched" momentarily on the side of a cliff, its function is to entice Lucy and precipitate her descent back into the world. This is not Gull Cottage with its "grey stone wall curved out into a round bastion," that suggests a solitary outward-focused battle with the forces of progress. In opposition to Gull Cottage, which has occupied its space for many years, and which has a long future ahead (as a home for retired sailors), Blane's house disappears when Lucy dismisses him.

There is an interesting subtext to the end of Lucy's affair with Miles. As Lucy dejectedly walks away from the tiny cottage, she fictionalizes Miles's character and his actions, thereby absolving herself from any complicity in this sad affair:

> Life was nothing but a play to him ... he could go from one play to another, always the central figure, always bringing down the curtain when comedy threatened to turn to tragedy ... leaving the other players stranded, to think out their own endings to their ruined plot ... but, thought Lucy, it was she who held the book of this play and she would end it in her own manner [p. 97].

As Lucy describes it, it is she (not the captain) who has written this story within a story, and she closes this book and this sorry interlude undiminished and unscathed.

But the captain cannot forgive himself for the pain he has caused Lucy. And the same night that Lucy dismisses Miles from her life, the captain's voice comes to her in the dark, solemn and sad:

> Nothing that I can say would be adequate.... All I do ask is that you try and forgive me, bloody fool that I am. I should have known better, because interfering unasked in other people's lives, whether from kindness or cruelty, is one of the greater sins, and I knew it. I am, indeed, a poor representative of either world, and I shall go away until I have learned greater wisdom. Shall I go away, Lucy? he asked humbly [pp. 97–98].

Lucy does not answer him "with her voice or her thoughts." And the captain, saddened by her silence, disappears into the night.

Portraits

Daniel Gregg, the sea captain who haunts Gull Cottage, exists only through his portrait. He is an aural ghost, one who is heard but never seen.

In the novel, the captain is a "thunder" in Lucy's head; to the rental agent, he is the sound of maniacal laughter, and to Miles Blane, he is the voice that urged him to return to the Cliff and rescue Lucy's dog. Captain Gregg lives only through speech—words are the vehicle by which he haunts, and the portrait connects the words to the man.

R.A. Dick does not give any particular distinction to the portrait. Indeed, she actually diminishes its importance by introducing it as "an oil painting of a sea captain in his uniform." And she adds "it was not a good painting" (p. 11). It is Lucy who lends form and substance to the aural haunting by initiating a link between the portrait and the words the invisible ghost utters.

Lucy Muir first sees Captain Gregg when she inspects Gull Cottage with the rental agent. The imposing portrait of the captain captures her attention because "the vivid blue eyes stared down at her with such intense vitality that for one moment Lucy thought one of them had winked at her." And when Lucy, "hoping to subdue the twinkling blue eyes to their proper status of dead paint," silently threatens to remove the portrait from its place, she is startled to see that, "some trick of light ... made him appear to move his eyes, for now they stared back at her, dull and lifeless and strangely less blue" (p. 13). When Lucy takes possession of Gull Cottage, she inexplicably moves the portrait from the living room to her bedroom; it is placed above the mantle surrounded by smaller paintings of schooners with large, billowing sails. By moving the portrait to her bedroom, Lucy creates an intimacy, an aura that foreshadows her relationship with the captain.

The uniqueness of Captain Gregg's portrait is that it is not a true likeness of the captain at all. In contrast to the 19th and early 20th century portrait in which socially or historically prominent personages commissioned well-known artists to paint their portraits, Captain Gregg's portrait is an amalgam of many people painted by a vagrant seafaring artist who painted the portrait in exchange for passage:

> "it's a very good portrait," said Captain Gregg.... "The hands are terrible," said Lucy. "They weren't my hands," replied Captain Gregg.... "Of course I couldn't always be sitting for him and wasting my time, so he'd paint bits of anyone that came along" [p. 44].

Rather than a portrait, the work is a history painting. Like the furnishings in Gull Cottage, which are described as "exotic relics of the past," bits and pieces from endless journeys over endless seas, Captain Gregg, the man, has not been immortalized, but his life and his time have. The portrait of Captain Gregg stands as a monument to ambiguity with the subject depicted as pieces and parts of many men painted by an artist who was a nameless wanderer.

Time

R.A. Dick marks Lucy's passage through life and her three valiant attempts at love in a most unusual manner—by the dogs that Lucy acquires throughout her lifetime. Lucy has always loved having a dog in the house but she was never able to choose one that suited her: "Not long after she was married, Edwin had presented her with a pedigreed Pomeranian that had yapped its delicate way into an early grave, regretted by no one" (p. 68). Lucy's description of the "pedigreed Pomeranian" is one that might well describe Edwin and his own early death. Lucy's happiness with her new home and her new-found freedom is reflected by the dog she purchases on her own: "this little creature, bought casually from a man by the curbside, was just a dog, partly Sealyham and partly terrier, and altogether amusing and companionable." The dog, Tags, a happy mix of breeds and "amusing and companionable," is a counterpoint to Cap'n Gregg's portrait and his persona. Lucy and Tags roam the beaches, climb the cliffs, and watch the sea. "With Tags, she went farther and farther afield ... coming home with glowing cheeks" (p. 68). This is Lucy's happiest time and Tags is the reflection of that happiness. It was Tags's unfortunate fall into a rabbit burrow (contrived by the captain) that brought Miles Blane into Lucy's life, and in the years that follow the remorseful captain's disappearance, Tags is her one comfort. After many years, however, Tags dies and Anna, Lucy's daughter, buys Lucy a "Pekinese of no certain pedigree." The dog reminds Lucy of Miles: "memory itself seemed to take on the ease of a lap dog, and she found that she could remember Miles with tolerance" (p. 99). And then, one night, the captain returns, booming his displeasure at the tiny Miss Ming who, as Miles had once hoped to do so many years before, is sharing Lucy's bed.

Lucy's final years, her old age, are now marked by the appearance of a "sedately stout fox terrier." This dog, like his elderly mistress, is content to sit by the fire and in good weather follow her into her garden. Lucy is now at the end of her life and her memory turns often to Tags, the dog that shared her new freedom and youth. Lucy mistakenly calls Spot, the stout old friend who now follows her about, Tags, in a fond and poignant reminder of her first and happiest year with Captain Gregg in Gull Cottage. The dogs represent three stages in Lucy's life: her life with Edwin, her strange and unforgettable interlude with Miles Fairley Blane and her lifelong love affair with the ghost of Captain Gregg.

Science: Blast the Enlightenment!

Julia Briggs in *Night Visitors: The Rise and Fall of the English Ghost Story*, explains the paradox between the ghost of the late 19th century, the pseudo-scientific/scientific communities, and the individual caught in between:

> The widespread interest in supernatural manifestations was in part a reaction against rational and materialist doctrines such as utilitarianism or "evolutionary meliorism" ... researchers set out to provide practical "scientific" proof of "forces beyond our knowledge" [p. 52].

Since Lucy was never quite sure about her dialogues with Captain Gregg (he was a "thunder in her head," a voice that she heard but could not see), she decides to turn to a psychoanalyst for an explanation:

> after a surprising conversation with this earnest specialist in human peculiarities ... he assured her that she was as normal as any woman could be, though there did seem to be this curious obsession in her subconscious, a craving perhaps for the ideal lover ... and if she were to continue her visits to him, at three guineas a time ... they could no doubt sublimate [a]nd rationalize it [p. 41].

Lucy finds this explanation quite unsatisfactory, and even more, too expensive to consider. The "earnest specialist" and science are summarily dismissed in favor of the inexplicable and irascible Captain Gregg.

But Edwin and Lucy have two children, a boy and a girl, and their early years were spent in London under the watchful eyes of Edwin's family. Edwin and his views of the "new" world live on in his son Cyril. Lucy has always been uncomfortable with her son, and when her mother-in-law comes to visit, she discovers why:

> the only one contented in her presence was Cyril, for Eva loved collections and so did he ... all the fleeting loveliness that fluttered like dancing flower petals in the sun was brought home in triumph, and their fragile wings were stretched out in stiff crucifixion ... and speared in a collection of death ... squashing the results flat between blotting paper ... labeling the faded corpses with dead Latin names [p. 55].

Eva brings science with her, and Lucy protests against this horrifying "taking of life": "oh, I know it's necessary for scientists to destroy life in order to preserve it, but I cannot see that it's essential for little boys to make morgues of bird eggs" (p. 55).

But Anna is her mother's child. Enamored of the sea, in love with nature—hair flying and rosy cheeks, she is the young Lucy Muir reborn. The world that is Gull Cottage is one in which she feels completely at home. The children, with their opposing predilections—one a budding scientist, the other a tiny free and uninhibited spirit—are representative of the incompatibility between science and progress and nature and mysticism—Gull Cottage and the outside world.

Who Wrote Blood and Swash?

References to books, novels, and plays occur throughout the novel: Lucy's father who "lived among the Greek poets," Lucy who marries Edwin because she had been reading a romantic novel in her father's garden and mistook Edwin for the hero, and the episode with Miles Blane that Lucy compares first to a play and then to a book that she is about to end. Lucy doesn't only read novels, she lives them, and her life with Captain Gregg is characterized by words, endless dialogues on varied subjects.

Blood and Swash is written because Lucy's finances have been depleted. Many years have gone by and her children have gone to school in London. Her son Cyril suddenly requires surgery and the cost of his operation has dissipated Lucy's small savings. In determining how she is to raise money, she immediately tells the captain what she cannot do: "I can't paint pictures or write, or do anything like that." The captain's cryptic answer is "Write books" (p. 110). When Lucy complains that she just said that she cannot write books, the captain responds, "I can" (p. 110).

Just as the strange episode between Miles and Lucy was seemingly devised by the captain and ultimately fictionalized by Lucy, so too is this psychic doubling projected onto the writing of *Blood and Swash*. Financial necessity is the driving force behind Lucy's need to write, and again Lucy allows the captain to devise the means by which she can achieve financial independence.

Blood and Swash is not a romantic novel, nor poetry or a play. It is, as the captain shouts, "the unvarnished story of a sailor's life" (p. 123). Like her earlier ambiguous description of the captain's portrait, "a sea captain," R.A. Dick plays with the question of an internalized and fantasized identity. Unlike the film, in which the captain is visualized and he and Lucy appear to be working in tandem, in the novel Lucy works alone, with the captain's voice shouting his words as Lucy pecks away on a typewriter. But every now and then, Lucy lapses into a reverie in which she "could hear his voice moving up and down the room as if he were walking a quarter-deck ... she tried to picture him as a young man and as a small boy" (p. 123). R.A. Dick sets the stage and provides the props and then leaves her heroine's imagination to embellish and expand on what she has seen and imagines she has heard.

Reality, if reality can exist in a ghost story, is in the exchange between Cyril and Lucy. Cyril ventures into Lucy's room late one night and discovers that his mother is writing a book. "Don't count on getting your book published," Cyril cautions, "so many women are writing books these days." "This is different," Lucy answers, "it's a secret, the whole book is a secret and I'm not writing it under my own name" (p. 126). Captain Gregg remains silent—he thunders no response to these words. In Lucy's emphatic response to Cyril's prying, one can almost detect the ghost of Mrs. Leslie/R.A. Dick in Lucy's words.

The Film

The adaptation of the novel to film is an almost total revision of the novel. Left behind is Lucy's son Cyril and all references to science and technology. And the voice of Captain Gregg, which was "like a thunder in Lucy's head," becomes the very visible and very attractive Rex Harrison. The "blasted in-laws" only serve as a momentary reminder of Lucy's life with Edwin, and they quickly disappear from the film. The film adaptation of *The Ghost and Mrs. Muir* is a remarkable and beautiful achievement. It is a film in which word, image, and music coalesce to project a fairy tale atmosphere. Gull Cottage belonged to a sea captain and the house is a reflection of the man. It perches on the edge of the sea surrounded by large, high cliffs. It is a lovely landlocked vessel that is metaphorically driven to unknown ports of call by Lucy's dreams and the words and stories told by the ghost of Captain Gregg. Bernard Herrmann's exquisite score is another voice in the film that movingly captures the sea sound of solitude, loneliness, and loss. The music becomes a major voice after the captain leaves Lucy, and the stories and conversations come to an end. The lonely tentative years are spoken by the music and the sea as Lucy endlessly paces the now deserted shoreline.

Houses and Spaces

The magic that encompasses Gull Cottage and the once-living man who built it is expressed in this exchange between Lucy and the captain:

The magic of Gull Cottage: "It reminds me of something, a poem or a song." Gene Tierney is Mrs. Muir and Rex Harrison is the captain in *The Ghost and Mrs. Muir*. (Film Stills Archive, The Museum of Modern Art, New York)

> Lucy: Edwin could never have designed a house like this ... it reminds me of something, a poem or a song.
>
> Captain: Charmed magic casements, opening on the foam of perilous seas, in faery lands forlorn.

"Keats," cries Lucy. "Ode to a Nightingale," affirms the captain.

To find a sea captain quoting Keats is an oddity, and Lucy wonders how the captain knows so much about poetry. In answer to Lucy's question, the captain answers that there was time to read during his long and lonely voyages.

That Lucy and the captain think in tandem, that one can recite lines from a specific poem and the other joyfully and quickly identify both poet and poem, evokes the spirit of the novel and its recurring references to novels, plays, and poems. This scene is not in the novel, but it does elicit the novel's suggestion of psychic doubling in which the captain is an extension of Lucy's own persona. The choice of Keats's poem appears to be a deliberate one in that while the two quoted lines are used to describe the house, other unquoted lines of the poem speak directly to Lucy's fantasy:

> Darkling I listen; and for many a time
> I have been half in love with easeful death,
> Called him soft names in many a mused rhyme,
> to take into the air [ll. 51–54].

The poem ends with these most appropriate lines: "Was it a vision, or a waking dream? / Fled is that music:—Do I wake or sleep?" (ll. 79–80). The use of Keats's poem foreshadows Lucy's lifelong but sterile obsession with the ghost of Captain Gregg. David Daiches explains that the poem's "true merit ... [is] of a higher kind ... it represents the escape from change and decay into eternity, but at the expense of eternal unfulfillment" (p. 920).

From this point on, until the captain speaks his wonderful farewell to the sleeping Lucy, their relationship becomes a blend of poetry and prose. The captain's own particular rough-and-tumble "seaman's" language that he interjects throughout his conversations with Lucy inexplicably seems to invade the entire household. This strange and fantastical union of art and words ultimately culminates in the writing of the book, *Blood and Swash*.

Miles Fairley has no house in Whitecliff. His home is in London with his wife and two children. Fairley, wonderfully played by George Sanders, loses the satanic dimensions that the novel gives him and becomes, in the film, a foolish but charming dandy. A man of little substance, with an almost childlike disdain of convention, he is appropriately depicted as a man of many talents and many names. As a writer of children's books, he assumes the name of Uncle Neddy. When he paints his pictures (usually of women or his wife and children) he prefers to be called Renoir. "And what do you do as Miles Fairley?" asks Lucy. "I play the fool," he responds.

Fairley's always transient state is depicted by having him appear to be in constant motion. He is always seen riding in horse-drawn carriages, on trains, or strolling in shaded glens. He is never seen inside a house. When Lucy, unaware that he is married, goes to his home in London, Miles's wife tells her that "Miles is not at home. He has taken the children for a stroll in the park." A foolish, moderately sinful man, he has no place to "drop anchor."

Both novel and film depict Miles Fairley as a man of many talents. The film interestingly portrays him, however, as a writer of children's books. Miles's and Lucy's connection to the world of letters is presented as a role reversal in which the children's book is written by a man, and the "unvarnished story of a sailor's life" is inexplicably written by a woman. *Blood and Swash*, Lucy's collaborative enterprise with the Captain, is the means by which Miles enters Lucy's life; they share the same publisher.

"Uncle Neddy" supposedly is loved by all the children in England. As Lucy excitedly tells Miles, "Uncle Neddy is my daughter's favorite author." Uncle Neddy, like his books, is not to be taken seriously either as a writer or a lover. But again, Lucy is duped by the suaveness, the facade, and the cajoling words that come to him so easily. In the film, however, Lucy does not appear as innocent as she does in the novel. The novel stresses the captain's motivation in bringing Miles into Lucy's life—he wanted to teach her a lesson; and after the affair draws to its unhappy conclusion, Lucy is able to fictionalize this liaison in a manner that absolves her from any complicity. Miles Blane becomes a "book" that Lucy is about to close. But in the film, Lucy and Miles are both duplicitous; Lucy first by telling Miles that Uncle Neddy is her daughter's favorite author (the captain later accuses Lucy of lying when he tells her that she knows that "Dead Eye Dick" is Anna's favorite book), and then by hiding her own authorship in a book supposedly written by the captain. But Miles Fairley goes a step further than Lucy's forgivable missteps—he hides a wife and children as well as his name.

Captain Gregg's bitter disappointment at Lucy's choice to "weigh anchor" with Fairley gives the film one of its most moving scenes, in which the captain says his poignant farewell to the sleeping Lucy:

> Don't trouble yourself, m'dear, it's not your fault. I should have known it was on the chart. You've made your choice, the only choice you could make. You've chosen life and that's how it should be. And that's why I'm going away, m'dear, I can't help you now. I can only confuse you more and destroy whatever chance you have left of happiness ... whether you meet fair winds or foul, make your own way to harbor.

Unlike the novel, in which the captain leaves Lucy in remorse for having caused her pain, the captain's words indicate that he is leaving because he knows that he has been displaced, that for the moment Lucy no longer needs him. The captain's poetic words thrust Lucy back into the world. Again, Lucy has fictionalized a deeply felt romantic liaison, and the captain, as Lucy experiences it, has relinquished his role in the writing of *Blood and Swash*:

> Lucia, listen to me, listen, m'dear, you've been dreaming, dreaming of a sea captain that haunted this house. The talks you had with him, even the book you both wrote together. Lucia, you wrote the book, you and no one else.

The Ghost and Mrs. Muir: **The Captain's farewell (Rex Harrison and Gene Tierney). (Film Stills Archive, The Museum of Modern Art, New York)**

> The book you imagined from his house, from his picture on the wall, and his gear lying about in every room. It's been a dream, Lucia, and in the morning and in the years after, you'll only remember it as a dream and it'll die as all dreams must die when waking.

The film is unlike the novel in that the captain never returns to Gull Cottage. He returns only when Lucy dies many years later to reclaim what he has lost.

Portraits

The film, like the novel, begins with Lucy and the rental agent inspecting Gull Cottage. The first room they enter is the sitting room. And as they enter, the portrait, which seems to lurk behind the door, leaps into focus. As though the portrait were alive, Lucy gasps, and then she murmurs, "oh, it's a only a painting." Lucy's reaction to this dark, brooding representation of Captain Gregg suggests the life force that lurks beneath

Portrait of Captain Gregg: Bits and pieces of many men. Gene Tierney in *The Ghost and Mrs. Muir*. (Film Stills Archive, The Museum of Modern Art, New York)

the painted surface. The portrait is, for all of the film, the dominant image in a world of cinematic imagery. In the novel, the painting embodies the fantasy, and the captain is an extension of that fantasy, a "thunder" in Lucy's head, an aural apparition. The film, however, requires a visible spirit and although the portrait is the means by which the Lucy begins her fantasy, it is no longer a mere painting; the portrait now has a striking, compelling, and very visible human counterpart.

When Lucy, at the captain's request, brings the portrait into her/his bedroom and begins to undress in front of the mirror, the viewer can understand her momentary hesitation as she sees the captain's painted eyes reflected in the mirror and modestly covers them with a shawl. As a constant eye within the camera eye, the painting is, as Angela Dalle Vacche suggests, "neither a mask or a camouflage ... it refers instead to a convoluted path of ideas, emotions ... and expectations" (p. 82).

Although Lucy has already encountered the now visible Captain Gregg in the kitchen of Gull Cottage, the portrait still retains its symbolic role; it is the repository of Lucy's "ideas, emotions, and expectations," her own extraordinary dream. The viewer and Lucy know that the captain is never far from Lucy's side; when he is not in the camera's eye, his portrait still contains the fantasy.

After the captain leaves Lucy, and before Miles's treachery is exposed, Lucy has the captain's portrait removed from her room. But after the affair with Miles has come to its sorry conclusion, the portrait mysteriously reappears on the wall. Although the captain never returns to Gull Cottage until Lucy's death, Lucy spends her remaining years trying to resurrect the dream that once brought her happiness.

* * *

The Ghost and Mrs. Muir is a fantasy born of a woman's need to redefine her place and her role in Victorian society. Her return to a Gothic environment, a haunted house, complete with the ghost of a sea captain, is the stuff that novels and films are made of, and this environment, this cottage, removed and distant from the rest of society, enables Lucy Muir to write *Blood and Swash,* her first and only novel. Lucy (or Lucia, as the Captain calls her) is a divided self, part child, part adult. Her choice of husband and lovers is unfortunate except for her fantasy lover, the poetic but irascible Captain Gregg. The sad and wonderful consequences of Lucy Muir's lifelong obsession with the captain are found in the last pages of R.A. Dick's novel:

> but I am so tired, and suddenly she fell back in her chair.... And now you will never be tired again, said the Captain's voice. Come, Lucia, come, me dear ... it was quiet in the room. Only the clock ticked on in the remorseless, mechanical minutes that men have made for themselves to measure away the joy and sadness of their earthly lives. The body of little Mrs. Muir sat very still in the chair, the face tilted sideways, looking without seeing into the painted eyes of Captain Gregg's portrait on the wall [p. 174].

Daniel Gregg, real or imagined, is/was an extraordinary ghost and an equally extraordinary man. A moderate, modified Heathcliff, Captain Gregg is precariously balanced between the ghosts of 18th century Gothic and 19th century romanticism. The novel puts his existence in question and the film shows us that he is real. Whether or not he is Lucy Muir's fantasy, he is possessed of an obsessive inexhaustible will. He guards and protects his wonderful anachronistic house against the intrusive destructive forces of modernity, and by extension, he protects and guards Lucy as well. He stands in stark contrast to Edwin Muir and Miles Fairley with his colorful personality, his heroism at sea (as he tells it), and his sexuality. Alive or dead, Daniel Gregg has/is passion. His human counterparts are rendered feeble and impotent by the unique exuberant aura of life that surrounds him. And yet, while Captain Gregg is a bit less than his Gothic predecessors and a great deal more than his current human counterparts, he fails to survive. His "flaw" is evidenced by a bit of "human" clumsiness when he inadvertently caused his own death. As he explains it to Lucy, he accidentally kicked on the "blasted" gas heater (while he was asleep) and died from the noxious fumes. And if he is Lucy's fantasy lover as both novel and film suggest, his life and Lucy's life are inexorably, eternally joined. When Lucy dies, the captain dies as well. Lucy is the catalyst that brings the captain into existence and she alone fosters his immortality by the book she writes. And if he exists independent of Lucy's dream, he and his exotic house—both relics of the past—still cannot survive in the modern world without Lucy's assistance. (She promises that she will turn Gull Cottage into a home for retired seamen.) With or without Lucy, the wonderful irascible ghost of Daniel Gregg is, in mid–20th century, the last of his kind.

CHAPTER THREE

Portrait of Jennie

a novel by ROBERT NATHAN
a film by WILLIAM DIETERLE

The Novel: Mutations of Gothic in the 1940s

Robert Nathan wrote two ghost stories that were made into films: *Portrait of Jennie* and *The Bishop's Wife*. Both films were produced in the mid-1940s and they are representative of how the gothic genre of the 19th century mutated from the classic Gothic depiction of the ghost story with its emphasis on the outward manifestations of horror into a more psychological form that emphasized the inner state of man/woman.

The film and novel *Portrait of Jennie* differ considerably from *Wuthering Heights* in that the ghost and the living are seen interacting almost as though they were living within the same time and space. The spatial disjunction between the living and dead in *Wuthering Heights* is replaced by a sense of an almost peaceful communion. This sense of communion is enhanced by the setting of the story, in which most of the scenes (in the novel and the film) take place outdoors. The confines of dark houses and castles give way to an openness that helps to convey a sense of timelessness—of past merging seamlessly with present and future.

The 19th-century Gothic horror that lived in the tower and the graveyard evoked a sense of confinement, entrapment, and finality. And the spectre that emerged from these places was empowered to frighten, torment, and cause misery. In the romantic ghost story genre of the 1930s and 1940s, the ghost sheds the horrors of the graveyard and the tomb to interact lovingly with its earthbound counterparts. Perhaps the most astonishing shift from the Gothic model is the gentleness of this novel. The frenetic elements of "excess and exaggeration, the wild and the uncivilized" that defined Brontë's *Wuthering Heights* are gone. This is a rational novel that quietly suggests that relationships with ghosts are possible.

The Dark Side of the Novel: States of Mind

The novel is, on the surface, a simple one. It revolves around a starving artist who comes upon a child in a park. The child has a dreamlike quality about her, and when the artist, Eban Adams, sees her, he notes that "the city sounds were muted and far away, they seemed to come from another time, from somewhere in the past ... as through the quiet arches of a dream" (p. 7). Adams is suddenly intrigued by "the little girl playing by herself in the middle of the mall.... I stopped and watched her, for I was surprised to see her there, all alone.... "It's getting pretty dark," I said, "Oughtn't you to go home?" (p. 7). Jennie responds by telling Adams that she doesn't "know time very well"(p. 7). The child asks whether she can walk along with Adams, and the two walk off together. There is a moment when the artist hesitates and wonders whether this chance meeting and walk with "a little girl no higher than my elbow" could cause him some difficulty. "I wondered if I could be arrested for what I was doing; I don't even know her name, I thought, in case they ask me" (p. 9). But the park is deserted—there is no one but Eban and Jennie. Eban studies the small girl carefully, "a child dressed in old fashioned clothes, a coat and gaiters and a bonnet" (p. 11). It is Jennie's strange appearance and her conversation—the references to places and people long dead but spoken of as though they were part of her present—that captures Eban's interest. The child seems to have been dropped from some distant long-forgotten world into the artist's unhappy present. As the child moves away into the darkness, she tells Eban, "I wish you'd wait for me to grow up ... but I guess you won't" (p. 14). Those last words and the chance meeting disturb the artist. When he returns to his studio, he looks at the paintings he has done, and he feels as though he has missed something—something terribly essential. Many days later, Eban sells a memory sketch he made of the child to the Matthews Art Gallery. It is a moment he has yearned for for many years—and it is Jennie who has given him that moment. From that day on, Eban becomes fixated on the child—his very existence, his emotional and creative powers become inexorably tied to the little elusive wistful creature he chanced upon in the park and whom he may never see again.

Most of the little book focuses on Jennie as a child and Eban's determination to capture her strange luminous qualities on canvas.

Jennie is a ghost. The how and why of her death (at sea in a shipwreck) are reserved for the very last chapter of the novel. The key to Nathan's work appears to be Jennie's influence on Adams's work—that without her sudden, inexplicable appearances, Adams would never have created the beauty that became the portrait of Jennie. In this novel, the ghost story is utilized to suggest a misplaced sexual drive, and art becomes the medium by which Eban externalizes, gives expression to, his inner conflict. The genre moves dramatically from depicting horror that originates outside the haunted to depict instead an inner state of mind. The sexual elements in this story are deftly camouflaged by the asexuality of the child ghost. David Punter explains the limitations of the Gothic genre with respect to psychology:

> gothic works can be complex and rich, but they will not be able to bring these qualities into the service of psychological unification ... unity is not a given property of the psyche; the mind is riven, fragmented, tortured ... the fundamental term here is taboo ... thus, surely, comes the formula of "dreadful pleasure," that pleasure which is felt when meddling with components of life ... outside the pale of "civilized discourse" [p. 410].

The novel's prototype appears to be Oscar Wilde's *The Picture of Dorian Gray*. The link between the two novels lies in how art and the artist are inseparable in depicting the underlying pathologies that drive their acts of creation. Basil Hallward, the artist who creates the portrait of Dorian Gray, explains that "every portrait that is painted with feeling is a portrait of the artist, not of the sitter" (p. 15). The passion that transposes Dorian Gray from life to art is Hallward's obsession with his subject. The form and scope of the passion that Hallward feels for Dorian is indicated in these words:

> I knew I had come face to face with someone whose mere personality was so fascinating that, if I allowed it to do so, it would absorb my whole nature, my whole soul, my very art itself" [p. 16].

The "living" Dorian Gray becomes the stationary, the fixed, and the unchangeable, and the portrait becomes the corresponding embodiment of the lad's corruption.

Nathan's book lacks the sophistication of Wilde's extraordinary imagination and prose, but his depiction of Eban Adams, the artist, parallels the obsessive qualities of Basil Hallward. Like Hallward, Adams's uneasy passion for Jennie is defined as one that both fascinates and repels:

> Caught in a mystery of good and evil, of blossom and rot—the mystery of a world which learns too late, always too late, which is the mold, and which the blossom [p. 89].

The binary oppositions, good and evil, blossom and rot, mold and blossom, are the signifiers that encompass and express the sexual tension that constitute the underpinnings of this strange story. Thus *Portrait of Jennie* transforms the Gothic ghost story into one in which the horror lies not in the haunting itself, but rather in the all too obvious sexual repression that causes the haunting to begin.

There also are several references in the novel to Lewis Carroll's *Alice in Wonderland*. Although at one point in the novel, Eban tells Jennie that "you sound like the White Queen ... the one in Alice" (p. 119), Jennie is Alice. The words *grow, growing, hurrying,* and *rushing* as they pertain to Jennie's size are peppered throughout the novel (and the film). In *A Critical History of English Literature*, David Daiches asserts that *Alice* has been analyzed and discussed for its "symbolic suggestiveness which can keep the most cunning modern analytic critic fully occupied" (p. 1086), and Eban's fascination with Jennie begins when she is a child and ends before she becomes an adult. It is of particular interest to note that when Jennie does "grow up," she is forced to die a second time. In the novel, Jennie is sent to finish her schooling in Europe. It is on her return home, ostensibly to rejoin Eban, that the ship on which she is traveling is destroyed by a hurricane. Had Jennie been able to return to Eban, she would have returned as an adult. The magic, the fascination, and the love would then assume another dimension, a dimension that would force Eban to redefine both himself and his work. The fury of nature is symbolically summoned to destroy Jennie's sexuality—the child ghost must die twice in order that she remain a child.

Art and Artists

There are two artists in the novel, Eban and his friend Arne. Eban's roots are in a small village in New England, and although he is now living in New York, his narrative constantly, almost imperatively, contrasts his past life with his bleak and joyless life in the city. Arne, however, works and lives in New England. The two artists share a love of nature and a lack of money. Eban affectionately describes Arne: "his voice, like that of an old sea captain ... his mind was a cave of winds, blowing from all corners at once, a tempest of ideas; he was in love with color; he was like a Viking gone berserk in a rainbow" (p. 91). Arne is a force of nature gone wild, and he is the outward manifestation of Eban's inner conflict. His canvases also are representative of the unpredictability, the volatility of nature gone awry, "unrestrained, wild and violent ... like scenes from an inferno" (p. 90). Arne thunderously appears at a critical point in Eban's life.

Eban had seen Jennie twice more since their first encounter in the park. It was winter and bitter cold. The large lake in the park had frozen and people were ice-skating. Eban had decided to join the skaters and suddenly, Jennie appeared carrying a pair of "round, old-fashioned skates" (p. 45). To Eban, Jennie appeared taller and a bit older. The two skated together and again Jennie spoke of places, people, and events that happened long ago. Eban told Jennie that he wanted to paint her portrait. The child was enthralled. For the first time in many years, Eban felt happy but the thought again occurred to him that "perhaps there was something strange about it; but just the same, it felt altogether right, as though we belonged just there, where we were, together" (p. 52). After she agreed to sit for Eban, Jennie disappeared into the fog. After this meeting, Eban made several memory sketches of Jennie in her skating costume, and again, the sketches were quickly sold to the Matthews Gallery.

Then Jennie made another appearance. One evening, Eban returned home to find Jennie "sitting in the old chair near the easel, prim and upright, her hands tucked away in a little muff, her toes just touching the floor. Jennie had appeared to tell Eban that she was going away to boarding school, a convent school somewhere "high in the hills." Eban asked Jennie if she could manage to pose for him before she leaves for the country. Jennie replied, "I was hoping you'd say that ... yes, I will" (p. 81). There was something in Jennie's face, a sadness, a longing that seemed to mirror Eban's own emotional state. And from that moment on, Eban "no longer thought of her as a child. She seemed to me to be of no particular age.... It was enough for me to believe that wherever in this world she actually belonged, in some way, for some reason, she belonged with me" (p. 88).

It is at this particular moment, when this odd friendship between Eban and Jennie leaps forward into obsession, that Arne makes his appearance. Arne's nature-driven persona, and his canvases that abound with violent color, "unrestrained and wild," mirror Eban's obsession. Blown in from the sea (like the ghost of Jennie), an artist who paints without form and feature, and whose vivid brush strokes emulate "scenes from an inferno," Arne's appearance and work depicts Eban's inner turmoil. Nathan returns to the Gothic "double," the psychological concept of dual natures, in order to clearly emphasize Eban's psychic division, his alienation from societal norms.

Eban's sexual pathology is particularly evident when Gus, another friend, tries to find work for Eban. Eban and Gus frequent a small bar when they have the money to pay for food and a drink. Gus, who is friendly with the owner of the bar, negotiates a bargain in which Eban will paint a mural on one of the walls in exchange for his meals. The mural Eban paints is a picnic scene that is "not unlike the lake in the park; and there, by the side of the water, under the trees, my women were gathered to tease and gossip on the grass" (p. 68). Gus notices that one of the women "looks drowned." Eban had "placed her under the trees which made her face seem dim and green with leaf-shadow; her dark hair gave the impression of being wet, and her whole body seemed shadowy with water ... it was that figure ... I imagined secretly to be Jennie—as she would be some day" (p. 70). In this mural, this painted surface, Eban has metaphorically murdered the adult Jennie and perversely buried her in an unholy place. Eban's inability to relate to Jennie's inevitable adulthood, her sexuality, is depicted in an artistic act of aggression in which the hated object is obliterated. In "Instincts and Their Vicissitudes," Freud explains this symbolic destruction: "when the object is the source of painful feelings ... we feel a repulsion from the object, and hate it; this hate can then be intensified to the point of an aggressive tendency towards the object, with the intention of destroying it" (p. 100). Eban therefore has painted Jennie twice. The portrait of Jennie, the child Jennie, sits in a respected museum, a work destined for immortality. The adult Jennie, however, one of those women who were "gathered to tease and gossip," is placed, like graffiti, on the wall of a bar. Thus does Eban utilize art in its "high" and "low" forms to depict the unfortunate little ghost.

In the film, the mural that Eban paints loses its sexual connotation and becomes a depiction of the Irish rebel Michael Collins, calling his men into battle.

Houses and Spaces

In the novel, the forces of nature are called upon to reflect Eban's conflicted sexuality; therefore, the settings, the park, the city, and the New England coast are inseparable from and essential to the plot of the story. This is a novel in which nature, both real and symbolic, assumes a major role. The settings therefore are depicted far away from the closed, contained, "civilized" world that, in the city portion of the story, exists on the edge, the periphery of Eban and Jennie's world. The two first meet in a park where "the city sounds were muted and far away" (p. 7). The city, alive and vibrant, and subject to laws and regulations, is reduced to silence in favor of the natural park setting where Eban and Jennie, man and child, can walk and talk, undisturbed, in the fading light of day.

Since the child ghost lives in spaces that have no boundaries, Eban's obsession with the small lost creature must also extend beyond any social and physically defined boundaries. The two therefore are depicted as children of the seasons, pushed and pummeled by the metaphoric fury of nature gone awry.

The final chapter, which places Eban at the edge of the world, between ocean and land, is the setting in which nature, in all its fury (the hurricane), reclaims Jennie for the last time and punishes Eban by thrusting him back into the world.

The Gothic model, in which the ghost and the haunted battle for supremacy or coexistence in confined and restricted places, shifts in this novel to allow the supernatural and the natural worlds to momentarily cease their struggle so that the ghost and the living, for whatever reason, may share a common space.

Jennie appears in Eban's studio for a second and last time. She has come to tell Eban that she is to leave, by ship, for Europe. Her education is to be completed in France. Eban and Jennie, somehow suspecting that this is the last time they will meet, spend their last remaining hours in the studio. They talk about Paris and poignantly plan for the time when they will finally be together. Suddenly, the door opens and Mrs. Jekes, Eban's landlady, bursts into the room: "oh no," she said, "oh no. Not in my house, not at night, you won't.... I've run a decent place all my life, and I mean to keep it so" Mrs. Jekes then points to Jennie and cries, "get out!" (p. 161).

This setting, inside the city and inside a dilapidated boardinghouse, is calculated to contrast the shabbiness and brutality of man against the silent vastness and mystery of nature. This moment, this savage moment, is Jennie's last and only view of the "real" world. And in response to Eban's plea, "don't listen to her," Jennie replies sadly, "it's too late now ... it's been said. It couldn't ever not be said again" (p. 162). Jennie, who has valiantly struggled against oblivion in order to regain her lost place in the world, disappears, for the last time, into the darkness.

The Film

Portrait of Jennie is a work that has translated beautifully from novel to film. The appeal of Nathan's story lies in its illusionary qualities—the fairylike child who appears and disappears in the mist and fog, the wonderful portrait of Jennie, and the terrifying hurricane. The director,

William Dieterle, lifts these elements out of the dark undercurrents that surround the story and with the help of a stellar cast (Joseph Cotten, Jennifer Jones, Ethel Barrymore, and Lillian Gish) adds an extraordinary dimension to the film that dispels any hint of sexuality in the relationship between the artist and the young Jennie. Hollywood's ever-vigilant board of censors would have disallowed any film that hinted of sexual deviance.

A prologue introduces and sets the mood of the film. It is filmed against a brooding sky and swiftly moving clouds. A voice speaks:

> Since the beginning, man has asked the eternal questions, what is time? what is space? what is death?... *Portrait of Jennie* is based on truth and hope. Time does not pass but curves around us and the past and the present are together at our side.

A quote from Euripides then appears on the screen:

> Who knoweth if to die is but to live ... and that called life by mortals be but death.

The key to the adaptation is in both the prologue and the quote that follows. The words "the past and present are together at our side," mystically spoken by a voice from the sky, almost suggest a 19th-century séance, in which a medium commands all skeptics (in this instance, the viewing audience) to suspend their disbelief in the hereafter. The mediumistic voice is emphatic in claiming that "*Portrait of Jennie* is based on truth ... that she lived and died, and that somehow, she was able to return to and communicate with the living world."

R.C. Finucane suggests in *Appearances of the Dead: A Cultural History of Ghosts* that in 1853, many Americans evinced a more than passing interest in mesmerism and spiritualism evidenced by the "claim that more than 300 'magnetic circles' in the city of Philadelphia were receiving messages from the dead." The renewed interest in spiritualism suffuses the ghost films of the 1930s and 1940s. Finucane explains why:

> the need for spiritualistic reassurance which moved so many Victorians is still with us ... ghost beliefs ... of the Victorian type continue to surface ... the great watershed of the spiritualist movement ... was the first World War and its appalling mortality ... the movement reached a peak in the 1930s. [p. 217].

This return to spiritualism is manifested by the film's depiction of multigenerational characters as they relate only to past and present. The three principal characters, Jennie, Eban, and Ms. Spinney, exist only in these two time frames. In the novel and its filmic translation, the future is an illusion, a dream that cannot be realized.

Jennie is the past; the aged Ms. Spinney is now what Jennie would have been had she lived. Thus Spinney is the key to Jennie's reappearance among the living—she is the medium by which Jennie is summoned to appear.

The opening scene of the film introduces the artist Eban Adams as he slowly walks through a park—he appears shabby, tired, and lonely. His thoughts are projected in voice-over and they express his depression: "New York is a cold place in the winter … it was no warmer in the winter of thirty-four. There is a type of suffering for the artist which is worse than any winter or poverty … it is a poverty of the mind, a dreadful feeling of the world's indifference." The city, which sits silently in the foreground, is depicted as an extension of Eban's sense of alienation. In keeping with an artist's point of view, the city is depicted as a painting, a textured canvas that is muted, faint, and unreal. There is a long black slash of a narrow bridge that stretches diagonally across the skyline. This long black line metaphorically creates a boundary between the reality of the city and the fantasy that is about to begin. The city, photographed as static art, a painting, rather than as a living active entity, creates an aura, an atmosphere that foreshadows Jennie's appearance.

The artist enters the Matthews and Spinney art gallery hoping to sell one of his pieces. He shows his ragged portfolio to Mr. Matthews, one of the owners of the gallery, who kindly but firmly disdains the artist's penchant for painting city landscapes and bridges. Ms. Spinney, Mr. Matthews's elderly partner, sits quietly, listening to the exchange between the two men. And then, just as Eban is about to leave, Spinney asks him to show her his work. She too looks through the portfolio and comments that Eban's work has "no love in them." "I'm an old maid and no one knows more about love than an old maid," but surprisingly, she offers to buy a small sketch—a vase of flowers. In gratitude, Adams tells Spinney, "You have beautiful eyes." The elderly woman stares thoughtfully at the artist as he leaves. Mr. Matthews remarks, "It's wonderful what a little compliment can do." And Spinney replies, "My first in twenty years."

Eban leaves the gallery and walks back through the park. As he moves along the snow-covered path, the city, now photographed behind him, becomes even more dreamlike and blurred. And then Jennie appears. She is a small, lovely child dressed in an old-fashioned long dark coat with an oversized wide-brimmed hat. Like Ms. Spinney, the child, who immediately introduces herself as Jennie Appleton, asks whether she can see Eban's

Portrait of Jennie: Jennie (Jennifer Jones) and Eban (Joseph Cotten) in the Park. "I wish you would wait for me to grow up," says Jennie. (Photofest)

paintings. She finds a small painting that disturbs her—a seascape with a lighthouse in the distance. Jennie grows pensive as she looks at this picture. The scene, she says, is familiar to her but she doesn't know why. Eban tells her that the picture was painted on Cape Cod in a place called Land's End. Jennie closes the portfolio and, like Spinney, suggests that Eban paint people instead of places. The child wanders away and Eban notices that she has left a small package behind—a lovely scarf wrapped in a decades-old newspaper. Eban calls after her, but she has disappeared. Eban is fascinated with the young girl: "there was something different about the child. I wondered if my pencil could capture it."

This first meeting between Jennie and Eban is taken almost intact from the novel. Jennie chatters about places and people long dead; she speaks of her parents who are high-wire artists and who are now appearing in a theater torn down long ago. And then, before she disappears into the darkness, Jennie repeats almost the same words that Nathan used in his novel, "I wish you would wait for me to grow up so we could always be together, but I guess you won't." In the novel, these words have a chilling connotation, for Jennie never moves beyond early adolescence. In the film, however, Jennie's words are utilized as a device that suggests the beginnings of a "real" love story in which romantic love will dominate. After this initial meeting, Jennie's appearances are marked by the difference in her appearance—she "ages" dramatically in each successive sequence.

The film adaptation of the novel also erases any trace of the sexually conflicted artist by using an adult (Jennifer Jones) rather than a child actress to portray Jennie. Although Jones, as the child ghost, changes from scene to scene to represent a child who grows (in cinema time) into an adult, she retains the aura of adulthood. A child actress, as was used in *Wuthering Heights* to depict the young Cathy, would have been morally unacceptable to the board of censors and would have thrust the film into the murky, sexual atmosphere of the novel.

The Medium

After seeing Jennie in the park, Eban returns to his shabby studio. He holds the child's scarf in his hands, and his thoughts return to the strange encounter in the park. He begins to sketch, and suddenly Jennie is resurrected.

Eban returns to the gallery, and again it is Mr. Matthews who greets Eban. The sketch of Jennie suddenly materializes on the screen. "What's this!" Mr. Matthews exclaims. Eban answers that it is a sketch of a little girl that he had seen in the park. "It's very good, isn't it, Ms. Spinney?... There's a quality about the girl; she reminds me of long ago." Spinney looks at the sketch and in a flat, almost amused voice, tells the artist, "Yes, I think you have something there, Adams." Mr. Matthews excitedly offers the artist twenty-five dollars for the sketch. And then Ms. Spinney asks Eban to join her for tea.

Ms. Spinney's room has a large window that faces the park. She has a lovely view of the ice pond where, in the distance, Eban can see the skaters on the ice. Spinney sits in her armchair next to the window, and as Eban watches the skaters, he tells Spinney that he's loved ice skating ever since he was a child in Maine. He then voices his doubts about his work, asking, "Of all the thousands of struggling artists, why do I think I'm one who has something worth saying?" Spinney muses, "Something about you appeals to me ... you remind me of a beau I wanted when I was young, when I was doubting myself." She then goes on to say that all Eban needs is inspiration, "someone like the girl in the park." Spinney's words seem to reassure Eban, and he decides to join the skaters in the park. He jokingly asks Spinney to come with him and "take a twirl on the ice." Spinney smiles at the suggestion and Eban leaves her sitting in her armchair by the window.

Eban is skating on the pond. The city skyscrapers form an unreal frame against which the skaters float like small, dark specks. Eban suddenly is alone; the skaters are no longer in the frame, and the large city buildings appear tilted and somehow out of balance. The camera moves to two large buildings, which stand like two huge pillars against the sky. A shaft of sunlight floats mysteriously between the two pillars, and then Jennie appears skating toward Eban. Jennie now appears as a teenager, almost full-grown. Eban's "inspiration, like the girl in the park" that Spinney had mentioned only moments before has suddenly reappeared.

Eban asks Jennie whether he can paint her portrait, and she agrees. Eban also mentions the scarf that Jennie had left behind on the park bench. Jennie looks pensive, and she tells Eban to keep the scarf for her "until she grows up." And then Jennie says that she has to leave. As she skates away, Spinney suddenly appears at Eban's side. She asks, "Looking for someone, Adams?" And Eban tells Spinney that he has just seen Jennie. The two look searchingly at the small figure that is skating toward the bright shaft of sunlight that still floats between the two huge buildings. As the girl disappears into the stream of light, Eban, in voice-over, muses that he suspects Spinney did not see Jennie.

This scene establishes the telepathic link between Jennie and Spinney. It is no coincidence that Jennie is able to materialize only moments after Eban and Spinney meet, for the encounters are similarly orchestrated throughout the film. Spinney's mediumistic ability manifests itself in scenes where she and Jennie appear and disappear almost simultaneously. The gallery itself, perched on the edge of the park and home to the elderly Spinney, juxtaposes reality, the immediate present, and illusion. Jennie is equally a manifestation of Spinney's thwarted desire and of Eban's search for inspiration. In this scene, Spinney has psychically summoned Jennie to give Eban the inspiration to continue his work and vicariously accepted his invitation to take a "twirl on the ice."

Spinney and Eban become inseparable. They go to concerts and the theater. And while Spinney enjoys her new happiness, Jennie does not appear. But with Jennie gone, Eban cannot paint. Again in voice-over, he expresses his frustration: "I needed to tell someone, and who else was

Eban (Joseph Cotten) and Spinney (Ethel Barrymore) in *Portrait of Jennie*: Spinney relives the ghost of her unfulfilled youthful dreams. (Film Stills Archive, The Museum of Modern Art, New York)

there but Spinney." The two are seen riding in a carriage in the park—Eban tells Spinney that he suspects that he is meant only to do one great work. "And that would be Jennie," Spinney replies. "I didn't realize how much you needed her. Better get that canvas ready for her." Eban returns home to find Jennie waiting for him, almost grown up and lovely in a white dress. She tells Eban that she is in her first year of college and that she is hurrying to finish growing so that Eban can marry her. That evening, Eban begins the portrait of Jennie.

The portrait is unfinished, but Eban is anxious to show it to Matthews and Spinney. Spinney and Matthews gaze in astonishment at the portrait and Spinney remarks with finality, "Well, Adams, you've found what you've been looking for." After Eban shows the unfinished portrait to Matthews and Spinney, Jennie appears for the last time. She is now full-grown, a woman, and there is a sense of finality in Jennie's demeanor—a sense of ending. Although this is the moment that Jennie has strived for in each of her previous meetings with Eban—she no longer has to ask Eban to wait for her to grow, to become an adult—there still is a sense of incompleteness, of movement that drives her. Jennie tells Eban that she must leave him one last time. She is to accompany her aunt to the New England coast for the summer. Now it is Eban who is anxious to marry Jennie, to keep her with him, but Jennie insists that this separation will be their last—that she will return to him after summer's end. Before this first and last romantic evening ends, Jennie and Eban return to Eban's studio so that he can finish the portrait. The novel and its filmic translation both disallow Jennie's adulthood—the novel centers on the artist's fixation on Jennie as a child, and the film focuses on Spinney's determination to provide Eban with artistic inspiration.

This last evening, in which Eban completes his "one great work," marks the end of Spinney's involvement with Jennie. The lessening of the telepathic communion is evident as Jennie's image is transferred to canvas. Her illusionary life force begins to diminish and dematerialize as Eban captures her essence on canvas. The camera focuses on Jennie as a fine white mist slowly surrounds her seated figure. Since Jennie's filmic image is inexorably tied to her portrait, the scene is lit from high above to give the seated Jennie an aura of liminality. With each finishing stroke of Eban's brush, the mist grows more intense and Jennie seems to fade and blur. When the portrait is completed and Jennie's essence has been captured on canvas, the transference becomes complete and Jennie falls into a deathlike sleep. Eban sees Jennie in this dreamlike state and rushes over to wake her—to bring her back. He shows her the finished portrait, and Jennie exclaims, "Oh, Eban, is it really me? I think someday it will hang in a museum and people will come from all over the world to see it." Jennie then puts on her cloak; the camera captures her as she stands alone in the darkened hallway—she is holding the scarf that she had left behind on the park bench, the one she told Eban to keep for her until she was grown. She sadly holds the scarf for one long moment and then vanishes.

The Storm

Both novel and film utilize the forces of nature metaphorically to depict emotional conflict. The novel, however, intertwines man and nature and man representing nature (the artist Arne) to capture Eban's misplaced sexuality. The film, as Angela Dalle Vacche insightfully suggests in *Cinema*

Portrait of Jennie. Jennie's spirit is captured on canvas and the telepathic link is severed. (The Theater Collection, The Free Library of Philadelphia)

and Painting, depicts nature's inexhaustible repertoire of natural phenomena so that, "the director ... underlines the entrance into a forest, or a meeting of land and water at the shoreline, precisely because his fantastic tale is about the unstable boundaries between what is real and what is imaginary" (p. 178). Dalle Vacche is discussing F.W. Murnau's "Nosferatu," but it would appear that William Dieterle has not strayed too far from Murnau's uncanny blending of the fantastic and the natural. Thus Jennie, who is an apparition in conflict with nature, and—as the film adaptation further suggests—with the church as well, is depicted in a final fatal reconfrontation with the same natural forces that had destroyed her.

Spring has passed and summer is at an end, and Jennie has not returned as she had promised. The only clue to Jennie's life is the convent where she had spent so many years. Eban decides to visit the convent, where perhaps he can find a clue to Jennie's whereabouts. Before he goes, however, he brings the portrait to the art gallery for safekeeping. He tells

Spinney and Matthews that he is going to the New England coast for a long vacation. Spinney evinces her prescience for the last time: "Paint me a little church while you're there with a big steeple ... don't get yourself drowned in the sea," she tells Eban. And to Eban's question, "Why did you say that?" Spinney replies, "I'm afraid of the ocean."

It is at the convent that Eban learns that Jennie is dead—that she died many years ago in a fearsome storm off the coast. The place where Jennie's small boat capsized is called Land's End, and the anniversary of Jennie's disappearance is only a few days away. Eban rushes to Land's End—his intent is to reconstruct Jennie's last day, to be there when the huge wave "hits the land," to rewrite Jennie's history, and to bring her back from her watery grave.

In the scene at the coast, the shoreline and the sea are shrouded in fog, and only the few characters that Eban briefly talks to are clearly delineated. The dense fog metaphorically suggests an inner blindness, an inability to penetrate the darkness and to see what lies beyond the immediate moment. Eban therefore is committed to sailing his small insignificant boat on a voyage cloaked in darkness and mystery to a place that is more dream than real. Eban has become a time traveler, one who is going backward against time and tide to effect an impossible rescue.

As Eban moves against the currents of time, he suddenly finds himself in the heart of a violent storm—his boat is thrust and then splintered as it smashes against the rocks that surround the Land's End lighthouse. The howling winds and ponderous clouds churn the sea into a maelstrom of violence. This storm scene is photographed/tinted a greenish hue—it is the first time that color is utilized in this black and white film. The color is confined to the atmosphere—the sea, the sky, and even the clouds take on this ghoulish tint. The color emphasizes the immense power of the elements and conversely accentuates the powerlessness of the man who is still symbolically photographed in black and white.

Eban shouts Jennie's name, and although the storm is at its most intense, his voice carries against the howling winds. He calls again, and suddenly the violence abates—the sky blackens, the sea smoothes and flattens into a glasslike surface, and Jennie's tiny boat glides on the mirror-like surface toward Eban. She reaches the rocks, and Eban tries to pull her up and out of the sea. But Jennie refuses to be saved. She tells Eban that "time has made an error," and that although they will be denied a present or future, they will have eternity. As she speaks, Eban sees the huge mountainous wave lift from the depths of the ocean—it moves swiftly and mercilessly toward them. Eban tries one last time to save Jennie, but the wave crashes against the rocks and Jennie disappears for the last time into the sea.

Eban has miraculously and mysteriously returned to the shore. The great storm in which he failed to save Jennie appears to have been a squall that destroyed his boat and tossed him onto the rocks of the lighthouse. Bruised and defeated, Eban lies in bed, and Spinney sits quietly by his side and listens as he tells her about the storm and Jennie. As he speaks, his grief overwhelms him—he now knows that Jennie will never reappear, that he has lost her forever. And then he sees Spinney holding Jennie's scarf. To Eban, the scarf is a personal triumph. Its reappearance provides testimony that Jennie really existed, that he hadn't imagined her, and that for a short extraordinary time, she and Eban were together. But for Spinney, who silently and stoically sits next to Eban, the scarf has come home.

The last scene of the film takes place in the Metropolitan Museum. A group of young girls cluster around the portrait of Jennie. "How beautiful she is," one girl remarks, and then Spinney suddenly appears. She and the girls stare at the portrait, which is photographed in full vibrant color. The camera lingers on the lovely painting and Jennie is heard, in voice-over, exclaiming, "Oh, Eban, is it really me?" The portrait and the final film credits are in color—the color of the setting sun. The sky is again depicted on screen, but now it is calm and serene. The conflict is over.

The film narrative pretends to a circularity in which, as the prologue suggests, "Time does not pass but curves around us and the past and the present are together at our side." This interpretation of the mutability of time and space no longer separates the living from the dead or the dead from the living; it guarantees a continuity of life in one form or another and in one place or another. Jennie existed and then she did not. Art, in the form of a talented artist and a determined telepathic art dealer, was the catalyst for Jennie's return. The portrait of Jennie, therefore, is the evidence of her short reentry into a living sphere where she inspires Eban Adams to create his one and only masterpiece.

* * *

The novel and film use Jennie badly—in the novel, she is the object of a sexually conflicted artist, and in the film, her peace is disturbed by an elderly woman who discovers love too late and needs the child/woman Jennie to fulfill her thwarted desires. In both novel and film, Jennie must die twice in order to fulfill the desires of these earthly taskmasters; however, this small spirit appears to be more than equal to the task.

Portrait of Jennie, both novel and film, presents a notable shift from the Gothic depiction of the ghost and the haunted in that both have lost the color, the intensity, and the power of their Gothic predecessors. Eban, the mid-century haunted, is an amorphous creature, more ghost than man. He collapses the image of the Gothic haunted, personified by the likes of Heathcliff and the more temperate Daniel Gregg, by his dreamlike, colorless, and nondescript appearance and attitude. He has no history and no home, and he never exhibits a violent, exaggerated display of emotion. He is less alive than Jennie, whose efforts to "grow and grow up" evince a determination of will that mocks the ineffectual introverted man. Introversion and introspection are the antithesis of the Gothic, which relies on fire and brimstone for both its verbal and physical effects. In *Jennie*, only the sea storm provides the sense of physical and psychical power that is now lost to man and ghost.

Eban and Jennie are now in a city, and their encounters smack of the physical and emotional boundaries imposed by an ever-watchful society. Ms. Spinney, however, lives comfortably and respectably in society while Eban and Jennie furtively meet in parks and in Eban's shoddy, shabby studio. In both novel and film, death becomes a metaphor for dealing with everyday existence, and Eban's dislocation, his separation and alienation from society, sets the stage for his interaction with and his love of/for death.

The film splits the ghostly power base in two, with Jennie and Ms. Spinney sharing equal time and equal status. Ms. Spinney is the catalyst that allows Jennie to interact with Eban, and the combined power of the two women even further neutralizes and diminishes the image of the haunted. The sole survivor of this triumvirate of art, life, and death is Ms. Spinney. Eban disappears from both novel and film when Jennie disappears back into the sea. Only Ms. Spinney remains—and the Portrait of Jennie.

CHAPTER FOUR

Letter from an Unknown Woman

a novella by STEFAN ZWEIG
a film by MAX OPHULS

If we consider the ghost story to be a living genre, then the concept of possession must be fluid enough to allow haunting to occur on levels far broader and subtler than the ghosts of Gothic literature. Gothic and Romantic ghost stories portray both living and dead as palpable forces. The Gothic particularly depicts life in its extreme—exaggerated, violent, and chaotic. The characters teem with emotion and the settings are charged with the combined forces of nature and man. The Gothic is a genre in which all passion, all emotion is externalized. The Romantic ghost stories and films place both living and dead in recognizable settings—the ghost assumes human form, has the power to love, and lives side by side with its human counterparts.

Letter from an Unknown Woman is a ghost story of another kind. It is a story that is not quite a story. The two characters are nameless; the writer of the letter, a woman, relates the history of her obsessive and desperate love to a man who is nameless, voiceless, and uncaring. What also sets *Letter* apart from its Gothic and Romantic predecessors is its form. In contrast to the novels under discussion, *Letter* is a novella, a short story, a form in which atmosphere and mood supplant the subject. In *The Theory of the Novel*, Georg Lukács describes the short story as

> the most purely artistic form; it expresses the ultimate meaning of all artistic creation as *mood* ... it is rendered abstract for that very reason ... it sees absurdity in all its undisguised and unadorned nakedness ... meaninglessness as *meaninglessness* becomes form [p. 51].

This description of the short story also perfectly describes Zweig's novella and the film adaptation, because both reader and viewer are presented with an unresolved antagonism whose only significance derives from the mood it evokes. The ghost story takes a dramatic turn in *Letter* by creating an atmosphere of haunting in which both ghost and haunted are metaphorically absent. *Letter* shatters the formulaic Gothic and Romantic ghost story by compressing both haunter and haunted into a spiritual and physical void.

The letter is the protagonist of the story, and it serves as the psychological surrogate for both writer and reader. In his essay "What Is an Author," Michel Foucault describes the symbolic absence of the writer:

> The essential basis of writing ... is primarily concerned with creating an opening where the writing subject endlessly disappears ... it is the kinship between writing and death ... writing is now linked to sacrifice and to the sacrifice itself [pp. 116, 117].

Because the subject, the writer of the letter, shades into a ghostly realm and never has a recognizable or substantiated presence, Foucault's and Lukács's theories of mood supplanting and displacing both subject and story indicate a ghost story liberated from the Gothic constraints of time and place. The woman is a free-floating apparition, as dedicated to her obsession as any of her Gothic predecessors; however, the Gothic notion of opposing forces, of active tension between the subject and object (the woman and her lover), disappears. What remains is the essence of the writer and the essence of the lover, a ghost story in its most disturbing and abstract form.

The Story

What is it that makes *Letter from an Unknown Woman* a ghost story? Perhaps it is the opening lines of the narrative:

> if you hold it [the letter] in your hands you will know that a dead woman is telling you the story of her life; the life that was yours all her waking hours [p. 218].

The woman begins her narrative by imparting some particularly devastating information:

> My child died today. For three days and nights I struggled with death over this small, fragile life ... he was your child too ... my child—ours—lies here

dead beneath the flickering candles ... don't be afraid of my words. A dead woman no longer wants anything—not love, or pity, or comforting words. There is only one thing I ask of you and that is to believe everything I tell you, everything the pain that flies from me to you reveals [p. 218].

The four words that begin the woman's story immediately set the tone of the narrative. The words evoke an uneasy atmosphere for the reader. The ambiguity of the words "my child" causes him to pause for a moment, to wonder whether this letter is meant for him or for some other. But then curiosity compels him to move on, to follow this opening thread to its conclusion. The relationship between the woman and the reader is paradoxical from the onset because the woman maintains that it is her child who has died, and the following words hesitate, "my child—ours—," before she reluctantly makes her final fatal proclamation. But once the woman identifies R as the father of her child, her narrative assumes the frantic tone of an abandoned hysterical woman. In relating the story of her involvement with the reader, the woman weaves in and out of past and present. Her tenuous link with R encompasses many years, and in her narrative, she compresses those years into one disjointed disconnected diatribe in which time becomes an abstract, as elusive and indefinable as the woman herself. Time has been the woman's enemy; it has not resolved her difficulties, it has enhanced them. And now, it has robbed her of her one reality, her son. Time, in both story and film, is manipulated to provoke memory, to abolish reality, and to allow this ghostly writer to move freely from past to present, and present to past, in order to force her solipsistic lover into remembering her.

The letter is unsigned. If the time/memory device fails, then R will never know more of this nameless and faceless apparition (and his dead child) than the fiction she has created in her letter of "a half-dozen pages." The woman will disappear; the man will continue; and the issues raised in the letter will be unresolved.

States of Mind: The Psychology of Namelessness

Like the novel *Portrait of Jennie*, which I have suggested has its prototype in Oscar Wilde's novel, *The Picture of Dorian Gray*, *Letter* also its underpinnings in another literary source. In *Notes from Underground*, Fyodor Dostoevsky gives an uncanny and disturbingly brilliant literary depiction of an obsessed and angry man. Framed within a monologic form, Dostoevsky presents an unseen and unnamed narrator, hidden beneath the floorboards of a house, who shouts and rants to an uncaring and unseen audience his perception of all the injustices and all the indignities of a life and a society gone awry. Richard Pevear, in the foreword to his translation of the novel, describes the hidden man:

> the nameless hero ... is not a professional man of letters ... but one whom circumstances have led or forced to take up the pen, to try to fix something in words, for his own sake first of all, but also with an eye for some indeterminate *others* [p. vii].

Both Zweig and Dostoevsky present a story in which their subjects evince such a cataclysmic display of emotion and despair that their collective efforts to consolidate their fragmented thoughts and emotions on paper culminate in an irrational self-accusatory diatribe. The act of writing, to both the woman and the underground man, is an effort to externalize their passion, to move from an inactive state to an active one. Zweig's letter writer "takes up the pen" in a final effort to gain recognition, and for a few minutes, the letter fulfills her expectations. The woman, therefore, has created a paper ghost in which she transforms her nonexistence into pages and pages of white cold paper.

The link between the two works is also evidenced by the anonymity of the two protagonists—"underground" and "unknown" are how they are described (one recalls Heathcliff in *Wuthering Heights*, who, at first, is also nameless—he is called "it" when he is first brought to the Earnshaws). Because the underground man and the unknown woman are never identified, their existence, their reality is thrust into a larger dimension. They both become the literary embodiment of passion carried to its extreme. The key appellations, "underground," "unnamed," and "it," are telling in that these words lend themselves far beyond their literary constructs to characterize the hidden emotions that are part and parcel of the human psyche. In *Stefan Zweig: A Critical Biography*, Elizabeth Allday describes how Zweig constructed the story to reflect the intensity of these emotions:

> the story is presented through the medium of the feminine first person.... Zweig moves the pen of a woman recalling her infatuation for an adored and thoughtless lover, who reads with growing horror of the dire results of his passion, ending with the death of a son he never knew. Zweig allows the woman full emotional rein in this, her first and last letter to her lover ... she swings from hasty recrimination to declarations of passion, feverish fantasy, and a pathetic jumble of irrelevant reminiscences which end in a denunciation of God [pp. 180, 181].

Allday's description of Zweig's story indicates how closely *Letter* mirrors

Dostoevsky's *Notes from Underground*. Both works share a displacement of subject and an unspecified audience; these stories also evoke a mood, an atmosphere in which disillusionment is mingled with hysteria and despair. And both stories end unresolved.

Zweig's R, the recipient of the letter, is introduced as a man of forty-one, a celebrated writer, who has just returned from a restful holiday in the mountains. His manservant brings him his tea and his mail. This is the only information that Zweig gives his audience. It is the woman's letter, her own fiction, that describes and defines him. We see him through her—without her, he has no intrinsic meaning. The film adaptation is faithful to Zweig's ambiguous description of the man by allowing Lisa's letter to give form and substance to this ghostly lover. Zweig, however, does use the initial R to identify the man.

"R" has an obvious Freudian connotation. R is, first and foremost, the (R)eader of the woman's letter. In the Freudian context "R" identifies the reader as (R)epressed, (R)estrained, and incapable of (R)emembering any person who exists outside the cerebral sphere of intellectual/rational pursuits. He stands as the polar opposite of the woman who has devoted her life to him. There is a peculiar unity that exists between the woman and her lover that is evinced in the singularity of the passion and *ennui* that define them. Both are one-dimensional characters—the one whose passion subsumes all sense of reality and all sense of community, and the other (R) who cannot sustain any passion beyond the momentary immediate experience. They (the woman and R) are two disparate forces equally intense in their commitment either to a passion or to a lack of passion, and it is this terrible irreconcilable contrast that culminates in the letter R receives.

The woman writes that her love began when she was only thirteen years old—when the writer moved into the building where she and her mother lived. She describes what she imagined the writer to be (an elderly man) and what she actually saw:

> I had imagined a bespectacled, kindly, old man, and then you appeared— you, exactly as you still are today, unchangeable ... you carried your hat in your hand so I was able to see, with amazement ... your open lively face and your youthful hair ... how young, how handsome, how willow-slim and elegant you were [p. 221].

Many of Zweig's stories deal with the adolescent's sexual and social estrangement from the adult world. Zweig's literary children are depicted as conflicted, alienated, and impotent in their efforts to understand the complex world of the adult. The adolescent, in Zweig's view, is forced to take comfort in a world of imagination and fantasy. The child/woman's description of her soon-to-be neighbor is a mixture of fantasy and reality. Reality would have been the kindly fatherly figure that the young girl so desperately misses (her father is dead); fantasy is the young handsome writer who appears in his stead. Either figure would have been embraced by the lonely young girl, but the writer more so—famous, handsome, unmarried, he is a fairy-tale figure, a prince in disguise.

The obsession that is the underpinning of *Portrait of Jennie*, the sexual obsession of man for child, shifts in *Letter* to that of child for adult. Both are unacceptable and unrealistic, but in both stories, it is the child who drives the narrative and creates the obsession. Because the woman's obsession is clearly grounded in childhood, she chooses to contrast the depth of a child's love with that of the unfeeling adult:

> Nothing on earth equals the unseen, hidden love of a child ... so servile, so submissive, so observant and intense, as the covetous and unconsciously demanding love of a grown woman never is [p. 123].

The words that describe the child's love: unseen, hidden, servile, and submissive, indicate the child's tentative furtive move toward sexuality. They indicate and characterize the woman as she was when she first saw R, and as she still is. Like Heathcliff in *Wuthering Heights,* the memory of the child's love continues through the rest of her short life with the same singular passion. The ensuing years sit heavily on her shoulders, but her fantasy (like Heathcliff and his love for Cathy) remains irrevocably bound in the realm of childhood.

The woman's description of her lover, his home, and the books he has written (and she has painstakingly read), are detailed and precise, but she reinforces her anonymity by her generalized and disturbing negation of the female image:

> a girl's or a woman's face must be extraordinarily changeable for a man, because it is mostly a mirror ... it is gone as quickly as a reflection in a glass ... a man can easily forget a woman's face because her age changes with the light and shade, and her clothes provide a different setting from one occasion to the next [p. 232].

In keeping with Foucault's theory of the disappearing subject, this passage serves to vaporize the letter writer's identity.

A Society of Exclusion

The story also reflects a segmented societal structure in which a great deal of the woman's seemingly deferential literary posturing can be attributed to her lack of social standing in the restricted society of "1900 Vienna":

> when you came into my life I was thirteen years old. You will certainly not remember us at all, the poor widow of an accountant ... and the thin, half-grown child immersed in our petty-bourgeois poverty ... perhaps you never heard our name ... we had no name plate on our door [p. 218].

Given the obvious wealth and fame of the writer R, the then child is overwhelmed by the physical ornamentations of a world that she knows exists but that she cannot enter (the film enhances this theme of social exclusion by depicting the girl (and later the woman) frequently hidden behind half-open doors as she waits to catch a glimpse of R). Indeed, this concept of exclusion remains a recurring theme throughout the story. The child shies away and draws back from any overt physical/social contact with the writer, thus indicating a prescribed "distance," a social threshold that the child/woman is instinctively aware that she cannot cross. This very same concept of social exclusion is also present in Emily Brontë's *Wuthering Heights* when Heathcliff (when he is quite young) is refused entry into the hallowed halls of Thrushcross Grange. Heathcliff's "status," his social nonexistence, is reiterated and reconfirmed by the physical and emotional deterioration of the inhabitants of Wuthering Heights (after Heathcliff takes possession) and of the house itself. The raw emotion, the singular destructive passion, that consumes Heathcliff (and the unknown woman) passes far beyond the confines of society—Heathcliff (after Cathy's death) becomes more beast than man, and the unknown woman spirals downward from respectability to social obscurity and to prostitution because she has obsessively devoted her life to the pursuit of an elusive and forgetful lover.

Setting

The woman has no home. There is no setting, no place that describes or defines her. She describes in detail only two physical settings. The first is the charity hospital where she gives birth to her son:

> I had to go to the maternity hospital. The child, your child, was born there—in the midst of the squalor of penury—where only the very poor, the outcast, and the forgotten drag themselves in their need ... it was a deadly place [p. 238].

And from R's home she has consigned every room, every detail, every furnishing, and every book to memory:

> I stood at the door to marvel at everything, for all your things were so very different from anything I had ever seen ... there were Indian idols; pieces of Italian sculpture; large pictures in dazzling colours; and then, finally came the books, so many and so beautiful, I wouldn't have believed it possible [p. 220].

This description of R's furnishings is reminiscent of Lucy Muir's description of Cap'n Gregg's house and his "relics." Like Cap'n Gregg's possessions, which smack of an exoticism, of a time long since passed, and which immediately fuel Lucy Muir's attachment to Gull Cottage (and its owner), so too are R's possessions descriptive of the opulence of old Vienna. There is enough fascination in the child's first view of this unusual establishment to generate and cement a lifelong obsession with the owner of all this beauty.

In contrast to the woman's lack of place, the writer R is depicted as living in serene comfort, and when the letter arrives, he settles in to read it in the security of his well-ordered home:

> his manservant ... brought him the accumulated post on a tray ... meanwhile tea had been brought. He leaned back comfortably in his armchair ... then lit a cigar and picked up the letter he had set aside [p. 216].

But the woman writes her last words in an undisclosed place alone with her dead child and "four candles—one at each corner of the bed ... and ... the fifth candle ... here on the table on which I am writing to you." The end of her letter indicates the end of her life—there is no postscript, no intervening hand to indicate the final resting place of the woman and her child (although in the film, Max Ophuls adds a postscript to the letter written by a nun who witnesses the woman's final moments). This contrast between Zweig's depiction of the comfortably situated, physically cared for gentleman and the homeless, transient, broken woman lends further credence to what David Turner calls the "spiritual isolation from the cosmic order" (p. 211).

Retribution

T.J. Lustig writes that "there is a very strong tradition for which, rather than representing crisis, chaos, and transgression (or indeed more interestingly, precisely *because* they represent crisis, chaos and transgression) ghosts preserve and sustain structure" (p. 24). This premise may well be valid in Zweig's story, since the letter serves to *shift* the balance of power from the man to the woman. All the indignities, humiliation, and loss move onto the reader R as the woman elaborates on the physical, moral, and social pain that her devotion has exacted. The imbalance of suffering corrects itself as it moves from the dead onto the living. The letter also serves as a moral catalyst in which memory and honor are prodded into a fleeting existence (in the film, the profligate lover goes off to fight a duel that he cannot win). The letter ghost extracts her justice by forcing a failed moral conscience to read and acknowledge that he has caused the death of his only son.

The Film

The film adaptation was written by Howard Koch, who felt that Stefan Zweig's story would be difficult to adapt to film. The story, he says in "Script to Screen with Max Ophuls,"

> was entirely subjective with only fragmentary incidents ... it was in the highly charged romantic tradition of Vienna at the turn of the century—definitely not the kind of story that Hollywood did well. I foresaw the danger of sentimentality, a so-called "woman's picture" awash with tears. Then I thought of Max Ophuls.

The film has been analyzed, discussed, and applauded *because* of Max Ophuls. Under his direction, the film loses the frantic Dostoevskian voice and adopts a softer, more reflective tone. The unknown woman, touchingly played by Joan Fontaine, speaks her letter to her lover and to the viewing audience. The adaptation removes the psychological and physical distance that Zweig imposed upon his protagonists by giving form and feature to the unknown woman and by visually connecting the lovers in flashback sequences. The woman and the man visually float between past and present in scenes so beautifully drawn and executed that the woman's misplaced passion becomes almost believable and the man's indifference almost forgivable. The extremes of emotion permeate the film but they are gently maneuvered to evoke a remarkably *intimate* and detailed portrait of a tragic woman, a ghost who has come back to tell her story.

In the film adaptation, the celebrated writer R becomes Stefan Brand, a famous pianist. His manservant, John (who appears only briefly in Zweig's story), becomes an almost constant (and necessary) presence in the letter's narrative, and the unknown woman is given a name, Lisa Berndle. The film begins with Stefan (Louis Jordan) receiving Lisa's letter immediately after he is challenged to a duel (supposedly by an irate husband). He begins reading the letter as he prepares to leave Vienna to avoid

The letter is the ghost of Lisa Berndle. Louis Jourdan in *Letter from an Unknown Woman*. (Film Stills Archive, The Museum of Modern Art, New York)

the confrontation but, as he becomes more and more absorbed in Lisa's ghostly narrative, he forgets the time and the film ends with Stefan keeping his appointment with death.

Bringing a Ghostly Narrative to the Screen

In keeping with the spirit of Zweig's story, the film concentrates on creating mood and atmosphere. Therefore, Lisa's narrative becomes the primary vehicle by which the illusion, the unreality, of the story is maintained. Therefore, the flashback sequences, the visual depiction of Lisa and Stefan, contain a minimum of dialogue. Simple short sentences (or equally simple anecdotes) are spoken at strategic moments to emphasize and reinforce the voice-over narrative that is the linchpin of each scene. Like the ancient Greek chorus in which voices provide an almost religious or moral commentary on the unfolding events, Ophuls's extraordinary "moving camera" becomes the voyeuristic all-seeing eye that reinforces Lisa's ghostly documentary. Since Lisa narrates her own story, she is visually depicted (as child and as adult) through flashbacks. And as her narrative (in voice-over) begins to fade and blur into an actual sequence, her on-screen dialogue is minimized to suggest her momentary resurrection among the living. Her only sustained lines are to Stefan (her lover) and to Stefan (their son); otherwise she moves and speaks throughout the film as a ghostly apparition—distant and removed. On the two occasions in which Stefan and Lisa are together, Stefan's dialogue is confined to the platitude, a device that affirms the shallowness of his character. The dialogue in the restaurant is a fine example of Lisa's reticence and Stefan's superficiality. Stefan has ordered wine:

>STEFAN: Do you like it?
>LISA: Yes.
>STEFAN: It's Valpolicella. The Italians say that it's such a good wine because the grapes have their roots in the valley and their eyes on the mountains.

This small anecdote serves as a metaphor for the distance that will always divide the two. The mountain metaphor also foreshadows Lisa's fall from grace. In the film's crucial Prater sequence Lisa asks Stefan about his love for mountain climbing: "When you climb a mountain, what then?" she asks. Stefan responds, "You come down again." In short, concise, seemingly frivolous dialogue, Ophuls and Koch depict Lisa's tragedy.

Because the story is told from Lisa's perspective, Ophuls organized each segment, each frame to visually recreate Lisa and each meeting with Stefan as she remembers them. Since memory-driven narratives are completely subjective, what the viewer sees and hears is Lisa's idealized version of her short and tragic affair. One subtlety that is added to the adaptation is Lisa's oblique reference to her identity. In contrast to the story, in which the woman is the disappearing subject, Ophuls inserts a small set of sequences in which Lisa is identified. Because this is Lisa's narrative, the scenes suggest that she is insisting on an identity, that it is only Stefan who fails to remember her. Therefore, in Lisa's recollection of her love affair, she is *known* and remembered (by everyone except Stefan) and her lover assumes the reverse role of having to identify himself. Since Stefan is a renowned musician, Lisa confines Stefan's search for recognition to her particular sphere of reference—the house in which both she and Stefan lived. In each scene in which Stefan enters this building, a distant voice calls out, "Who is it?" and Stefan answers, "Brand." Lisa however, is always admitted without having to identify herself. In one particular scene she runs away from the train station (and her parents) in order to return to Stefan. She stands at the gate, rings the bell, and the concierge greets her with "Oh, Lisa, it's you!" These scenes, in which Stefan must give his name when he enters his building, serve as a reminder that Stefan's identity (as it is firmly entrenched in the house where Lisa first saw him) is entirely dependent on Lisa's point of view.

Time: Only the Present Counts

The concept of time, of past, present, and future, plays a significant role in Zweig's story and its filmic adaptation. To Zweig and Ophuls, time is the ultimate corrupter in which the promise and desires of childhood and adolescence ultimately give way to the ache of reality. The doubling of time and death and love and death are integral to the story of the unknown woman. Zweig creates a circular narrative that begins with the child's death—"My child died today"—and ends with the woman's death. Ophuls follows Zweig's lead but softens Lisa's opening lines: "by the time you read this I will be dead." These lines are equally disturbing, but they gently ease the viewer into Lisa's story and create the atmosphere, the illusion that drives the adaptation. Because death begins the narrative (in story and film), all concept of time, like life, is nonexistent. Ophuls encodes all reference to time in repetitive phrases and scenes that signal (to the viewer) that shortly Lisa will experience another loss. One of these phrases is "two weeks, two weeks," repeated each time someone leaves Lisa to travel outside her sphere of consciousness.

The first person who speaks these words is Lisa's stepfather, and they serve to foreshadow other travel sequences in which Lisa will experience a loss. The words are spoken at a train station that will take Lisa away from Vienna to Linz. Lisa stands alone at the edge of a counter listening and watching while her newly married parents maneuver the mountain of baggage that must be sent on to their new home. "How long if we send these third class?" asks Lisa's new father. "Two weeks, two weeks," replies the stationmaster. "Two weeks then," agrees the father, and the luggage is sent on. Like a tolling bell, these words reverberate throughout the film in order to connote a final irrevocable departure.

This train sequence foreshadows a later scene in which Lisa sends her small son Stefan back to school and to his death. Unaware that the train compartment she and the small boy have chosen for the trip is infected with typhus, Lisa and the boy sit together and say their farewells. "Two weeks, Mother, I'll see you in two weeks" are the words that drift back toward Lisa as she uneasily waves goodbye to the small Stefan.

Ophuls utilizes train and travel as a metaphor for death and desertion. Both Stefans, father and son, journey by train only to disappear from Lisa's life. And as they say their goodbyes to Lisa, they echo the prophetic "two weeks, I'll see you in two weeks." In both instances, father and son do not return. In the film, the train is a vehicle of death, a conveyance that carries people from the safe and the familiar to some unknown destination. In the film both Lisa and her son have been infected with typhus. Her death follows some days after his and before Stefan, Sr., receives the letter.

The absence of time, specifically the concept of future time, is encoded in a small but significant scene that centers on the word *tomorrow*. When Lisa and Stefan finally spend their only evening (and night) together, Stefan walks into the corner café to leave instructions with the manager to cancel his prearranged appointments for that same evening. As he is about to leave the café, Stefan is stopped by a small dark man who pleads with Stefan to look at a piece of music. Stefan impatiently dismisses the intruder by telling him to "send it to me, I'll look at it tomorrow." As Stefan and Lisa leave the café, the intruder fades from the scene, but as he disappears from the frame, he repeats the word "tomorrow," which then echoes and hovers about the departing couple. This fleeting, and seemingly inconsequential, intrusion is strategically placed and its meaning is abundantly clear. For Stefan and Lisa there is no tomorrow nor will there ever be. The small, dark man is a timekeeper, a human clock, whose disappointed echo "tomorrow" indicates that it is the moment, the now that is the essence of this small history. And because this timekeeper ostensibly addresses himself only to Stefan, he indicates Stefan's monumental flaw—that he cannot see beyond the present moment.

It is interesting to note that Stefan (in Lisa's point of view) *emerges* in the film (and story) as a finished product, full-grown and established. And where Lisa indicates a past (the childhood scenes), Stefan has none. Only once does he refer to himself in a time frame other than the present—he explains to Lisa that he was once considered a child prodigy and that he is no longer "prodigious"—a child who never fulfilled his promise. The death of his own child Stefan is perhaps metaphorically representative of the death of potential and the nonexistent future.

The Orphic Myth Revisited

John, Stefan's manservant, is mute, and in his inability to speak, he doubles Lisa's self-inflicted silence. Physically bound to silence, he, like

Lisa, can communicate only by writing (in answer to the mover's question, "where do these go?" he writes his answer on a pad of paper while Lisa watches—a foreshadowing of her eventual letter). And in the last scene of the film, after Stefan has finished the letter, it is John who identifies Lisa by writing her name on a slip of paper. In his essay "Max Ophuls' Letter from an Unknown Woman," George Wilson suggests that by writing Lisa's name (in answer to Stefan's astonished, "you knew her!"), John signs the unsigned letter.

In contrast to the shy, reticent Lisa and his mute manservant, Stefan Brand is permitted a vast spectrum of expression—he is a renowned musician and his audience is all Europe. He is a womanizer and his successes depend (in part) on his ability to charm and seduce his victims. The gifts of music, charm, and grace are what define him and place him in opposition to the silent, worshipful watchfulness of Lisa and John.

One cannot help but compare this character to the legendary Orpheus who, as Mark P.O. Morford and Robert J. Lenardon claim, "represents the tradition for the tragic story of music, enchantment, love, and death that has been re-created again and again with imagination, beauty, and profundity whether it be in an opera or in a movie" (p. 287). Orphic motifs abound in the film beginning with Lisa's fascination with Stefan's music. His artistry, his music is the underpinning of Lisa's emotional involvement. And in the scene in which Stefan plays the piano for Lisa (their one evening together), a music stand in the shape of a lyre (the Orphic lyre) is strategically placed directly in front of the piano. The lyre is kept in full view as Stefan plays and Lisa rapturously listens. The lyre was introduced in the beginning of the film when Stefan moved into Lisa's apartment building. The continuity script for the film indicates that "in the opening scene, the man is lifting a large antique lyre ... the man moves forward ... removing the lyre from the truck" (p. 36). As the ultimate enchanter, Stefan's mystical power over Lisa is manifested and then maintained through the magic of his music.

In contrast, Lisa and John exist on the periphery of Stefan Brand's radiant world—their silence is significant because it connotes the nonrole they play in Stefan's world. Bereft of speech (or any creative expression), they can evince only a silent animal-like devotion to the famous musician. As David Turner explains:

> The heroine repeatedly describes herself waiting for long periods of time at the door of her apartment, lying on the floor, or outside the house of her adored young writer, in search of a glimpse of him. Again the scene is a metaphor of exclusion, but one which [recalls] the position of a loyal dog awaiting its master [p. 209].

The magic of music. Joan Fontaine as Lisa and Louis Jourdan as Stefan in *Letter from an Unknown Woman*. (Film Stills Archive, The Museum of Modern Art, New York)

The musician's fall from grace is documented in the opera scene where Lisa and Stefan meet after a lapse of almost ten years. When Stefan tries in vain to remember where he has seen Lisa before, he admits that he cannot have seen her at one of his concerts because he no longer gives concerts. And when Lisa goes to Stefan's apartment for the very last time, she finds that the piano has been locked. Stefan has now been transformed from someone who possessed the ability to charm the soul and delight the ear, to one who is merely a seducer of women (not unlike Miles Fairley in *The Ghost and Mrs. Muir*). The music is gone, and as Lisa shortly discovers, so are her illusions—Stefan does not, cannot remember her. It is precisely at this point, when Stefan admits that he too has become silent, that the balance of power shifts and begins to rest equally between the three protagonists. Lisa fatally implicates Stefan in her deathbed confession, while John, as the sole mute survivor of the tale, holds the keys to the now silent piano in his pocket. The ghostly silence that has always defined Lisa and John now surrounds all the players, and silence is all that remains.

Since many of Zweig's novellas are concerned with the adolescent and the uneasy sexual transition from childhood to adult, the Prater sequence (which culminates in the first and only night Lisa spends with Stefan) is a unique scene in which the adult Lisa is depicted in the hesitant state between childhood and the threshold of sexuality. In the tiny pseudo train compartment, where Lisa and Stefan take their only (pretend) journey together, Lisa assumes a childlike persona and Stefan reinforces Lisa's tentative step backward by telling the "stationmaster" that "we are going to revisit the scenes of our youth." This stationary train trip, this fantasy of movement, coupled with Lisa's reminiscences of her "pretend" travels with her father, indicates her momentary reluctance to relinquish a remembered time for an uncertain unknown experience. It is of interest to note that although this is the only train sequence that does not appear to end tragically, the train maintains its aura of death. As Lisa and Stefan "travel," Lisa remarks that her "real" father was also a pretend traveler who enchanted her with his nightly question, "So where would you like to go tonight?" Her father's only "real" voyage was his final one, his death. In this context, this pretend trip foreshadows Lisa's death and the death of her son.

This scene in the Prater (like the outdoor park scenes in *Portrait of Jennie*) is conspicuous in its strange atmosphere of dueling worlds—the conflict of childhood and the onset of sexuality embedded in a dreamlike carnival sequence (although it is winter, there are vendors selling candy apples and taffy to a nonexistent crowd of children; Lisa is the one child who buys an apple). The pretend train in which Stefan and Lisa travel also indicates the disparate worlds that Lisa now inhabits. Her ghostliness, her physical death, now allows her to replay her past. And her happiest time was/is her childhood. She writes of the Prater and of the train trip with the eye of a child. And in this magical moment she has created, Stefan becomes the magical lover she has dreamed of—attentive and caring; enchanted, bewitched, and enthralled with the elusive childlike Lisa.

Setting

The settings are also predicated on Lisa's recollection (as they are in Zweig's story). Stefan's apartment is depicted as exotic and sumptuous—his rooms (the ones that Lisa and the viewer sees) are filled with paintings, tiny statues, wonderful carpets, and memorabilia from his concerts.

His piano occupies a large sunfilled space—it is the core, the heartbeat of Lisa's obsession. In contrast to Stefan's apartment, Lisa's own living quarters (in the same house) are drab and ordinary and they are visible only in the early scenes of the film. The last time Lisa's apartment is seen is when the family prepares for their move to Linz and Lisa frantically rushes back to try to find Stefan. Her apartment is empty; all vestiges of her past and her identity are gone. Lisa wanders through the empty rooms and speaks through her narrative. "These rooms where I lived had been filled with your music. Now they are empty. Would they ever come alive again? Would I?" The stark, empty rooms serve to emphasize Lisa's lost identity, her despair, and her own sense of emptiness and loss.

Retribution and Judgment

In Zweig's story, the letter shifts the balance of power from the man onto the woman, and the letter becomes the means by which the woman recounts in painful detail all the indignities and loss she has endured. There is no resolution to Zweig's story. The writer R struggles vainly to remember something of the woman he has wronged. He cannot. "Shadows flitted to and fro, yet no picture formed. He felt recollections of emotion, but still he didn't remember" (p. 250).

The film adaptation remains faithful to the original story in that John (Stefan's manservant) is the only person who remembers Lisa. The film depicts Stefan grasping at remnants of recollection. Tiny images begin to emerge as Ophuls utilizes faded blurry flashbacks of Lisa in the Prater sequence and finally, of Lisa as a child, hiding behind an open door and smiling at Stefan as he walks away. In the film, Stefan remembers the woman, but it is John who gives Lisa a name.

But where the novella argues for an eternal distance between the two protagonists, the film suggests that the distance has been bridged. Their indiscretions (Lisa's illegitimate child and Stefan's profligacy) demand a collective judgment and resolution. The opening scene of the film, which introduces Stefan before he receives the letter, tells the viewer that he has been challenged to a duel. As Stefan enters his apartment, he is prepared to flee the country. But as he begins to read Lisa's letter, he forgets the time. This time, Stefan's forgetfulness will cost him his life. His own flaw, forgetfulness, is his final judgment; he is obligated to take part in the duel. Lisa's letter arrives after her death, indicating that she has already paid a heavy price for her indiscretions. The letter is the uncanny vehicle by which Stefan is made to own up to his part in the tragedy. Therefore,

Letter from an Unknown Woman: Trying to remember Lisa. (Film Stills Archive, The Museum of Modern Art, New York)

the irreconcilable separateness that is the heart of Zweig's story moves (in the film) toward a unity of guilt—a guilt that finally unites the lovers.

Ophuls/Koch add an interesting religious commentary; the end of the letter contains a small notation written by a nun who witnessed Lisa's final hours and her death: "This was written by a patient here, we believe it was meant for you as she spoke your name just before she died. May God be merciful to you both." These final words written and signed by a member of the church are Stefan's final judgment. An honorable death (a duel of honor) becomes the means by which he can obliterate a dishonorable life and settle his debt to Lisa and their son.

* * *

The film adaptation of *Letter from an Unknown Woman* both shatters and embraces the romantic ghost films of the 1940s. The film co-opts the singular obsessive passion of the Gothic ghost story (*Wuthering Heights*), bypasses the touching communal flavor of *The Ghost and Mrs. Muir*, and seems to draw on the dreamlike illusionary mood and setting that is the hallmark of *Portrait of Jennie*. But here, all similarity ends. Although *Letter* is an amalgam of its romantic contemporaries, the film dismantles the sense of cohesiveness and community that began to take root in the romantic ghost film of the 1940s. This is a one-sided love story in which there is no shared past, no moment in which the two lovers occupy the same sphere of conscious emotion. The story belongs solely and entirely to the unknown woman—she has created the situation that both begins and ends the tragedy. The film adaptation and Zweig's story touch at the end in the vague sense of something or someone lost and in the voice of a ghostly shadow forever silenced:

> [I]t seemed to him as if a door had been flung open suddenly by an invisible hand, and a cold current of air from another world flowed into his peaceful room. He became conscious of a death and conscious of undying love ... he strove ardently to reach out in spirit towards the unseen presence, as though he were hearing distant music [p. 250].

The short story, as Lukács suggests, is creativity in its purest form, where mood supplants plot and where a fragment of life is presented as whole and complete. The letter, written by a woman who has died, constitutes the whole of Zweig's novella, and it embraces haunting in its most abstract and compelling form. The recipient of the letter, the reader(s), and the viewers are thrust into a dimension where love and life are illusionary and death even more so. And because the reader(s) and viewers share in the reading of the letter, we are, by implication, all guilty of the same indifference that caused her death. The dead woman and her reader(s) never connect; therefore, to the reader and the viewer, her life and death remain unresolved. It is the type of haunting, the letter as ghost, that guarantees the woman's oblivion, for once the letter is read, the woman's reality fades and disappears. Her life is a piece of paper, as brief and unreal an apparition as a fleeting image on the screen.

Foucault in "What Is an Author?" discusses the relationship between writing and death. The written or spoken word, he claims, was once a guarantee against obscurity. Now, he argues, writing has "the right to kill, to become the murderer of its author" (p. 117). If one accepts Foucault's reasoning, then the ghostly letter, the novella's written word and the film's spoken adaptation, guarantees the woman's final leap into obscurity. The letter is finished, her life is over, and the film and her story end.

CHAPTER FIVE

The Uninvited

a novel by DOROTHY MACARDLE
a film by LEWIS ALLEN

The Uninvited is an amalgam of terror, romance, and comedy presented as one of the favorite film genres of the 1940s, the ghost story. Instead of adhering to the traditional escapist aesthetic, this film parodies many of the genre's characteristics in order to create an uneasy contrast. By doing so, *The Uninvited* is able to offer the viewing public an alternative to the purely romantic depiction of the ghost story. Rather than re-create the imagery of two separate worlds inhabited by two unequal lovers, the dead and the living, *The Uninvited* offers an alternative, a brother and sister team of ghostfighters who do battle with the spirits of the dead. In contrast to the traditional romantic ghost story, both film and novel place the love interest as secondary, the ghostfighters' reward for their efforts in freeing their small world from malevolent forces.

This restructuring of the basic characteristics of the romantic ghost story combines other new elements as well—it permits a comedic element to be interjected in a heretofore semitragic genre, and it thrusts the ghost story into the immediate present. The Fitzgeralds are a brash, young, down-to-earth team who take on the task of solving a particularly disturbing mystery. This rearrangement of priorities—battle first, reward second—mirrors the time frame of the 1940s in which a global war is being fought. In this film, the ghost story is no longer pure fantasy, set in a time period far removed from the present, but fantasy juxtaposed with current social and global issues.

The Novel

The Uninvited, in true Gothic form, is the story of a haunted house. The story is set in Devon, England, in "one of those villages that run headlong to the sea in cleeves of the Devon hills" (p. 4). Like *Letter from an Unknown Woman*, *The Uninvited* is also a book of second sight; the story of Cliff End is Roderick Fitzgerald's story, and he is the narrator of the novel. His letter to a friend begins the story:

> Dear Garry,
>   Here is your book. It was you who insisted on my writing it. I understand your pertinacity. The extraordinary events of that summer will never be credited—we shall even doubt our own memories, unless the facts are recorded without more delay.... What strange interweaving of destinies began with the reckless mood of that April morning when Pamela and I first saw Cliff End!

The house, Cliff End, is perched on "the top of the world," with nothing arround it, "not a building ... in sight except a lighthouse and a coast-guard station away on the left" (p. 6). Brother and sister Roderick and Pamela Fitzgerald stumble upon the house during a weekend house-hunting trip. The two have shared living quarters in London—Pamela came to live with her brother after spending some difficult years caring for their invalid father, and after his death, she accepted her brother's invitation to share his flat in Bloomsbury. But London living began to pall on this small family, and Roddy (as he is called) suggested that the two pool their resources and find an affordable house far from the noise of London and near the sea. In *The Ghost and Mrs. Muir*, Lucy Muir leaves London to "settle things for herself." Bullied by an overprotective mother-in-law, and in defiance of her restrictive social role dictated by her "widowhood," Lucy rents the enchanting Gull Cottage even though she knows it is haunted. When Lucy Muir moves into Gull Cottage, her relationship with the rest of society ceases to exist.

Pamela and Roddy Fitzgerald are not looking to withdraw from the world. They are both young; Roderick has a career as a theater critic (and he wants to write a novel), and Pamela is a strong-willed young woman who fondly remembers the joy of living in a large house by the sea. Born and raised in Ireland, she simply wants to return to a life she once cherished, a simple life away from the hustle-bustle of London.

Roddy gives no time frame for his story (Macardle published the novel in 1944), but Roddy drives a motor car, and references are made to airplanes and air travel. The novel appears to be precariously balanced between the wars (post–World War I and pre–World War II). The brother and sister are part of a colorful group of artists, writers, and theater people, and their London flat significantly is in the heart of Bloomsbury.

They have an impetuosity of manner and speech that immediately sets them apart from the "locals" who inhabit the tiny hamlets they have been visiting.

Cliff End sits near the village of Biddlecomb, high in the Devon hills. It is in shabby condition, badly in need of repair. But its location, high on a cliff with the sea shimmering just below, quickly steals the Fitzgeralds' hearts. Roddy and Pamela love the house, and when they see a "for sale" sign, they quickly drive to the owner's home to talk to him. They arrive at Commander Brooks's house and ring the bell; the door is opened by the commander's granddaughter, who "looked at us with dismayed dark eyes ... her hair enveloped in a turban of pink toweling ... her cheeks pink from the heat of a fire" (p. 7). This is how Roddy introduces Stella Meredith to the reader.

Stella gives the Fitzgeralds the key to Cliff End and the brother and sister return to inspect the inside of the house. The house exceeds their expectations. As Roddy tells it: "it was a fine entrance, broad, balanced, ample ... the dining room ... was a long room, high ceilinged, with a beautiful marble mantelpiece.... I crossed the wide hall to the door opposite, opened it, and stood silent. I had seen no lovelier room ... the beauty of the cornices and of the mantelpiece" (pp. 9, 10). The house is a small wonder except for a tiny studio that had "the east window blocked up ... the fireplace was too small ... and the room struck cold. It was dim, graceless, wholly without charm" (p. 10). With the exception of this small, cold room, the house suits the Fitzgeralds perfectly. They return to Commander Brooks's home to negotiate the sale.

The dialogue between the Fitzgeralds and Commander Brooks reads like a battle between the past and the present—the commander disdains motoring in favor of the "vehicles of his early days" (p. 14), and at lunch, he takes special pains to extol the fine qualities of the Devonshire men. And when Pamela asks whether there is a "celtic strain in North Devon, you would expect it here ... between Cornwall and Wales," the commander's answer is curt and sharp, "the Welsh are an entirely different race" (p. 18). Stella, who has been listening quietly to this exchange between her grandfather and the Fitzgeralds, suddenly recalls Pamela's famous ancestress of the same name, and she impetuously adds that this ancestress of Pamela Fitzgerald was "said to have been a daughter of the Duc d'Orleans ... she married Lord Edward Fitzgerald who led the Irish uprising of 'ninety-eight" (p. 19). The commander is not impressed with this information. "I am afraid ... that I am not well acquainted with Irish rebel history" (p. 18). The battle lines are drawn during this small luncheon.

The Fitzgeralds, young, articulate, and Irish, have locked horns with a member of the English old guard, an old naval warrior who is remarkably intolerant of any "race" other than the English (he is especially fond of his Devonshire men). Indeed, the commander's undisguised contempt for "foreigners" sets the tone for the extraordinary events that are soon to unfold at Cliff End.

The commander agrees to sell the house to the Fitzgeralds for a very nominal price, but he feels compelled to tell them first that a previous tenant had experienced "disturbances" there. The two young people are not deterred by this information. And so, having both been fed and warned, the Fitzgeralds become the owners of Cliff End.

Pamela and Roddy, in record time, restore the house to its original beauty, and they bring their old Irish nanny, Lizzie (and her cat Whiskey), to live with them. Under Pamela's sure and swift hands, the house is painted, old family furnishings are brought out of storage, and the house begins to glow with a sense of warmth and comfort. But the cold little studio defies repair. The paint will not dry, the wallpaper will not stay on the walls, and the room seems to resist any attempt to make it livable.

Pamela and Roddy have taken a great fancy to the delicate, shy Stella. But Stella, who has led a cloistered life with her grandfather, and who has a great love for Cliff End, is forbidden ever to visit the Fitzgeralds. The commander, it seems, has included the Fitzgeralds in his list of "undesirables"—"they're not our sort," is the explanation he gives to Stella. But there is another reason that the commander will not allow Stella to visit Cliff End. Stella's mother, the commander's only daughter, died a most unfortunate death while living at Cliff End when Stella was a little girl. The commander, fearing that Stella is too fragile to withstand any sort of emotional shock, does not want her to revisit her mother's house. The beautiful, isolated Cliff End is a house with an unhappy past and an uncertain future.

Who Haunts Cliff End?

Cliff End is haunted and it is haunted by two ghosts, not one. The story appears to turn on a simple case of mistaken identity—the ghost who is presumed to be Stella's mother (Mary Meredith) is not her mother at all, and the second ghost, Carmel, who is Stella's mother, is unable to rectify this terrible injustice. The two dead women, one proud and defiant, the other sad and abused, continue a battle that rages on, unresolved, in death as it had in life. The two ghosts are polar opposites. Mary Meredith is English, beautiful, cold, and proud. Carmel doubles Heathcliff in *Wuthering Heights* in that she has no last name, and like Heathcliff, she is described by the villagers as a "dark, Spanish gypsy" (p. 221). In this context, Carmel retains the Gothic notion of the "other," a nebulous, now feminine "foreign" power whose very presence seems to threaten the small English village.

Carmel met and fell in love with the artist Llewellyn Meredith in Spain and lived happily with him for a good while. As one of the Fitzgeralds' neighbors tells it, "then Mary Meredith comes, all cool and English and exquisite—with some money, too, and a home ... they marry [and] rather than lose sight of him, she [Carmel] becomes Mary's servant ... and his model ... he seduces her" (p. 315). When Mary learns that Carmel is pregnant, she takes Carmel to Paris. After the child is born, Mary takes the child away from Carmel and returns to England, where she claims the child as her own. Carmel is left in Paris destitute and alone. But soon, despondent over the loss of her beloved child, Carmel manages to return to England. Ill and weak, she finds her way to Cliff End. The villagers tell of Mary Meredith's goodness and compassion—how, when the sick and broken Carmel returned to Cliff End, Mary magnanimously took her in and cared for her. The villagers do not hesitate to comment on Carmel's exotic appearance:

> Who was she? God only knows. An artist's model folks did say. They brought her back with them from foreign parts. Supposed to be a sort of lady's maid to Mrs. Meredith, she was, but a queer sort of maid, if you ask me; wild as a gypsy in her ways. She'd dress up in her shawls and ribbons and dance on the lawn, then she'd break out in passions and weep and give out curses in her foreign lingo [p. 41].

The disdain and dislike of the "other," the foreigner, already evidenced by the commander, is apparent throughout the village. It is this "difference," measured against Mary's own family background, that brands Carmel from the time she sets foot on English soil. Carmel's return to England is seen not only as a marital threat to the Meredith family, but a national threat as well. *The Uninvited*, therefore, is a story of a small personal war that mirrors both the Gothic and postwar (World War I) paranoia of the foreigner, the other. The commander's disdain of any nationality other than his own "fine Devonshire men" encompasses the Irish-born Fitzgeralds as well. The story of Cliff End becomes a parody of English colonialism in which the enemy is a lone and abused Spanish gypsy, a metaphoric aggressor. The territory or soul at stake in this battle is Stella

Meredith, the commander's only grandchild. Also involved in this ghostly battle is an unlikely multitude of factions: artistic, religious, and theatrical, each of whom claim to hold the solution to the conflict.

Carmel's haunting is confined to a room in the house that was once the nursery. Her presence is always accompanied by the scent of mimosa, her favorite perfume. Her weeping and moanings are heartwrenching—and once Carmel begins her night's lamentations, the malevolent Mary quickly appears, bringing with her a deadly paralyzing cold that drives the sobbing ghost away. The clash between these two unequal enemies is a nightly occurrence and one that seems never to be resolved.

The fact that the house is haunted becomes apparent to the Fitzgeralds not long after they settle into their new home. And although the villagers do not know that the house is haunted, they are all aware of the story of Mary Meredith and her "servant" Carmel. The villagers are most anxious to relate how the women died. And when Roddy asks for the details, this is the story he is given:

> No living soul knows what happened, Mr. Fitzgerald, or ever will know. Unless ... the nurse knew more than she'd say ... she said she saw them there at the edge of the cliff. It was dark night and a gale from the south-west. It was as if the wind took Carmel and flung her into the tree; she could see her, in her black dress, clinging to it.... Mrs. Meredith couldn't stop herself on the slope; 'tis steep there, she flung herself sideways, making a grasp at the tree, but fell back and went down [p. 42].

Carmel survived her "mistress" only by one week. She died of pneumonia while being cared for by Mrs. Holloway, Mary Meredith's friend and confidant. This is the story that has been circulated by the commander and kept alive by both the commander and Mrs. Holloway. The true story of this life-and-death confrontation is that Mary Meredith refused to relinquish the child to her mother, and rather than have Carmel take the child, she ran with the child to the cliff's edge. Carmel, frightened that Mary might harm the baby, tried to take her from Mary. The two women struggled at the edge of the cliff, and Mary accidentally fell to her death. Mary's death was an accident, but the story was embellished so that Mary Meredith was depicted as a heroine who died to save her servant.

The New Warriors

The story of Stella, Mary, and Carmel unfolds gradually during the course of the narrative, and the mystery of Stella's parentage is not resolved until the end of the novel. Yet the story is also the Fitzgeralds' story. It is their bravery and their inventiveness simply in surviving the horror of the visitations, and in mustering their collective forces to defeat the evil spirit that controls their house, that adds a special dimension to this ghost story. A small village, high in the hills of Devon, and protected by the sea on all sides, would appear to be impervious to any outside malevolent forces.

But Macardle shows that this is not the case. The English and the "foreigners," personified in the skeletons of the two ghosts, and locked in an eternal battle fought in this single small arena, mirror a national paranoia. The Fitzgeralds, brother and sister, and the remaining Merediths (Stella and the commander) are the living counterparts of this divisive conflict. The Fitzgeralds are not ordinary people. Born and raised in Ireland, their Celtic sensibilities are both repelled and entranced by the spirits with whom they are forced to coexist. And because this family has developed an attachment to Stella, they evince a nobility of mind and action in their attempts to save her that is supposedly absent in the rest of the village (and presumably the rest of the Empire). This is not war on a grand, epic scale, but it is, nevertheless, a war that is to test the resourcefulness and ingenuity of these two "foreigners." The fact that we are told of Pamela's famous ancestress (of the same name) who played a small part in the Irish uprising of 1798 is not coincidental. The spirit of this brave woman apparently lives on in the "new" Pamela, in the bravery and resilience she shows in solving the mystery of the ghosts of Cliff End. Pamela's ancestress, it should be noted, was a "foreigner" herself (a daughter of the Duc d'Orleans) who married the Irish nobleman Lord Edward Fitzgerald. Pamela and Roddy's family background are given as examples of tolerance and bravery, qualities that appear to be missing in Commander Brooks's family. Since the story is told from Roddy's point of view, we are to assume that the Irish are the true nobility, the heroes of the novel.

The battle between the two ghosts occurs every night without interruption. It does not matter who occupies the house—indeed, whether the house is occupied or not. The haunting itself is never in doubt; it is the resolution to this unfortunate problem that is the underpinning of the story.

The Fitzgeralds decide to have a housewarming. Some of the guests are from London, and they are Roddy's friends. They reflect Roddy's cultural, social, and artistic interests. The friends are an amalgam of cultures: Max is a painter and Roddy's dearest friend. He is married to Judith; Peter and Wendy Carey are two very young actors (also married), and the two other guests reflect the Fitzgeralds' new life—Stella Meredith and Dr.

Scott, the village doctor. Persuading the commander to let Stella visit Cliff End was left to Pamela and to Dr. Scott, the commander's personal physician. The group who is to assemble at Cliff End inadvertently become involved in the nightly hauntings that have terrorized the house's inhabitants.

The first night of the reunion begins uneventfully. The house looks warm and splendid. The friends gathered there are enchanted with its beauty. Max and Judith are given the old studio, where attempts have been made to drive out the ghastly cold that still seems to permeate the very walls. Max, Judith, and the Careys arrive a day early; Stella and Dr. Scott are to complete the party the following night. Before retiring, Roddy and Max have a long chat. Roddy mentions the artist Llewellyn Meredith and Max recalls some unpleasant information about the artist: "Lyn Meredith! That's he! Llewellyn, and called Lyn. By Jove, that man painted a picture—he made himself famous with it for a season; notorious rather; but not through its merits" (p. 73). As Max gives a description of the picture—a woman painted both in youth and old age—a cry stops Max's narrative, "a gasping, long-drawn sob ... it was Judith ... weeping, babbling, hysterical" (p. 73). Pamela, who rushes to Judith, is able to get Judith to tell what she saw, "when she sat down to cream her face in front of the mirror, she thought she looked old ... stark old age—death's-head old age" (p. 75). Judith's encounter with the apparition is an interesting one because the vision she sees in the mirror is both a manifestation of her own fears and a doubling of the story of Lyn Meredith's painting. Judith is a beautiful woman some years older than her husband, and the loss of her beauty is something that would physically depict the difference in their ages—something that she fears. And Max, in relating the subject of Llewyllen Meredith's most famous painting, a woman painted both in youth and old age, gives form and substance to Judith's fear.

Art enters into this conflicted arena by Meredith's horrifying representation of Carmel. The portrait is one that depicts Carmel before Mary Meredith entered and destroyed her life. The "young" woman is Carmel as Meredith first found her in Spain. The death's-head figure is Carmel after she has returned to England, defeated, desperate, and in search of her child. The painting therefore is a metaphor for the politically and emotionally conquered, and Judith doubles Carmel in her fear and vulnerability.

But rather than fleeing the house in terror, Max and Judith join forces with the Fitzgeralds in trying to drive away the ghosts of Cliff End. Judith bravely offers her solution to the haunting. When asked by Roddy how she would deal "with these miseries of the past," Judith replies, "simply by living in the house as you are living in it" (p. 95). And Roddy and Pamela concur and state the credo that will hopefully defeat the intruders, "it would be strange indeed, if the vigor and content of the living could not banish the lingering sorrows of the dead" (p. 98). Max offers to tap into his resources in the art world to discover more information about Llewellyn Meredith. It is now Stella's encounter with the ghosts and her extreme vulnerability in the face of this nameless danger that draws her tightly under the protective wing of the new warriors.

The next evening brings Stella and Dr. Scott to the house. Roddy, already half in love with the girl, notices how lovely she is. She wears a faint scent of mimosa, a scent she mistakenly believes was Mary Meredith's perfume. She is drawn to the nursery and stands there, silently remembering a time long past when a gentle voice would come to her in the dark and murmur loving words. The evening passes; the guests are finally asleep when Roddy hears a sound in the nursery where Stella had stood only a short while before. Roddy explains: "I became aware that there shone, very faintly, a pale, pulsating gleam. It was not moonlight; it moved ... somebody moved and sighed there; somebody moaned ... the scent of mimosa lingered, potent still" (p. 93).

Stella's presence in the nursery prompts Carmel's appearance. After all these years, her child, now grown, has returned to the room where Carmel waited and yearned for her. Stella's return to Cliff End intensifies the nightly visitations, and the Fitzgeralds resolve, even more vehemently, to find a solution.

The Church

Lizzie, the Fitzgeralds' faithful nanny, has not been spared the nightly battles. She refuses to sleep in the house, and each night Roddy drives her to a neighboring farm where Lizzie has had the good fortune to find in the kindly matron an Irishwoman like herself. But Lizzie has not only confided in her new friend, she has also turned to the church for help. At Lizzie's request, Father Anson, half-Irish, a Catholic and a resident of Biddlecomb for well over twenty-five years, arrives at Cliff End to offer his assistance.

Father Anson listens sympathetically and carefully to the Fitzgeralds' description of the haunting. To Pamela's question, "Father, can nothing be done?" he reluctantly offers exorcism as the only solution. Much to their astonishment, the Fitzgeralds learn that Carmel was a member of Father

Anson's parish, that she faithfully attended services, and that at the time of her death, the priest was not called to administer last rites. Carmel and the Catholic Church, both "others" in Anglican England, were joined from the time Carmel came to the village. The notion of battle, now from the perspective of the Church, continues the parody of subversion, now a threat to the survival of the English ghost. An exorcism, however, is something that the Fitzgeralds assure Father Anson is the very last thing that they would consider.

The Séance

Stella pays an unannounced visit to Cliff End when Roddy and Pamela are away. She ventures into the nursery, and Roddy, returning home with Pamela, hears a scream. "The bay of the nursery lit up by a bluish gleam, then its window burst open and someone ran out—ran frantically, straight for the edge ... it was Stella" (p. 178). Had Roddy not given chase and caught Stella as she plunged forward, she might have met the same fate as Mary Meredith—she would have plummeted over the cliff to her death. In shock and despair, Roddy forbids Stella to return to the house. But now, the battle has intensified; its obvious purpose is Stella's destruction.

The Fitzgeralds mention Father Anson's offer to Stella, and she recoils in horror. "'[T]hat's what they do to devils,' she stammered, 'to drive them down to hell ... you've got to swear to me—to swear ... that you will never do that'" (p. 145). Pamela then suggests trying to communicate with the enemy. She proposes a séance, a practice she recalls hearing about when she was a child. Roddy, aware that the practice of summoning the dead usually turns out to be fraudulent, turns to his friend Max for help and advice. Max discovers Garrett Ingram, "member of the Irish Bar, a man of thirty with a curious variety of achievements ... published plays for the Abbey Theater and published verse ... and a book called *Parapsychic Phenomena, an Analysis*" (p. 242). Ingram, another Irishman, evinces talents that are almost comedic in scope. The description of his extraordinary achievements mocks the bucolic sleepy English village. And now his talents include communing with the dead.

The séance is attended only by the Fitzgeralds, Ingram, and Max. Ingram's method of communicating with the dead requires a pack of alphabet cards spread around a large table and an inverted wine glass. The group is asked to touch the rim of the upturned glass with their fingertips and then ask their questions. The spirits, if they are so inclined, spell out their responses by moving the glass to the appropriate card.

The séance produces some disturbing results. With each question, it becomes more apparent that the two ghosts are deadlocked in battle, with one ghost seemingly exerting more power than the other. After several attempts to make sense of the frantic spelling and then misspelling of words, the glass begins to spin frantically around the table and then it crashes onto the floor and shatters. Pamela appears to have fainted, and as everyone gathers about her, Roddy notes that "her breathing grew deeper ... the syllables which Pamela uttered were as strange to me as the voice in which she was speaking—a light joyous voice, soft and lilting.... I heard tender little sounds repeated over and over ... then she began to moan ... she wept with abandonment. This was the helpless sobbing that we so often heard" (p. 295).

Single Combat

The séance has given Pamela the answers she and Roddy have been searching for. The reason for the haunting of Cliff End has finally been discovered. The words that Pamela uttered while she was in the trance were in Spanish. And when they were translated, the words were found to be tender loving words of endearment from mother to child. It was Carmel who spoke through Pamela—Carmel is revealed to be Stella's mother, and Mary Meredith is the unrelenting villain. What remains is to rectify this terrible wrong.

The last chapter of the novel is titled "Single Combat," and it describes how the ghosts are finally driven from Cliff End. The title of this final chapter indicates that the battle will be won only by a one-on-one confrontation between the spirits of the house and the Fitzgeralds who have, from the very beginning, been determined to undertake this challenge. But it is left to Stella to right the wrong that has been done to Carmel. And when Pamela quietly and gently tells Stella the truth—that it is Carmel who is her mother and not Mary—Stella firmly moves to rectify this terrible wrong. She walks into the nursery:

> I could hear her quick, eager breathing and Carmel's sobbing breath, as if there were two women in that room; then Stella began to speak. She began with fragments of Spanish, little words, broken phrases; then phrases of English ... there was such tenderness in her voice, it rose and fell, soft, persuasive, a little lyric of pity and love. When she was finished, there was quiet in the nursery. I could hear no sound but the wind; the sighing had ceased. "Rest in peace," I heard her say gently. "She is gone! Oh Roddy, I believe she has gone in peace" [p. 334].

Stella's act of bravery and love frees her as well as Carmel. Her parentage, half–English, half–Spanish, and her youth reveal her to be as "foreign" as the brother-and-sister team who have befriended her, and her singular and poignant bravery in freeing Carmel from her years of despair shows her to have the same compassion and strength as the Fitzgeralds. But suddenly, the joy of the moment is challenged by Mary Meredith. Roddy describes the scene:

> the sudden cold made me gasp ... I looked up at her. She stood, taller than I had seen her before, expanding and gathering form, palely luminous. She began to float down towards me [p. 335].

Roddy, almost paralyzed by the deadly cold and Mary's menacing expression, does the unthinkable: "Step by step, I mounted up against her, pouring out my derision in blades and shafts ... 'you pitiful trickster, you are finished!... Your mummery and your poses are done with, you shallow fraud!'"(p. 335). Roddy sees the form begin to dwindle and diminish. As he continues to climb up the stairs for his final angry thrust, the form begins to cower, "breathing and writhing like smoke under a downward wind ... 'there is nothing left of you Mary,' I mocked, 'but a story to laugh over, a tale for maids to giggle at'" (p. 335).

The ghosts have been defeated, and Cliff End is free. This tiny war has come to a happy conclusion. The victors of this tale are the "invaders," both alive and dead. Carmel, the original "other," has reclaimed her lost daughter, and the Fitzgeralds, aliens and "others" as well, have vanquished the enemy. The death of the English Mary Meredith and the triumph of the foreign invader suggests a political allegory, a fable in which the oppressed, real or perceived, manage to defeat their enemies.

The Film

Although Macardle's novel contains all the elements that define the traditional ghost story—a house by the sea, a portrait of the dead, night hauntings, and a young girl threatened by the ghosts of the past—the author broadens the scope of her novel by manipulating these elements to mock the concept of national identity. In *Rabelais and His World*, Mikhail Bakhtin explains the role of laughter/comedy in parody: it "does not deny seriousness but purifies and completes it ... laughter purifies from dogmatism, from the intolerant and the petrified; it liberates from fanaticism ... from fear and intimidation" (p. 123).

The film adaptation of *The Uninvited* parodies the very popular romantic ghost story of the 1940s by introducing the innovative concept of the ghostfighter (the new warrior) to the screen. The warrior aspect of Dorothy Macardle's novel is carried over in the screenplay with the brother-and-sister team of Roderick and Pamela (played by Ray Milland and Ruth Hussey) retaining the brashness and bravado that characterized them in her novel. *The Uninvited* subverts the romantic ghost story by reenacting scenes from several revered ghost films and then placing the brother-and-sister team of detectives/ghostfighters within the scene. The team of ghostfighters adds a dimension of impudence and brashness to the action so that the distinctive elements and specific characters that figured so prominently in *Rebecca, Portrait of Jennie, The Ghost and Mrs. Muir,* and *Wuthering Heights* assume a comedic tone that they never previously had.

Although the adaptation retains the basic components of the novel, the most notable changes are reflected in the names of the house and of two of the characters—the name of the house inexplicably changes from Cliff End to Windward, Commander Brooke becomes Commander Beech, and Roddy is Rick (perhaps an oblique reference to the film *Casablanca* in which Rick/Bogart becomes a freedom fighter at the end of the film). Rick's occupation also changes from writer to pianist/composer and one cannot help but recall *Letter from an Unknown Woman,* in which Stefan Brand, a concert pianist, mesmerized Lisa with his music. Rick's occupation as a budding composer gives the film an exquisite score by Victor Young in which the popular song "Stella by Starlight" became its signature piece.

Like the film and novel *Rebecca, The Uninvited* begins with a narrative prologue spoken by Rick: "they call them the haunted shores.... Mists gather here and sea fog and eerie stories ... they listen to the pounding and stirring waves.... There's life and death in that restless sound and eternity too." Rick's voice is juxtaposed against a long, sustained view of a restless, angry sea. Rick speaks with the measured sonorous tones that are the hallmark of the classic film actor, and his prologue emulates the prologue that introduce the films *Rebecca* ("Last night I dreamt I went to Manderley again") and *Portrait of Jennie,* which utilizes a written prologue. After the spoken and reflective prologue, Rick and Pamela revert to a sparkling rapid-fire dialogue that is always laced with a touch of sarcasm. The prologue, therefore, begins the parodic effect of juxtaposing past with present in order to create a sense of imbalance in which the genre of the ghost film is mocked.

The Uninvited: Stella by Starlight. Gail Russell as Stella and Ray Milland as Rick. (Film Stills Archive, The Museum of Modern Art, New York)

Doubles

Before a new order can be established, it is necessary to represent the old and to juxtapose it alongside the new, either as a corresponding or as a discordant double. In *The Uninvited*, the old and the new are continually, and parodically, contrasted. The heroes of the film (as in the novel) are a brother and sister—a pairing not usually utilized in a romantic film. The two act in concert; their thoughts, ambitions, and general demeanor evince a solidarity and strength that sets them apart from the other characters—indeed, these two characters form the center of a circle of doubles that are eventually rearranged. Stella is initially paired with her grandfather, Commander Beech; the two ghosts, both women, are paired to represent the age-old contest between good and evil; but Dr. Scott, whose role has been expanded in the film, lives alone. He is later drawn into the group by the appearance of the Fitzgeralds' dog Bobby, who runs away from Windward when he becomes frightened by the ghosts—thus Dr. Scott is no longer alone even though his pairing is quite unusual.

These doubles, as they are initially presented, live in an unfinished state — a state of potential rebirth and growth. They also are asexual pairs who have yet to find their respective life partners. And in this context, these pairs are representative of this new genre of ghost film — as yet untried and in the process of becoming. The film itself is paired with, and pitted against, the traditional romantic ghost story. Ultimately, the doubling is rearranged so that a new life situation is born: Stella and Rick fall in love, as do Dr. Scott and Pamela; the two ghosts are banished from the house, one to heaven and the other to hell. And the old guard, Commander Beech, dies. The film itself creates a new outgrowth of the old ghost story by establishing a new dimension for the genre, the ghost fighter.*

Alfred Hitchcock's *Rebecca* is a film not easily mocked. Its masterful blend of suspense and terror combined with the wonderful performances of Laurence Olivier and Joan Fontaine assure it a secure place in the canon of film classics. But it is the performance of Judith Anderson as the demented Mrs. Danvers that gives the film its specific touch of horror. The portrait of Rebecca is the heartbeat of the film — an icon of beauty, her face and form are forever captured in a magnificent portrait. The portrait is one of the driving forces that depict Mrs. Danvers's malevolence and the new Mrs. de Winter's feelings of inadequacy. *The Uninvited* diminishes and subverts the Gothic staple of portraiture and evil housekeeper by creating a parody, a comedic representation, of both. In contrast to the one portrait that is one of the hallmarks of the ghost film (*Portrait of Jennie, Ghost and Mrs. Muir*) *The Uninvited* has three extraordinarily oversized portraits of Mary Meredith (Stella's supposed mother); one portrait hangs in the living room of the commander's house, another in Stella's bedroom, and still another in the study of Mary Meredith's companion and confidant, Mrs. Holloway. Mrs. Holloway, played by Cornelia Otis Skinner, bears an uncanny resemblance to Judith Anderson (Mrs. Danvers), and she exhibits the same manic devotion to her friend as Mrs. Danvers to her mistress. But where Mrs. Danvers took every opportunity to extol the dead Rebecca's beauty and accomplishments to the cowering and frightened new Mrs. de Winter, Mrs. Holloway is fixated on the painted image; she speaks to the portrait addressing it as "my darling." The meetings between Mrs. Holloway and Rick and Pamela parody those between Mrs. Danvers and Mrs. de Winter. Unlike the frightened Mrs. de Winter, the Fitzgeralds are not easily intimidated and they are quick to identify madness when they see it. The scenes between these three characters

---

*A modern day parody of the ghostfighter is Ghostbusters *(1984).*

diminish the Danvers character by exposing her to the ridicule and bravado of the Fitzgeralds.

Another oblique reference to *Rebecca* is presented in the very last scene of the film, where Rick confronts the ghost of Mary Meredith. As he ascends the stairs toward the menacing spirit, he carries a lit candelabra (something that Mrs. Danvers was noted for). As he shouts his final admonition to the ghost, he throws the lit candelabra at the spirit—there is a small fire, in which only a small room and a bit of carpet are damaged. In *Rebecca* Mrs. Danvers also carries a candelabra, which ignites the fire that destroys Manderley. Mrs. Danvers destroys a formidable estate; in comedic contrast, Rick Fitzgerald manages to scorch only a tiny room and leave the house essentially undamaged.

Houses and Spaces

Again, in contrast to the traditional haunted house, which is the hallmark of *Rebecca, Wuthering Heights,* and *The Ghost and Mrs. Muir, The Uninvited* depicts (in parodic spirit) three houses—each more formidable than the other. There is Windward, the haunted house which the Fitzgeralds occupy; Commander Beech's house, which contains the two oversized portraits of Mary Meredith; and the Gothic castle that belongs to Mrs. Holloway and which is aptly named the "Mary Meredith Retreat." All three houses are, in one form or another, tied to the ghost of Mary Meredith. And because Mary Meredith is evil, the houses are symbolic of her malevolence. "The Mary Meredith Retreat" is an asylum where wealthy inmates are referred to as "guests" and where they are ministered to by the equally mad administrator, Mrs. Holloway; Commander Beech's home is his granddaughter's prison, and Windward House is the place where Mary Meredith once lived and still occupies. Windward is the only one of the three houses that survives Mary's evil influence, and it survives because of the Fitzgeralds' success in driving her away. The house, now free, takes on a new life and it is carried forward into a new ghost-free era. The two other houses disappear (like Manderley in *Rebecca*) when their caretakers' flaws are exposed.

In the films *The Ghost and Mrs. Muir* and *Wuthering Heights* the space surrounding the houses is vast and limitless, with the houses depicted as passages or passageways to somewhere far beyond what is depicted on screen. In these films, the future is death because only in death can disparate souls (the living and the dead) finally be united. This particular concept of a space beyond the present is eliminated in *The Uninvited*. The

The Uninvited: The séance. *Left to right:* Barbara Everest, Ray Milland, and Ruth Hussey. (The Theater Collection, The Free Library of Philadelphia)

Fitzgeralds are firmly grounded in the present, and their future lies in the space they now occupy. The ghosts who share the Fitzgeralds' space (and house) have merely to be disposed of in order to set the Fitzgeralds' world right—and when they are driven away, the Fitzgeralds, victorious and triumphant, remain to begin their respective futures.

Stella

The film, like the novel, presents Stella as the unknowing haunted; the Fitzgeralds experience the wrath of the two ghosts on her behalf. Because Stella has not been permitted to enter Windward House (Cliff End) since she was a small child, she is unaware that the house has become a battleground in which two ghosts are fighting an eternal battle over her parentage. Since Stella's past is obscure and her present life a cloistered one, she is depicted on screen (as in the novel) as "otherworldly," childlike and tentative. Even her speech differs from that of the Fitzgeralds in that it is stilted, formal, and hesitant. Rick gives his impression of Stella to his sister: "there's a kind of sleeping-beauty magic about the kid." And indeed, the sleeping-beauty metaphor is carried forward in the film, when Rick gives Stella her "awakening" kiss and the two fall in love. In the film, the séance scene is altered so that it initiates the final confrontation between the dead and the living. And in contrast to the novel, the film adaptation depicts Stella and not Pamela as the medium—it is through her that Carmel, her real mother, speaks. The séance segment (in the film) also involves all the characters who will, at the end of the film, become life partners, Rick and Stella, Pamela and Dr. Scott.

Stella's character is an amalgam of some of the more famous women depicted in the film adaptations of the romantic ghost stories: she evinces the childlike shyness of the unnamed Mrs. de Winter, Lucy Muir's air of detachment, and Jennie's (*Portrait of Jennie*) aura of otherworldliness. But where these other characters retain their respective personas throughout their films in order to present a constancy of characterization on which the movie depends, Stella subverts these static characterizations. Her persona is ambivalent, one that shifts in every scene. She is first depicted as a shy child afraid of her grandfather, then a disobedient girl who defies her grandfather, then Rick's lover, and then a woman who is able to confront a ghost and vanquish her. The Stella character parodies the other haunted hero/heroines by being initially unformed—a character who is in the process of being created. Her final finished persona is predicated on the resolution of her parentage, and once the Fitzgeralds solve that mystery, Stella emerges complete. She is, like the Fitzgeralds, prepared to begin another phase of life.

* * *

By creating a comedic parody of the romantic ghost story, Dorothy Macardle allows reality and fantasy to coalesce into a newer, less restrictive dimension. The romantic ghost story is weakened and diminished so that a more positive, realistic, and modern version of the genre can emerge. As Bakhtin explains:

> Laughter has a deep philosophical meaning, it is one of the essential forms of truth concerning the world as a whole, concerning history and man ... the world is seen anew, no less (and perhaps more) than when seen from the serious standpoint [p. 66].

Thus does the romantic ghost story move forward into the modern world.

III
THE THEATER GHOST

CHAPTER SIX

Liliom

A Legend in Seven Scenes and a Prologue by FERENC MOLNÁR
a film by FRITZ LANG

The Play

Ferenc Molnár's *Liliom* is an ambitious play. In Bernard F. Glazer's introduction to his English translation of the play (it was written in Hungarian), he writes of its complexity of structure and the reception the play received when it was initially produced in Budapest: "What did [Molnár] mean by killing his hero in the Fifth scene, taking him into Heaven in the Sixth and bringing him back to earth in the Seventh? Was this prosaic Heaven of his seriously or satirically intended? Was Liliom a saint or a common tough? Budapest was frankly puzzled" (p. ix). Indeed, the entire play is a study in contradiction in which each character, each setting, and each dramatic development has a corresponding and discordant other. As Glazer explains: "the amazing virtuosity of *Liliom*, [is] its imaginative daring, its uncanny blending of naturalism and fantasy, humor and pathos, tenderness and tragedy into a solid dramatic structure" (p. xiii). Who and what the character Liliom is (saint or sinner) is perhaps the dilemma on which the play turns—even his name evokes the enigma of his identity—the playbill reads, "Liliom is the Hungarian for lily and the slang term for a 'tough.'"*

Liliom (like *Letter from an Unknown Woman* and *Portrait of Jennie*) introduces yet another variation of the traditional Gothic ghost story—that of a time-defined ghost, a "qualified" ghost, and a task-driven ghost. Liliom becomes a spectre who is permitted to return to earth, in his original human form, for only one day. And in this one day, he is to do one

---

**Playbill for the production by the Theater Guild on the night of 20 April 1921 at the Garrick Theatre, New York City.*

good deed for his family so that he may be released from the "fires of damnation" where he has been condemned to burn for "sixteen years and one day" (p. 121).

In order to understand Liliom's ultimate destiny, that of a sinner condemned to the fires of purgatory, the play is structured to depict Liliom in three starkly disparate settings: the world of Carnival, the world of reality, and the afterlife—all these worlds are seen from Liliom's point of view. Heaven (as Liliom experiences it) becomes a mirror image of earth, where the "angels" who come to escort Liliom to heaven are called "God's police," and the soul who insists on hearing Liliom's story in order to dispense judgment is known as the "magistrate." As Glazer explains, "Liliom's Heaven is the Heaven of his own imagining. And what is more natural than it should be an irrational jumble of priest's purgatory, police magistrate's justice, and his own limited conception of good deeds and evil" (p. xiv). Liliom's earthly travels finally lead him to this dark afterlife, in which there is no redemption for the transgressor and where the dead must endure the same punitive judgments they experienced on earth. Liliom's three worlds constitute his journey through life: his childhood (the world of Carnival), his marriage to Julie (adulthood), and his death. His first world, the world of carnival and childhood, is the one in which he is firmly and forever grounded. In *Rabelais and His World*, Mikhail Bakhtin describes a particularly relevant concept of Carnival:

> This double aspect of the world and of human life existed even at the earliest stages of cultural development ... but the basic carnival nucleus ... is by no means a purely artistic form ... it belongs to the borderline between art and life. In reality, it is life itself, but shaped according to a certain pattern of play ... because of their obvious sensuous character and their strong element of play, carnival images closely resemble certain artistic forms, namely the spectacle [pp. 7, 8].

Bakhtin's notion of "this double aspect" of the world, as it applies to Carnival, is the underpinning of Molnár's play. It is the way in which Liliom's unique character can best be explained.

In this exaggerated world of Carnival, Liliom is a wondrous sight. He is a vibrant, larger-than-life life force. He is a unique spectacle: a barker on a carousel, a seller of dreams, a bully, and a womanizer. Liliom loves life—*this* particular life—and the prologue is the device by which Liliom's vibrant and distinctive character is projected to the audience. The prologue is as swift and fleeting as childhood itself; it quickly establishes Liliom at the peak of his powers—the pinnacle of his "career" and his life.

This exaggerated display of Carnival, where the child (Liliom) rules, and "play" is the order of things, is the theatrical device that explains Liliom's later inability to adjust to any other environment. In the prologue, the carousel (and Liliom) are displayed prominently:

> Right Center with barker's stand at the entrance.... Liliom stands ... cigarette in his mouth, coaxing the people in. The Girls regard him with idolizing glances and screech with pleasure as he playfully pushes them through [the] entrance.... Liliom mounts the barker's stand at the entrance *where he is elevated over everyone on the stage.* Here he begins his harangue. Everyone turns toward him. The tumult makes it impossible for the audience to hear what he is saying, but every now and then some witticism of his provokes a storm of laughter which is audible above the din [p. 4, *emphasis added*].

In this stage of Liliom's journey, in this particular place and time, he is a supreme being. He is the seducer who draws the tired factory "girls" and overworked housemaids to the carousel to watch and listen to his familiar call, "step right up ... room for one more on the zebra's back." Just as the animals on the carousel are bound to the wooden revolving platform, so too is Liliom bound and defined by the carousel and the sense of complete power and youthful abandon that he shares with the whirling animals, the tinkling music, and the bright lights. The carousel epitomizes the idyllic world of childhood; it is a large slice of fantasy that is perched on the edge of reality. The carousel, this spectre of fantasy, figures prominently in the ghost story as a poignant reminder of the lost world of childhood. The "Prater" (carnival) sequence in *Letter* also features a large "silent" carousel as a backdrop. Liliom's role in this magical kingdom (and throughout the play) is best defined by Bakhtin:

> The rogue, the clown and the fool create around themselves their own special little world.... These figures carry ... a vital connection with the theatrical trappings of the public square, with the mask of the specific, extremely important area of the square where the common people congregate [p. 159].

Liliom is the rogue (the bully) and the clown who has created his own "special little world," and the "common people" who crowd around him and hang on his every word and gesture authenticate Liliom's importance in this tiny kingdom. Whether Liliom is a saint or a sinner has yet to be established.

Julie and the World of Reality

Liliom's idyllic life as barker on the carousel is depicted only in the prologue. Once the prologue is ended, the carousel slips out of sight—only the tinkling sounds of the calliope (which continue to be heard throughout the play) remind us that it still exists. The first scene after the prologue introduces Julie and the cast of characters who will plunge Liliom into the next phase of his life. In contrast to the vibrant and exciting prologue in which the chaotic world of Carnival is enacted on stage, the stage is now bare. Julie and her friend Marie are depicted in a "lonely place in the park, half hidden by trees and shrubbery" (stage directions, scene one). This lonely place, devoid of color and life, interjects a discordant and jarring note—the empty stage stands as a contradiction to the raucous and rowdy sounds of Carnival—a representation of two worlds torn asunder.

The two girls have just left the amusement park and Julie is arguing with Mrs. Muskat, the owner of the carousel. Mrs. Muskat* (who is in love with Liliom) has accused Julie of allowing Liliom to "fool with her" while riding the carousel. The two women argue, and Mrs. Muskat forbids Julie to come to the carousel. This quarrel between the owner of the carousel and Julie, "a common servant girl" from the city beyond the park, is the incident that inadvertently precipitates Liliom's departure from the world of Carnival. And the park, "half hidden by trees" and perched between the amusement park and the city beyond, metaphorically serves as the passageway between the familiar present (carousel) and the unknown (the future). Mrs. Muskat and Julie, who stand on this pathway and argue about Liliom, represent the choice that Liliom will be forced to make—whether to remain safe and secure in the combined world of fantasy and reality, or to follow Julie into a solitary sphere in which fantasy has no place.

As the women argue, Liliom suddenly appears accompanied by "four giggling servant girls." Mrs. Muskat notices the four girls and jealously demands, "What have you been doing now?" Liliom dismisses the question, and then he notices Julie. At first, Liliom appears to be concerned about Mrs. Muskat: "What's the matter? What has she done to you?" But when Mrs. Muskat, in her fury and desperation to keep Julie away from her carousel (and Liliom), demands that Liliom obey her command—"You can touch as many girls as you want and as often as you want ... *but not this one*" (emphasis added)—it would seem that Mrs. Muskat senses that Julie is the one person who can seduce Liliom into leaving the carousel. Liliom, in a sudden act of defiance, tells Julie, "You come to the carousel

---

As part of the world of carnival and owner of the carousel which features varied and fantastic animals, Mrs. Muskat's name (which is suggestive of muskrat, a small, furry animal) places her squarely in the world of carnival.

as often as you want to, little girl, and if you haven't got the price, Liliom will pay for you. And if anyone dares to bother you, you come and tell *me*." Angrily, Mrs. Muskat fires Liliom—it is an idle threat and quickly withdrawn, but Liliom's pride has been hurt. Mrs. Muskat has humiliated him and Liliom refuses to return with her.

Marie (who has silently watched the unfolding events) reminds Julie that they must return to their employer's house or they too will lose their jobs. Julie refuses to leave, and Marie quietly leaves the stage. Julie and Liliom remain together silently seated on a park bench—Liliom has been forced (either by circumstance or his own bravado) to choose. He has now entered another universe, Julie's world, and the next step of his journey begins.

A small warning slice of reality (and foreshadowing of things to come) occurs while Julie and Liliom sit innocently on the park bench. Two policemen arrive. They demand to know "what are you doing there?" As Liliom attempts to answer, one policeman barks, "stand up when you're spoken to!" Liliom rises and then the officer demands to know Liliom's name. Liliom answers, "Andreas Zavoczki," and as he gives his name, Julie "begins to weep softly." No longer Liliom, no longer the larger-than-life carousel barker, Liliom has, for the first time, been forced to adopt a name consistent with the rest of society. The rogue who had created and lived in his own "special world" has suddenly assumed a different persona. This name, this "real" name, is starkly inconsistent with the Liliom of only a few minutes ago—it is an ordinary name used by ordinary people—the "common" people who thronged the carnival grounds and cheered and admired the man known as Liliom.

After the police leave the stage, Liliom falters, "All I have to do—is to go back to her ... she'll be glad to get me back—then I'd be earning my wages again ... she'd take me back the minute I asked her." The stage directions indicate that Julie is silent. And then, after a pause, Julie murmurs, "Don't go back to her.... Don't go back to her." The scene ends on a mournful note: "They are silent. The Merry-Go-Round is heard in the distance. There is a long pause before the curtain falls."

Houses and Spaces

The ground plan for the prologue of the play indicates that the carousel and the barker's stand are positioned as a stage within a stage and a spectacle within a spectacle (theater presenting theater). These impressive structures (carousel and barker's stand) are surrounded by smaller, seemingly insignificant booths: a juggler (in the forefront), a Punch-and-Judy show, and a novelty stand. This theater of Carnival, which shares the same space in which representations of daily life (fighting, arguing, flirting) are being enacted, is a commingling of fantasy (Carnival) and reality. And when Liliom mounts the barker's stand, "elevated over everyone on the stage," he is (for the moment) the undisputed ruler of these combined worlds. Bakhtin, in his explanation of spatial and temporal worlds, gives a fine example of the superiority and influence that these larger-than-life people (and structures) connote:

> everything of value, everything that is valorized positively, must achieve its full potential in temporal and spatial terms, it must *spread out as far and as wide as possible* and it is necessary that everything of significant value be provided with the power to expand spatially and temporally [p. 167, *emphasis added*].

Before Liliom entered Julie's world, his position within the space of Carnival was one of fearlessness and bravado. His name was Liliom—he needed no other. But now Liliom has married Julie and his move from one realm to another is a rapid downward spiral. Suddenly, Liliom finds himself an ordinary man with ordinary cares. Life and living are reduced to simple economics—food on the table and fuel to warm the house. And all the while, the tantalizing music of his lost happy world continues to cast its spell over the frustrated and angry Liliom. The home that he and Julie share is in stark contrast to the world he left behind: "a dilapidated hovel ... a brown-curtained entrance to Julie and Liliom's room ... there is a washstand and a bucket, a table and two chairs" (stage directions, scene two).

Liliom's world has shriveled—it has been reduced in size and in stature. Bakhtin explains this inversion of size and its implications: "everything evaluated negatively is small, pitiable, feeble and must be destroyed ... the bad ... does not grow but rather degenerates, thins out and perishes" (p. 168). In the space that Liliom and Julie now occupy, Julie has assumed the dominance that once belonged to Liliom. (She has a job as a photographer's assistant while Liliom remains without work.) And as Liliom blindly stumbles through his now mundane and demanding role as Julie's husband, his inadequacies and his confusion become quickly apparent. Liliom's new life (and new surroundings) have adversely affected an already volatile temperament—always prone to anger, always quick to use his fists. Childlike in his quick and angry response to any unwelcome criticism, Liliom has begun to strike out at the people and the place that have destroyed his well-being. Julie describes the new Liliom to her friend

Marie: "Yes, they arrested him, but they let him go the next day. That makes twice in the two months we've been living here that Liliom's been arrested." Julie's aunt (who owns the house where Liliom and Julie live) also has negative comments about Liliom: "He won't work, and he won't steal ... a big strong lout like that lying around all day ... he ought to be ashamed to look decent people in the face."

If we compare Liliom's fall from grace with the other novels and film adaptations under discussion, we realize that none of the other novels or films address the diminution of character, space, or place. The houses (Gull Cottage, Wuthering Heights, and Thrushcross Grange) appear to exist on the periphery of "something bigger," something greater than the houses themselves. And it is precisely the place in which the houses are situated (mostly on the edge of the world—the sea, the moors) that metaphorically suggest a pathway to a great and wondrous world beyond.

What we now see is Liliom's diminishment defined by the space he now occupies. The carousel is gone—the exaggerated fairy-tale kingdom has disappeared from sight. This wondrous structure and all it represents has been relegated to the realm of memory. What remains is a *solitary* world of squalor populated by the poor and the wretched. As an inverse of Carnival, some of the people who inhabit Liliom's new world have animal names. Marie's husband-to-be is named Wolf and Liliom's soon-to-be partner in crime is Fiscur, the Sparrow. And Liliom, who now lives in this colorless, joyless world, has become a figure to be ridiculed (a big, strong lout) and pitied. Unable to leave Julie and unable to provide or care for her, Liliom has taken to gambling, drinking, and fighting. And gentle, quiet Julie has become a beloved taskmaster.

In the remakes of *Liliom*—Rodgers and Hammerstein's *Carousel* and the 1956 film adaptation of *Carousel*—Julie has been portrayed as long-suffering and physically abused. Not only is Liliom unable to provide for her, but Julie asserts (to Marie and her aunt) that Liliom beats her: "He won't work at all ... he never learned a trade you see—so he does nothing—Last Monday he hit me" (scene two). And when Marie urges Julie to leave, Julie quietly describes Liliom's obvious torment: "He's gentle now, sometimes, very gentle. After supper, when he stands there and listens to the music of the carousel, something comes over him—he gets thoughtful and very quiet, and his big eyes stare straight ahead of him." Julie's description of her "beating" is flat and matter-of-fact. The emotional displays of anger and dismay are left to Marie and Julie's aunt: "Strike a poor girl like that! Ought to be ashamed of himself! And the police just let him go on doing as he pleases."

Liliom's "brutality" and Julie's passivity must be judged, once again, by the upside-down, bizarre world of Carnival to which Liliom is inextricably bound, and which subtly mirrors the world in which he now lives. Liliom and Julie are the living counterparts ("double aspect") of one small booth in the amusement park, the Punch-and-Judy show.* The stage plan for the prologue indicates that this attraction was a small part of the Carnival scene. This tiny side-show, once obscured by the splendor of the carousel, assumes a new relevance when Liliom and Julie marry.

With the disappearance of the carousel, the main (and benign) attraction of the carnival, the remaining sideshows, the grotesque and exaggerated by-products of Carnival whose main attraction carries an extreme but direct relation to the real (the aspect of wife-beating in Punch and Judy carried to outlandish proportions), assume dominance. And Liliom, a product of Carnival, cannot help but adopt and emulate these shoddy remnants of the world he left behind. Liliom and Julie are the actors solely involved in this interplay of fantasy and reality. And if we assess Julie's flat, unemotional response to the blows she receives from Liliom against the real anger demonstrated by Julie's aunt and Marie, we can see that Julie and Liliom (in their roles as husband and wife) bear little resemblance to the world around them. They have become mere puppets, manipulated by the many strings of fantasy. The most poignant and memorable lines in the play, spoken by Julie, attest to the puppetlike (Judy-like) nature of her character. In answer to her daughter's question, "Is it possible for someone to hit you—real loud and hard—and not hurt you at all?" Julie answers: "It is possible dear—that someone may beat you and beat you and beat you—and not hurt you at all" (scene seven).

The Third World

The one thing that Liliom is able to steal successfully is a glittering star from the heavens—it is a small piece of wonder that Liliom tries to capture and give to the child he has never seen and will only see for one short earth day. The star metaphorically describes Liliom's past—it is a poignant reminder of the role he once played in the theater of Carnival where he was the star, the main attraction of the carousel.

In *Meyerhold on Theater*, Meyerhold explains the concept of puppet theater and the dilemma it presents when applied to modern drama:

---

*The Oxford English Dictionary *defines the Punch-and-Judy show as a "traditional puppet show in which Punch, a grotesque, hook-nosed, humpbacked character is shown nagging and beating and finally killing a succession of characters, including his wife Judy."*

One director wants his puppets to look and behave like real men ... here man strives just as hard as the puppet to imitate real life ... the other director wants to make his puppets imitate real people too, but how could he part with the puppet which had created a world of enchantment with its incomparable movements, its expressive gestures achieved by some magic known to it alone [p. 128].

Meyerhold's second puppet, the one who strives to retain a sense of "otherness," of magic, even when forced to "imitate real people," describes Liliom in his present state. And the rhythm of Molnár's play turns on this interplay between naturalism (as Glazer wrote in his introduction) and fantasy.

Mrs. Muskat supplies the tempo, the time pattern that controls Liliom's movements (in puppet fashion) from place to place, from this world to that. Mrs. Muskat, who manipulates this fantasy world, strikes a meaningful note when she reminds Liliom that in her world, he is an "artist" and a "star." Mrs. Muskat's appearances serve to remind both Liliom and the audience that the naturalistic setting in which Liliom now finds himself is merely an artistic ploy—that Liliom is merely "playing" at life, and that this momentary step away from theater into reality is a long step out of character and must come to an end.

As Liliom hesitantly begins to agree and bargain over the terms for his return, Julie appears and tells Liliom that she is pregnant. With Julie's announcement, Mrs. Muskat, who cannot compete with the absolute reality of life, children, and responsibility, leaves Liliom and Julie to their fate—the "star" falls for the last time; and the half-open door that leads back to the carousel closes forever. Liliom's very last call as a barker (and as a star) is touchingly enacted as he tries to announce to an uncaring world that he is to become a father; he leaves the room, goes outside, and jumps on an old broken-down sofa that sits outside the door, and "in a voice that overtops the droning of the organ, he shouts as if addressing the far-off carousel, 'I'm going to be a father!'" But this time, there is no audience, no adoring crowd, and no one applauds.

Fiscur has devised a plan to accost and then rob a wealthy business man. He tells Liliom of his plan and Liliom reluctantly agrees to join him. The robbery presents itself as a parody of theater with two inept actors (Liliom and Fiscur) fumbling and stumbling with lines they cannot remember:

LILIOM: What do I say?
FISCUR: You say, Good evening sir, can you tell me the time?
LILIOM: I'll say—Good evening—excuse me sir—can you tell me the time?

The only stage props in this poorly developed side show, are a knife that Fiscur insists that Liliom carry and a deck of cards. Liliom's last moments on earth are a sad jumble of events—a card game in which Fiscur cheats Liliom of his promised share of the robbery; the robbery itself in which the robbers are foiled by the victim; the raucous sounds of police whistles; and the shouts and threats of years in prison. In the din, Fiscur manages to disappear and Liliom, knife in hand, stands alone to take both blame and punishment. This whirl of activity, the threats of years in jail, the thoughts of Julie and his unborn child swirl around and about Liliom. Suddenly, "He bursts into laughter, half-defiant, half self-pitying." He says, "Julie," and "he thrusts the knife deep in his breast."

A View of the Afterlife: Through a Glass Darkly

Liliom experiences the afterlife as an extension of his life on earth. Liliom is led (by God's police) into an ordinary-looking but "heavenly" courtroom where an ordinary-looking (but heavenly) magistrate hears Liliom's case and then dispenses punishment. Liliom's last conversation with Fiscur (right before the robbery) sets the stage for his bleak view of the afterlife. When Liliom asks Fiscur what he should say when (or if) he comes before God, Fiscur replies: "the likes of you will never come before Him ... the highest *we ever* get is the criminal court ... for us, my son ... there is only justice ... and where there is justice there must be a police magistrate" (p. 111).

Liliom's death experience is another stage setting, another piece of theater that now parodies the conventional religious depiction of a benevolent afterlife. In this heavenly courtroom, the stage entrances and exits (which mirror an actual stage setting), now signify exits and entrances to heaven and hell. And Liliom's "purification by fire" has been predetermined by the magistrate who "sees through Liliom as through a pane of glass." The jumble and furor of the robbery, his suicide, and the guilt he feels about "beating" Julie all translate into a bizarre depiction of heaven. Liliom's guilt and shame for his roles in the botched robbery, the wife-beating episodes, and his abandonment of Julie and his soon-to-be-born child filter through the facade of bravado that Liliom assumes, and the magistrate is unrelenting in his judgment. He decrees that Liliom must be punished. He will be allowed to return to earth for one short day to perform a good deed for his family—the deed may be small and insignificant, but it must be something that will be meaningful to his family. This deed, if well performed, will release Liliom from hell and permit him to gain entrance to heaven. But for now, and for the next sixteen years, Liliom is condemned to purgatory, where it is hoped that his faults and his flaws will be burned away.

Liliom accepts his judgment with a shrug, but as he is escorted to the mouth of hell, he falters, and like the caricature of the condemned man about to die, asks the escort for a last cigarette. The escort gives Liliom his last request; the door opens, and Liliom plunges forward into the fires of hell.

Ghost for a Day: The Good Deed

Liliom returns (after sixteen years and one day) to a world that has changed. Without him, the world he knew has become orderly, clean, and "modern." Julie and her daughter live in a "small neat house with a porch and [a] tiny garden." The music of the carousel that once tinkled brightly in the background is gone. Liliom drops silently back to earth and stands in front of Julie's house, the star he has brought for Louise (his daughter) tucked in his pocket. His sixteen years in purgatory have beaten and changed him—the anger, bravado, and intense "color" have disappeared. Actually, Liliom now resembles this new world—stripped bare and clean, molded into a model of conformity.

Julie and Louise mistake Liliom for a beggar and offer him food. Liliom tentatively touches Louise's arm and she draws back from his touch. The three sit together, and Liliom, his eyes never leaving the two faces before him, quietly asks about Julie's husband. Julie replies that she is a widow, and Liliom asks how her husband died. It is Louise who answers, and she answers with a story that Julie has told her since she was small— that *Andreas* had gone to America and died there—no one knew where or how. As Liliom asks his few questions, the women become apprehensive and angry. But then, Liliom tells Louise that he knew her father. Louise excitedly asks for details about the man she has never seen or known. And Liliom, cowed, tells Louise the truth—that Liliom was a carousel barker, that he told funny stories, that he was handsome, and that he was a bully and that he hit Louise's mother. Julie calls Liliom a "shameless liar" and orders Liliom away.

Liliom, who must do his one good deed, begs for a few minutes more. He reaches into his pocket and pulls out the star. He tries to give it to Louise, but Julie forbids Louise to take it. Liliom pleads, "please, Miss— I've got to do something good—or—do something good." Louise and Julie refuse to listen and angrily demand that Liliom leave. Louise extends her hand to point the way out. For one brief moment, Liliom's old self reappears and he slaps Louise's hand. The moment has passed—Liliom's chance for redemption has ended. His day on earth is over and Liliom has failed in his task. Liliom and his heavenly escort move silently toward the door on the right. The two women have provoked Liliom into an act of violence; and in doing so, they have deprived him of heaven. As Liliom moves slowly and sadly toward darkness and oblivion, a remnant of Carnival, a solitary organ grinder, begins to play.

Saint or Sinner

Although Liliom is depicted as a bully and a wife-beater, the punishment he receives (eternal damnation) seems disproportionate to the "crimes" he has committed. Throughout the play, Liliom is shown to be in constant conflict with the world around him. And his conflict is that of a soul who has wandered outside the unpredictable world of Carnival into the predictable sphere of the real. The real world contradicts the world of Carnival, where all things extreme and aberrant are never judged—they are always expected. If a saint may be judged as one who is long-suffering, then Liliom's travels and trials might grant him sainthood. In the play, Liliom never sees the face of God—he never sees heaven. He sees and is condemned by a facsimile of an afterlife that he himself invents. Liliom's contest with life and death is theater-driven—it is a distortion of the real, and by extension, a distortion of the unreal. The sadness of Liliom's last glimpse of his wife and child, and the horror of his final walk into the perpetual darkness, attests to a world out of balance and his own inability to set it straight.

The Film

Two versions of *Liliom* were adapted for film in the 1930s. One version was made in 1930 and directed by Frank Borzage. An advertisement for the film reads

> The Ference Molnár play which later was made into the musical "Carousel," is congenial material ... about a trouble-prone hero who dies and is permitted by heaven to return to earth for a single day. Director Frank Borzage unifies the lovers across time and space to add a dimension of visual profundity.

This short description of Borzage's version of *Liliom* is indicative of the then "homegrown American tradition of sentimental melodrama and rural romance" (Cook, p. 218). And embedded in this first version of *Liliom* lie the seeds of the future (1956) filmic adaptation of the musical stage version, *Carousel*, which moves the action to the Maine seacoast and where all semblance of fantasy and Carnival (except for Agnes DeMille's "dream sequence" dance) disappears. The second adaptation of the play was filmed in 1933 and directed by the great Austrian director Fritz Lang. The film was subsidized by the European subsidiary of Fox studios (S.A. Fox) and filmed and released in France. In her book *Fritz Lang*, Lotte Eisner describes Lang's approach in adapting Molnár's play to the screen:

> the life of the colorful little fairground is presented with popular humour and much comic detail, at once playful and homely. The joy and suffering of ordinary people are depicted with a lightness ... which mingles earthy reality with the seductive, ephemeral atmosphere of the fairground [p. 149].

The film is constructed in picture-book style with tiny frames situated within the larger frame of the screen, thus preserving the fantasy atmosphere of Molnár's play. Mrs. Muskat sits in her booth at the carousel and looks out at the crowd through a tiny square frame; small heart-shaped or star-shaped windows open or begin a scene and then expand to a larger scene inside. Julie and Liliom's living quarters are not enclosed by walls or doors but retain a stage effect by being presented on a raised platform open on all sides. Unlike Lang's contemporary Max Ophuls's *Letter*, in which Ophuls's famous moving camera is utilized to create a fluidity of motion and movement that portrays Lisa's movement from one stage of life to another (childhood to adult), Lang depends upon elaborately structured miniaturized sets that create a fairy-tale aura (the picture-book style). Liliom and Julie are one-dimensional characters (as are all the players) and there is no attempt to endow these unfortunate lovers with any more depth or feeling than this tiny miniature world allows. (The only scene not in the picture-book style is the prologue. The carousel and the rowdy, noisy crowd surrounding it stand full-sized. The crowd all appear mesmerized by Liliom's joyful exuberance and playful, and boisterous demeanor.)

After the carousel scene (when Liliom and Julie leave together), the world becomes small and tight and the scenes are scaled down to ordinary size. And in keeping with Molnár's stage directions, the tinkling sounds of the carousel are kept as background music throughout the rest of the film.

Julie is small, blond, and angelic in appearance. She is cool and

Liliom: Liliom (Charles Boyer) and Julie (Madeleine Ozeray). Remnants of Carnival, the Punch and Judy Show. (Bibliothèque du Film, photographed by Walter Limot, courtesy of Limot)

detached with an almost otherworldly appearance. She moves and speaks her lines woodenly and without passion. And when Liliom leaves the carousel to live with Julie, the contrast between the husband and wife becomes even more exaggerated. Liliom retains the passion, the vibrancy that initially defined him in the opening carousel scene while Julie becomes more silent, more ephemeral, and more otherworldly. In keeping with the story-book fantasy aspect of the film, Alfred (Fiscur of the play) has the look of a bear. He is grotesque in appearance, hairy, dirty, and lumbering. He remains as Liliom's companion and eventual partner in crime (the fatal robbery).

The sense of unreality, of fairy tale, pervades the film and is driven by Julie's Judy-like demeanor (which never changes even when she is slapped by Liliom); by Liliom's exaggerated Punch-like character diminished (but yet distinctive) by his unhappy new life away from the carousel; and by the tiny frames that open and close like the small curtains in the boxlike structures of the sideshows.

Through a Glass Darkly

When Liliom, in a fit of anger and frustration, strikes Julie, he is sent to the police station to explain his actions to the magistrate in charge. Alfred accompanies him. And the two obviously poor and downtrodden men sit and wait for hours and hours. Signs on the walls and doors, "No Smoking," "No Talking," "No Spitting," "Knock before Entering" spin around the two unfortunates as they wait to be received. Liliom's low social status is emphasized when a well-dressed "gentleman" enters the waiting room and is immediately received by the magistrate while the long-suffering Liliom is ignored and kept waiting.

At this point in the film, Lang introduces a subtext to his adaptation that Lotte Eisner describes as a "factor already present in *M*, and which will play a still larger role in Lang's [later] films ... the selectivity of justice ... [a] comment on social reality" (p. 152). The magistrate's deference to the wealthy man and disdain for the poor (Liliom) in the police station scene is replayed in exact detail when Liliom is escorted to heaven. This added subtext suggests that Liliom's life is manipulated by adverse forces: poverty and the social bureaucracy that has no time or pity for the poor. Liliom is a victim, and the film particularly stresses this even though Liliom is initially portrayed as a bully and a rogue. He has physical and social power only within the confines of the amusement park. And the police station and heaven scenes connote how fragile he is outside of his designated place in the world.

When Julie tells Liliom that she is pregnant, Liliom reenacts his final barker role in much the same manner as in the play: he stands on the small stage that is now his home and leaps upon a wooden box and then upon a well-worn sofa. He swings his arms to the rhythm of the distant carousel music, and shouts his news to unhearing ears. In the film, Julie hears Liliom's shouts and hesitantly asks him "What's wrong?" Her quiet (and inappropriate) question shocks Liliom into silence. He turns and throws himself onto the battered, broken sofa—his back toward the audience. Julie silently places a blanket around him and slowly moves off camera.

The Robbery

As in the play, it is Alfred (Fiscur) who suggests that Liliom participate in the robbery. The robbery scene is notable for Charles Boyer's acting style, which, in this scene, is completely Chaplinesque. He begins the scene acting sheepishly—more pathetic clown or buffoon than robber. He approaches his victim holding his hat in his hand and bowing formally. And because he has forgotten his lines, he repeats "good evening, good evening" almost pathetically. He assumes the "little tramp" persona with complete ease and grace, and in doing so, interjects a mixture of comedy and pathos into this completely grotesque farce. When the police arrive, the Chaplinesque persona disappears, and Liliom kills himself rather than humiliate Julie (and his unborn child). The film adds a poignant note to Liliom's death. Lotte Eisner describes the scene:

> In the fairground, Mrs. Muskat bursts into tears; and requests a few moments silence: One of "our own people" has died she says. Everything stops—movement and sound. Like a dark and heavy cloak, a sinister silence settles, almost audibly, upon the fairground ... it is a scene, in terms of visual effects and sound, such as few directors could bring off today [p. 154].

Liliom's Heaven

Liliom's body is placed on a cot in front of Julie's house. Two candles placed at Liliom's head (reminiscent of Ophuls's depiction of the child's death scene in *Letter* where four candles are placed around the child's bed), and Julie drops her wooden doll-like persona as she kneels by the cot and proclaims the love she was always afraid to reveal. Poignantly, pathetically, she holds Liliom's hand, and in a torrent of emotion, talks to him. Then, the words spoken and all emotion spent, the old Julie reappears: wooden and silent, she leaves the body and walks into the house. The role she has played in Liliom's earthly life has ended.

Lang's fantastic depiction of Liliom's ascent towards heaven is best described by Eisner:

> Raised up to make a journey through the sky, Liliom looks around him with curiosity and pleasure ... falling stars and rotating planets mingle with the mist and luminous light in a harmonious fugue ... heavenly armies showing their baby bottoms and Fra Angelica's heavenly prospects charmingly paraphrased as a great airy auditorium made out of clouds [p. 156].

The spectacle that Liliom sees on his ascent upward is brought to an abrupt end when he suddenly finds himself in a waiting room that replicates the police station on earth. Although this heavenly room of justice is presented in comic fashion—a burly magistrate who now has angel's wings attached to his suit, and a beautiful secretary (with a star in her hair) who types on a tinkling glass typewriter while powdering her nose—a sense of

Liliom: Liliom (Charles Boyer) ascends to heaven. (Film Stills Archive, The Museum of Modern Art, New York)

irony pervades this odd glimpse of the afterlife. The glory that Liliom experiences on his ascent has disappeared (as did the carousel in Liliom's earth life) and falls away only to be replaced with a mundane hall of justice. Eisner explains Lang's dual heavens: "where is innocence and where is guilt? Is there a social justice, and who is permitted to cast the first stone?" (p. 156). Liliom's most heinous crime, that of striking Julie, is replayed for Liliom on a movie screen (film depicting film), and this is the crime that dooms Liliom to purgatory. Liliom again assumes a Chaplinesque demeanor as he hears his sentence: he shrugs his shoulders, asks for a cigarette, and then plunges forward through a door marked "purgatory."

The Return to Earth

Lang's depiction of Liliom (after sixteen years and one day in purgatory) differs from Molnár's in that Liliom's appearance is ghostlike. White-haired and gaunt, a shadow of his former self, Liliom drops silently onto a street that leads to Julie's house. A young and beautiful Louise (played

Liliom: Liliom (Charles Boyer) asks for a cigarette before descending into the fires of hell. (Bibliothèque du Film, photographed by Walter Limot, courtesy of Limot)

by Julie) walks by this sorry apparition. Touched by his appearance and assuming that he is a beggar, Louise offers him money. Liliom follows her home and stands silently in the small garden in front of Julie's small house. Inside, an equally gaunt and ghostlike Julie lights two small heart-shaped candles that stand on either side of a photograph of a smiling, insolent Liliom.

In the film, it is Louise and Liliom who speak together while Julie remains in the house.* And when Louise throws away Liliom's glorious gift, the star falls silently onto a sewer grating—its glitter fading as it touches ground. A ghostly passerby lifts the star from the ground and flings it upward. It flies toward the heavens and then takes its place among the other stars (this small scene within a scene is a foreshadowing of the outcome of Liliom's day on earth).

As the star flies upward, a large scale of justice appears in the heavens attended by a now completely scorched and burned Alfred. A heavenly

---

*This same scenario, an exchange between Liliom and his daughter, is carried over in the 1956 film adaptation Carousel.

eye watches Alfred as he in turn watches Liliom on earth and then balances the scales either for or against him. When Liliom slaps Louise's hand, the scales of justice tilt heavily toward purgatory, but in a deviation from the play, Julie saves Liliom from an eternity in hell. After Liliom strikes Louise, he sadly moves to a window of the house and peers inside. Julie sees him (as he hoped she would) and then clutches her heart. She looks again, but the ghostly apparition has disappeared. When Louise asks her mother whether someone can receive a blow and not feel it at all, tears flow from Julie's eyes. And as she answers her daughter, these tears, Julie's tears, tip the heavenly scales in Liliom's favor. The now gaunt, white-haired, ghostlike Julie has given Liliom his heaven.

* * *

Liliom is a dark play, one that offers the carousel barker no mercy. It would appear that Lang has acquiesced to the Hollywood style in which happy endings must prevail. Or perhaps, Lang holds fast to his storybook fantasy approach and simply prefers heaven for his long-suffering puppet.

In a sequence of ghost stories and films, *Liliom* deserves a special place. In the long trajectory from the Gothic ghost to the more modern depictions of ghosts and hauntings, *Liliom* manages to straddle the worlds of folklore and fantasy and still interject the disturbing issue of social injustice. As lovers, Julie and Liliom are different from their predecessors. In order to understand Liliom's ghostliness, and the reason he must return to earth, we must first follow his (and Julie's) life path and their struggles. In order to understand his death, we must first know Julie and Liliom as they lived. Liliom is a ghost for one short scene in the play and one short sequence in the film. The ghost does not dominate the play and film; it supplements it. And the concept of the task-defined ghost—one who is instructed by the heavenly powers to do a good deed, is the means by which the story can be told before the ghost enters the picture. The trajectory is a realistic one; before there is death, there is life. And where there is life, there is a wondrous story to be told.

CHAPTER SEVEN

Our Town

a play in three acts by THORNTON WILDER
a film by SAM WOOD

The Play

Where *Liliom* attests to the artistry and sophistication of the European stage and its penchant (especially in the early to mid-twentieth century) for dramatizing "the aspects of daily life ... depicted in some ingenuous farce" (Meyerhold, p. 264), Thornton Wilder's play *Our Town* is painted on a small canvas. There is no artifice and no elaborate staging. And where *Liliom* is a prime example of a fantasy, arcanely tailored to depict the problems of social injustice, and staged and filmed in an extraordinary and fantastical style, *Our Town* is presented as a disconcerting slice of reality, an ordinary town, with ordinary people who live all their lives in one seemingly idyllic village.

The underpinnings of *Our Town* may be traced to an earlier Wilder work, his novel *The Woman of Andros*. In *Thornton Wilder: His World*, Linda Simon writes a description of Wilder's vision of the novel:

> [Wilder] meant society in Brynos as a metaphor ... it was a world in which "the living too are dead" ... it was a world in which the "highest point toward which any existence could aspire was to be a member of an island family, living and dying on one farm, respected, cautious" [p. 74].

If Simon's assertions are correct, then Wilder's vision of an idyllic town (an island setting) is bleak and unsettling. The characters in the play (long dead) are one-dimensional—flat, dull, and emotionless. The Stage Manager's (played by Frank Craven) description of the three acts, "the first act is called 'Daily Life,' the second, 'Love and Marriage,' there's another act coming after, I reckon you can guess what that's all about" (Act II) gives evidence of the town's philosophical structure, to live and to die in one particular place without experiencing the excitement, challenge, and exploration of life and other lives beyond Grover's Corners. There is no magic, no movement, just a mundane passionless "living" existence that at some point in time culminates in the town graveyard high on the hill.

Even death holds no mystery. There is no great beyond or glimpse of heaven. The graveyard is an extension of the town itself—the same people, the same flat observations by the dead about the living. They, the dead, are depicted as waiting. Some have been dead for many years, but still they sit and wait. Doomed never to rise to great heights either in life or death, and never to leave their community, they sit, in the same stultifying numbness that defined their lives—fading ever so slowly and silently into nothingness. There is a dystopic aspect to this play, a sense of hopelessness and despair that is especially evident in this community of ghosts who are as earthbound in death as they were in life. The play contradicts the aura of excitement, suspense, and passion that is the hallmark of the traditional ghost story. In Grover's Corners, life and death are indistinguishable.

In contrast to the highly stylistic *Liliom*, Thornton Wilder's play *Our Town* depicts a hallowed segment of Americana, an "archetypal town ... a small, white New England village." Mr. Webb, the town's newspaper editor, comments, "It's a very ordinary town, if you ask me, little better behaved than most. Probably a lot duller" (Act I). The town itself suggests an idyllic space, a space that conveys a neverending continuum of stability based on a sense of kinship. Oblivious to the outside world, the town is presented as a microcosm of sheltered security where life is predictable, where the same families have lived (in the same houses) for generations, and where small, seemingly insignificant daily routines (milk deliveries, newspaper deliveries, breakfast scenes, walks to school), assume the high status of a ceremonial occurrence.

The outside world exists (for the inhabitants of Grover's Corners) only as a thought, a whimsy—sometimes desired, sometimes mentioned fleetingly, but never acted upon. There is a 5:45 train that leaves Grover's Corners for Boston every morning, but the train and its departure only serve as a means of marking time; the 5:45 train is merely a signal that morning has come and that the town will soon be awake. The town is a tiny closed world, "just across the Massachusetts line: latitude 42 degrees 40 minutes; longitude 70 degrees 37 minutes" (Act I) with the cemetery as the most notable boundary; "it's on a hilltop ... you can see range on range of hills ... and of course, our favorite mountain, Mt. Monadnock's right here" (Act III). The boundaries of Grover's Corners are so tightly drawn that it is difficult to realize that there is a vast universe swirling about and around this small town that is waiting to be explored.

Time

The sense of isolation, of distance and separation from an ever-growing and changing world, is the most pervasive theme in the play. Time has stopped in Grover's Corners, and with its end, all meaningful activity, all creativity and growth, has stopped as well. Grover's Corners is "idyllic" in a most destructive sense; it is a tiny island caught in the swirling currents of its own space and time. It bears no relation to a living world other than the clearly defined space it occupies; therefore, the activities, the "happenings," that define the lives of the people of this town bear little resemblance to the existing world. "Our town," this town, is no more than a picture postcard; it is a one-dimensional depiction of a lovely space that is finished and completed. Time is measured against itself, it has no substantive relevance to the living universe except to establish a chain of parochialism that even death cannot break.

Because time is absent in Grover's Corners, its absence is constantly referred to. It (time) serves as a marker of life rather than the catalyst that helps to produce life. The Stage Manager notes that a bank is being built in the town and questions what should be put in the cornerstone for people to "dig up—a thousand years from now." "We're putting in a Bible ... and the Constitution of the United States—and a copy of William Shakespeare's plays" (Act I). Because time has disappeared from Grover's Corners, nothing that designates the immediate present is deemed worthy of preservation. What will be buried in the cornerstone is a living cultural, religious, and literary legacy whose significance has been lost to the town and its people. The burial of this legacy characterizes the town's failure to incorporate this living history into the fabric of their lives.

Wilder plays with time in order to establish a sense of stasis. The Stage Manager, in his interactions with the audience, represents the present. On this level, he and the audience share common time; he is as much a spectator as the spectators. But then he steps backward, into the play itself, and becomes part of the past; "the day is May 7, 1901" (Act I). He plunges even further back to establish that the past itself has a past, "the earliest tombstones in the cemetery ... say 1670–1680—they're Grovers and Cartwrights and Gibbes and Herseys—same names as are around here now" (Act I). This narrative technique of subverting present into past serves to establish a historical time as opposed to a living time. The shades in the graveyard may be viewed as the particles of tradition locked by virtue of their lineage into a descriptive narrative of the town's history.

The Stage Manager, the narrator of the play, is also the town historian or chronicler. As narrator and historian, he manipulates and controls the action. He introduces the characters, charts their relationship to the town, and deftly maneuvers the dialogue and the action so that actor and audience appear to interact. On one occasion, he encourages mock questions from the audience. The questions are asked by actors seated in various sections of the theater. This interaction with the audience projects an intimacy and the illusion that he and the viewers are participating in the action that is occurring on stage. And in introducing the players to the audience, the Manager inverts the accepted form of introduction by telling the audience the date, place, and time that each character died. The player is then presented as a living being reenacting his or her life role. What the audience is seeing is essentially a community of the dead, resurrected to reenact a small portion of their lives. The idyllic, small, close-knit community is one that has long vanished.

Setting

Portraying a New England village tucked neatly away from the outside world—and whose population is culturally, spiritually, and physically distanced from the rest of society—must have presented a difficult challenge for Wilder. He conveys this detachment by the use of colloquial speech, by simple costumes, and by eliminating scenery. The stage directions in Act One indicate how Wilder created this effect:

> No curtain. No scenery. The audience, arriving, sees an empty stage in half-light. Presently the Stage Manager, hat on and pipe in mouth, enters and begins placing a table and three chairs downstage left, and a table and three chairs downstage right. He also places a low bench at the corner of what will be the Webb house [Act I].

The setting, or lack of it, is as much the story as the story itself. The bare stage, the plain unattractive costuming, the exaggerated colloquial speech peppered throughout with platitudes, metaphorically depicts the banality and isolation of this small town. George and Emily's wedding scene was constructed so that the audience would be part of the ceremony:

> the Bride and Groom come down the aisle, radiant, but trying to be very dignified ... [they] reach the steps leading into the audience. A bright light

is thrown upon them. They descend into the audience and run up the aisle joyously [Act II].

What Wilder had written did not conform to "standard" theater fare. Simon writes of Wilder's desire to bring a more naturalistic approach to American theater:

> For Thornton, American theater was still very much in the nineteenth century, aspiring toward "verisimilitude instead of reality. The box set encouraged the anecdote," he wrote. "The unencumbered stage encourages the truth operative in everyone. The less seen, the more heard ... I look forward to the time when actors will be able to play not only without scenery but without specific costume ... and thus the audience can clothe the actors in their fitting garb as well as the stage with its fitting scene [p. 136].

It is the interaction of audience and players—Emily and George running down the theater aisle into the theater itself and the questions and answers from the audience—that gives the play its remarkable effectiveness. But it is the locale of the action (Grover's Corners, New Hampshire), a small, very traditional slice of Americana, that could not be rendered in conventional staging. And integrating a community of the dead, the ghosts of Grover's Corners, within the same physical space as the living, presented a challenge that would ultimately stretch the boundaries of traditional theater. In one sense, Wilder had created a theater of the mind in which the audience experiences each shift in action and staging as it occurs; the play is both an intrusive and a collaborative experience between actor and spectator. The Manager leans against the "right proscenium pillar" (Act I) and watches and waits patiently until the audience is seated and the lights have dimmed before he begins his story.

The play relies on the interaction between actor and audience to supply the illusion of movement, of action that the sparse dialogue and bare stage cannot. And the Stage Manager is called upon to act on several different levels: as narrator, spectator, actor, and someone who has to communicate with the audience. He also acts as the moderator who directs the dialogue between the actors who are placed in the audience and the actors on stage who are called upon to answer the questions.

The graveyard scene is most compelling in that the stage is bare except for "three openly spaced rows facing the audience. These are graves in the cemetery" (Act III). Most of the actors seated on the chairs (graves) are those we have already met. The Stage Manager assumes his place on stage and begins a particularly contradictory narration: "beautiful spot up here. Mountain laurel and li-lacks. I often wonder why people like to be buried in Woodlawn and Brooklyn when they might pass the same time up here in New Hampshire" (Act III). The rows of the dead who face the audience and who "pass the same time up here" both demystify and abolish any sense of an afterlife. As they look outward at an expectant sea of faces, the dead gossip and comment on what and how they feel and what they are experiencing. This uncanny exchange serves to destroy any illusion of a passage from the state of life or living to a "higher," better, or different existence. The dead do not leave the stage of life, they continue on it. And each day, more and more people take their place on the rows of chairs and balance and comment on their concurrent roles as past and past/present. The growing community of the dead metaphorically have established a town of their own that mirrors "our town" and stunningly illuminates the futility or illusion of escape.

Life Cycles

Emily Webb and George Gibbs represent the youth of Grover's Corners. Their relationship provides the framework by which the life cycles that define the town—life, love, death, and the afterlife—are depicted. The play, therefore, is structured around them and their relationship to each other and to the town. In the two young lovers in the play, one notes that love is not a grand passion, it is perceived as a natural uneventful occurrence not unlike the changing of the seasons. In this play, any sense of the traditional Gothic with its aura of exaggeration, obsession, and passion disappears and mutates into the very ordinary persons of Emily and George, who are simply two very young people who have always lived next door to one another, whose parents have been lifelong neighbors, and who both have no particular desire for any other life than that which they have always known.

George's ambition is to graduate from high school and then work on his uncle's farm. For one fleeting moment, he thinks about going to a state agricultural college, but it is a brief digression that is quickly put aside in favor of marrying Emily and remaining in Grover's Corners. George explains to Emily his decision not to go away to school: "being gone all the time ... in other places and meeting other people.... I guess new people aren't any better than old ones ... they almost never are ... I don't need to go and meet the people in other towns" (Act II).

Emily has much the same temperament as George. She is a mere seventeen years old when she and George marry. A conscientious girl and an unremarkable student, Emily's scholarship is predicated merely on her good memory, and education to Emily and George is merely an extension of their daily lives:

> GEORGE: You certainly do stick to it, Emily. I don't see how you can sit still that long. I guess you like school.
> EMILY: Well, I always feel it's something you have to go through ... it passes the time [Act I].

Emily's description of the emptiness and lack of inspiration that mark her school years mirrors the barrenness and the banality that are the hallmarks of the town. Only one young person managed to do well in school and move away from Grover's Corners. The price extracted for this show of individuality and creativity was a heavy one. The Stage Manager matter-of-factly describes his fate:

> Joe was awful bright—graduated head of his class.... Got a scholarship to Massachusetts Tech. Graduated head of his class there, too.... Goin to be a great engineer, Joe was. But the war broke out and he died in France—All that education for nothing [Act I].

In Grover's Corners, acceptance is predicated on conformity. Those who attempt to break the mold, to achieve more than his or her neighbors, pay the penalty of dying far from the comforts of home and friends. Even Mrs. Gibbs (George's mother) is not spared the fate of an adventure away from home:

> She went out to visit her daughter ... in Canton, Ohio, and died there—pneumonia—but her body was brought back here. She's up in the cemetery there now [Act I].

Mrs. Gibbs's fate was kinder than that of Joe (who died in another country). She was brought back home and buried with family and friends on the hill beneath the mountain.

On the morning of their wedding (Act II), Emily and George experience some doubt. In a panic of indecision, George tells his mother that "I don't want to grow old. Why's everybody pushing me so? All I want to do is to be a fella." Emily too is frightened of the future: "Why can't I stay as I am? I never felt so alone in my whole life ... Papa, I don't want to get married." The Stage Manager (who has observed this slight deviation from the traditional wedding in this town) reminds the audience that their hesitation is merely part of the courtship and marriage cycle, but then he adds a disconcerting view of Emily and George's future: "the cottage, the go-cart, the Sunday-afternoon drives in the Ford, the first rheumatism ... the deathbed, the reading of the will" (Act II). The Manager's observations are matter-of-fact. He has noted, for the record, that this is life's inevitable progression in Grover's Corners. And Emily and George, in their only moment of rebellion, have tried to break loose from the inevitability of their future (as the Manager foretells it). They have failed; the moment has passed. They marry and join their community as husband and wife.

Art and the Artist

Since creativity belongs to the individual, it has no place in Grover's Corners. Whatever creative streak motivates the artist, it must be sacrificed in order to sustain the community's order and balance. In an exchange between the audience and Mr. Webb (Emily's father), Mr. Webb is asked, "Is there any culture or love of beauty in Grover's Corners?" His response is

> Well, ma'am, there ain't much in the sense you mean ... there's some girls that play the piano ... but they ain't happy about it.... *Robinson Crusoe* and The Bible, and Handel's "Largo" we all know that ... those are about as far as we go [Act I].

Simon Stimson is the organist of the church. As an artist, Mr. Stimson is given no special recognition and no introduction. He appears on stage in his role as conductor of the church choir. Mr. Stimson provides the town with its sole source of gossip and worry. He is the town drunk and his drunkenness is a source of disgrace and displeasure to the ladies of the choir. Oblique mention is made of Mr. Stimson's "troubles," but they are never defined or explained. Mr. Stimson was/is a musician who has chosen, for whatever unnamed reason, to remain in the town, and consequently his life has been stunted and deformed by the rigors of conformity. His creativity and his passion for music have been abandoned and he performs only at weddings and funerals.

It is only at the end of the play, in the graveyard scene, that we learn that Mr. Stimson committed suicide (he hanged himself). His tombstone is one that defies explanation to the residents of the town. Notes and notes of music adorn his tombstone—they are his epitaph. So unique is this strange final gesture that we are told that "it was wrote up in the Boston papers" (Act III). The horror of Mr. Stimson's suicide is that death has not given him the release he yearned for. He sits, with the other shades in the graveyard, waiting. Dr. Gibbs offers a feeble, but telling, explanation of Mr. Stimson's unhappy end: "Some people ain't made for small-town life" (Act I).

A Community of Ghosts

The dead, we are told, are buried in the graveyard that borders the town. They are a community of people whom we have already met. They (the dead) are seated onstage in rows of chairs, and they look as they looked when they were alive. The Stage Manager speaks of them as though their hold on life still exists: "gradually, gradually, they lose hold of the earth ... and the ambitions they had ... and the people they loved ... they get weaned away, weaned away" (Act III). The Manager's description of the plight of the dead disdains any religious doctrine; there is no heaven, no eternal peace, and no God. This "decline" of the dead metaphorically emphasizes the sense of captivity and of imprisonment that pervades the town and its inhabitants. There is no distance between life and death; therefore, there can be no release from earth—just a "weaning away," an eternity of waiting.

After nine years of marriage, Emily Gibbs has died while delivering her second child. As the funeral procession stops at Emily's open grave, the dead begin to question who is coming to join them. The conversation between them, the questions and answers, smack of the same gossipy banter of "living" conversation. They determine that it is Emily who has died, that she died in childbirth, and then, as the group begins to reminisce about Emily's wedding, Emily suddenly makes her appearance among the dead.

All the faces Emily sees are the faces she has known all her young life. She takes a chair next to Mrs. Gibbs (George's mother, her mother-in-law) and greets the people she once lived with. As the newest member of this community, Emily speaks "with a touch of nervousness." She rambles on about her son, her farm, and the car that George just bought. The dead, especially Mrs. Gibbs, listen but their responses show little interest. Again, the dialogue among the dead mirrors their "living" dialogue—flat, uninterested, dull, and gossipy.

The graveyard scene is particularly forceful in its oblique statement that nothing distinguishes the dead from the living. Emily's death is perhaps the most tragic aspect of the play. Because of her youth, she is unfinished. And while it is true that she has a living child (a projection of the future), we are not told whether her second child survived.

Emily, the new and very young ghost, still feels the pull of life. She turns to the Stage Manager, who has stood silently by listening and watching, and insists that she still feels alive and that she knows she can go back and "live ... back there ... again." The dead (and the Manager) try to dissuade her, but Emily insists. Emily, like Liliom, is permitted to relive one earth day. In her sad search to find this idyllic day, she chooses to relive her twelfth birthday. Her request is granted, and Emily returns to Main Street and moves excitedly to her house. She sees the newspaper boy and the milkman performing the same familiar rituals. She enters her house and is astonished at how young her parents look—the sight of their youth brings her pain.

This vision of her suddenly young parents who have been mysteriously recreated by Emily's now twelve-year-old persona indicates to Emily that what she is now reliving is lost forever, and the interaction between this ghost of the present (Emily) and the ghosts of the past (her family) clash like loud, discordant, irreconcilable notes between the two times. Emily's parents see her as she was, a very young girl, when she desperately needs them to see her as she is. Emily is spoken to and embraced by people who once were young and caring but who now, distanced from her by time and death, can only woodenly repeat the same dialogue of that "special" day as though it were a memory exercise at school. It is too much for Emily to bear. She pleads for the Stage Manager (who has accompanied her) to "take me back—up the hill—to my grave."

Emily returns to the graveyard and takes her place among the dead. She and Mrs. Gibbs silently sit side by side and stare at a distant star in the heavens. Suddenly George (Emily's husband) appears and in despair, throws himself at Emily's feet. A female ghost declares, "Goodness! That ain't no way to behave!" Another ghost replies in agreement, "He ought to be home!" Emily does not react. She now sits, like the others, still and waiting. And when George visits her grave and brokenheartedly falls at her feet, Emily has no reaction. She has, like the others, become part of the history of Grover's Corners.

The play ends with the graveyard scene. The community of the dead nullify the living. The town disappears while the dead remain seated until the Stage Manager obliquely reminds the audience that what they are now seeing is their own inevitable fate: "There are the stars—doing their old, old crisscross journeys in the sky. Scholars haven't settled the matter yet, but they seem to think there are no living beings up there.... Just chalk ... or fire." He silently draws the curtain across the stage and informs the audience that according to Grover's Corner's time, the play is over.

The Film

The film adaptation of *Our Town* was produced in 1940 by Sol Lesser (United Artists). Thornton Wilder, Frank Craven (who played the Stage Manager), and Harry Chandlee collaborated on the film adaptation of the play. The film, like the play, becomes a vehicle that is constructed to fit a specific medium. In the theater, the lack of scenery and the interaction between actor and audience gave the play a sense of realism.

What was most effective and innovative, however, was the simplicity of language and dress that defined this setting and the actors as part of a specific slice of Americana, a small village in New Hampshire. In the play, the town itself was given no defining scenery, so that the narrator's description of place and time (as opposed to an elaborate stage setting) served to construct a mental and verbal image of what the town of Grover's Corners was supposed to look like. In his review of the play in the *New York Times* (5 Feb. 1938), Brooks Atkinson wrote "by stripping the play of everything that is not essential, Mr. Wilder has given it a profound, strange, unworldly significance. This is less the portrait of a town than the sublimation of the commonplace ... in contrast with the universe that silently swims around it"

The film, directed by Sam Wood,* retains the same sense of simplicity, of unworldliness, as the play. In keeping with the theater setting, the film's sets were constructed to depict the sense of enclosure and confinement that characterized the town and its inhabitants. Like Fritz Lang's *Liliom*, windows, doors, and mirrors abound in each scene, with each window sectioned into even smaller framed panes of glass. This illusionary mechanism is structured to metaphorically convey a vision that is filtered and distilled in order to depict the townspeople's distorted concept of life. Wood's depiction of the town and its inhabitants becomes one of interior spaces.

As narrator of the film, Frank Craven retains the role he created for the stage. In the opening scene of the film, the narrator (Craven) appears to be climbing up from some undefined place or depth onto a long road that leads into the town. A long, continuous fence lines both sides of the road—it is broken and in a state of disrepair. As the narrator strolls along, he stops every now and then to replace a broken piece of fence that has fallen onto the road. The narrator's appearance from an undefined place far below the road and the long span of broken fence suggest that both

---

*Wood's film credits include Kitty Foyle *(1940)*, Kings Row *(1942), and* Saratoga Trunk *(1945).*

Main Street of *Our Town*: a descent into the past. (Film Stills Archive, The Museum of Modern Art, New York)

the narrator and the town itself no longer exist. The narrator comes to life briefly so that he, along with the viewing audience, will revisit a town long dead and forgotten.

Above the narrator is a cloud-filled sky that disappears as the town comes into view. The sky—which narrows and then disappears as the town comes into view—imparts a sense of dislocation, isolation, and darkness that indicates that the town was never a part of a living, vibrant universe but merely a slice of time that has long disappeared.

The narrator stops and leans on the fence; he looks out at the audience (this time the film audience) and begins to describe the town and its inhabitants. As he speaks, he turns toward the town and points out various points of interest (the churches, the train station). The lights of the town twinkle in the darkness and then the narrator turns to his unseen audience and points out that although the year is now 1940, the town we are about to enter is locked and sealed in the year 1901.

The narrator then asks "the operator" to roll the film backward. In keeping with this descent into the past, the narrator appears to struggle

Interior spaces show crypt-like enclosures in *Our Town*. **(Film Stills Archive, The Museum of Modern Art, New York)**

down a steep and difficult decline as he enters the town. As the "operator" moves the film back in time, the open space that first introduced the narrator (and also produced him) becomes narrow and focuses (as the town comes into view) onto a tiny valley of space that has suddenly become the present.

The film, like the play, continues to utilize the viewing audience in order to project this time shift from past to present; the narrator speaks directly and familiarly to the camera at all times maintaining the intimacy that was present in the play. The players also direct their opinions and their observations about the history of the town to the unseen audience, speaking not to each other but only to the camera.

The players' nonliving state is emphasized by the narrator, who must summon them to appear so that they may be seen and heard. When they are called to speak, the dead (the past) become visible only when they open a window or a door. The players are always depicted inside a house or a store (an interior space) that metaphorically suggests a crypt and the window or door becomes the vehicle by which their resurrection is accomplished. The actor opens the door or window, leans on the window frame, peers out at the unseen audience, and in puppetlike fashion, speaks directly to the camera.

One may describe these characters as pictures within pictures—photographs that have suddenly been brought to life. Because they can speak only when they are summoned, and because they inhabit Grover's Corners only for a short space of time, they appear as one-dimensional characters. They project no emotion other than a sense of pride in their descriptions of the town; they speak only when spoken to, and they stop speaking when the narrator has determined that the information they have imparted to the audience is sufficient.

In the film, the town has one street, the street where the Gibbs and Webb families live. Their two houses are situated side by side and are surrounded by white picket fences. The action in the two houses is confined to one room, the kitchen. It is always morning and it is breakfast time. The dialogues between the two mothers (in the two separate houses) and their families are mirror images one of the other. It is of interest to note that the colloquial speech so prominent in the play is missing in the film. Except for a word here and there, the dialogue, sparse though it is, is lyrical—the regional accent is missing. By avoiding colloquial speech, the film broadens its audience appeal. *Our Town*, this town, becomes a global possibility as opposed to a mere oddity of Americana. The same milk deliveries begin the day; the children are then summoned to breakfast; the two mothers repeat their calls to the children until the children finally rush downstairs, gobble their food, and then simultaneously leave their houses and walk to school.

In the film, the sense of interior space, of confinement and enclosure, dominates both dialogue and scenery. This sense of enclosure is most apparent in the scenes between Emily and George. Their bedroom windows face one another, and as the light fades, and the town grows dark, Emily and George are depicted sitting by their open windows looking out at the evening sky. Emily remarks about the moon, how large and wonderful it is. And it is Emily who can hear the train in the distance, "if you hold your breath and listen" (in the play it was the narrator who mentioned the 5:45 to Boston). But all George and Emily can do is look out at the world from behind their windowpanes. And their seemingly inconsequential remarks serve as reminders of the physical limitations that have been imposed on these characters; as one-dimensional characters, they speak, they wonder, but they have no agency. Their lives have been scripted and cannot be altered. The moon that floats high in the heavens covers an area far wider and far broader than the small space that George and Emily now occupy. And the train speaks of distant places and of movement—all of which connotes a living present and a world far beyond the two small open windows in Grover's Corners.

The Choir and Mr. Stimson

The scene that introduces Mr. Stimson (the church choir director) is the most highly detailed and disconcerting scene in the film. The scene is constructed to visually depict Mr. Stimson's feelings of entrapment. The women in the choir are seated in an area separate and away from Mr. Stimson. And as the tormented musician pounds away at the organ, his shadow, black, distorted, and menacing, is superimposed on the wall behind the women. The shadow is in sharp contrast to the plain, composed, and rather dignified women who prophetically sing the hymn, "Art Thou Weary?" And as the music continues, the shadow remains visible on the wall like a malevolent spirit.

Mr. Stimson, disheveled and angry, shouts his instructions to the women, and it is apparent that he has been drinking. When choir practice is over, and the women return home, Mr. Stimson is seen lurching blindly down the street. His face, white and filled with despair, is briefly illuminated by the moon. He stumbles to a door, hesitates for a moment, and then plunges inward toward whatever lies behind. His character retains the same mysterious sense of futility and despair that was so disconcerting in the play. This character stands distinctively apart from the town. In the film, as in the play, he retains the persona of the unfulfilled artist.

Interior Monologues

The filmic depiction of Emily and George's wedding deviates sharply from the theater production. In the play, the wedding scene is presented as part of the town's narrow and pessimistic view of a life cycle, "the cottage ... the Sunday-afternoon drives in the Ford ... the grandchildren ... the deathbed ... the reading of the will" (Act II). The wedding scene, therefore, became the means by which Emily was propelled from childhood to adulthood and then to her early death. In the stage production, the universal doubts and fears that the young bride and groom experience were part of the dialogue with the Stage Manager, who offered his own comments

Mr. Stimson (Phillip Wood) leading the choir: "Some people ain't made for small-town life." From *Our Town*. (Film Stills Archive, The Museum of Modern Art, New York)

on the proceedings. In the play, therefore, the wedding scene was an inverse of chronological time; it was presented as an end rather than a beginning.

Lesser, in contrast, wanted to film the wedding scene realistically. He felt that "it won't be interesting enough, and ... it will reduce many of the surrounding scenes to ordinary-ness" (Simon, p. 153). Lesser also wanted to "give the picture more appeal for the forty millions" (p. 154). And so he argued (with Wilder) to consider an ending, a rewrite, that would allow Emily to live. Lesser believed that in film, the relationship between the characters and the viewers changed from what they were on stage. Filmic relationships become more concrete; "Emily was more real; and her death would seem 'disproportionaly' cruel" (p. 155). Thus, the wedding scene in the film was altered to reflect Hollywood's insistence (again) on the happy ending.

Rather than have the narrator speak for the characters, the characters were permitted the added dimension of private thought. The prewedding fears and doubts that the Stage Manager had initially commented on would now be silently generated by the character herself or himself in voice-over and then float outward to the audience beyond the screen. There would be no intermediary, no narrator, to comment on what was now, for the moment, two living, introspective people.

In the wedding scene, the narrator is replaced by a minister who will preside over the ceremony and provide his own perspective on the various life cycles. The minister has a moment of reflection before he assumes his duties. He stands before a full-length mirror and, as he puts on his ministerial robes and prepares for the ceremony, his thoughts on love and marriage, life and death, are spoken in voice-over as he looks at his mirrored reflection. His weariness and solemnity are reflected in his reflection and his words as they drift around him and then float outward toward the viewer.

As in the play, Emily and George have their moment of hesitation in which they again express the usual premarriage doubts of the very young and very vulnerable. But in the film, these doubts are also expressed in voice-over. The two young people face the camera while their thoughts and fears flow outward beyond the moment toward the silent and listening audience. These inner doubts, these silent soliloquies, add a dimension to the film that the play lacks. They give the characters the poignancy and the sense of reality that Lesser felt was so necessary in the film adaptation. The three people intimately involved in the wedding ceremony—minister, George, and Emily—become universal voices of fear, doubt, and hope that transcend the limitations of Grover's Corners.

The voice-over effect also adds the dimension of immediacy. And since doubt and reflection belong solely and entirely to the realm of the living, and the characters who are experiencing these moments have long since died, these moments of reflection establish a sense of timelessness and eternity. They exist as the world exists and they are repeated and replayed every day. And so, unlike the play, when each ghost replays his or her specific moment in the history of Grover's Corners (Emily, George, and the minister as well), they are reliving and reenacting a universal theme that connects them with the living world.

Community of the Dead

After the wedding scene, the narrator stands on the same road he traveled when the film began. He points to the cemetery and describes how the graveyard is structured. The "old" part of the cemetery contains the shades of those who fought in the Civil War and then there is the "new" part where Mrs. Gibbs, Mrs. Soames, Mr. Stimson and various other characters we have met are seated. The narrator tells us that the ghosts of the past are now awaiting a new addition to their ranks: Emily, who is having a difficult time delivering her new baby.

The scene shifts to Emily's room. We enter her room through a large, open window crisscrossed with many smaller panes of glass. A despondent Dr. Gibbs watches over Emily's still form. Emily's eyes open and her gaze falls onto the open window. "I want to live, I want to live," are her thoughts in voice-over that echo silently and then drift out the open window into the night. Emily's eyes then move to a group of photographs arranged neatly on a far wall in the room. The photographs begin to blur and fade and then suddenly reappear, alive, in the graveyard. In keeping with Lesser's decision to allow Emily to live, the graveyard scene is depicted as part of Emily's illness, her delirium. The scene unfolds as a dream state in which Emily imagines her death and her return to earth.

The shades begin to speak (mostly about Emily's wedding) and their voices are projected back into Emily's room. Then suddenly a group of mourners appear and are seen walking, in a driving rain, to Emily's grave. The minister begins his prayer for the dead and Emily's voice is then heard greeting the seated and familiar ghosts. Since the graveyard scene is depicted as Emily's dream or fantasy, Emily stands high above the seated shades; she is all in white and a luminous white light surrounds her standing form. Emily's struggle to "go back," because "I can feel my baby in my arms," attests to her battle with death. Emily's figure becomes more shadowlike, a superimposed figure photographed against a vast endless sky juxtaposed against the stationary seated figures of those already dead.

Emily "visits" her family to relive her one happy day, but she enters her house as an aural spirit, one who can see and hear but cannot be seen or heard. "Momma, I'm here," she cries. "I'm grown up." Emily sees herself as she was on that special day and she sees George as well. She tries to make her family (and George) see her as she stands before them but they cannot. As she fails in her efforts to be seen and heard, her shadowlike figure becomes fainter and fainter—it seems to dissipate and disintegrate as she prepares to go back to the cemetery. The last lines we hear are, "I want to live!" And suddenly, a baby is heard crying. The graveyard disappears and we are projected back into Emily's room, where she is holding her new baby. George timidly enters her room and sits beside her; Emily has won her battle with death.

With Emily's return to life, the narrator's story ends. He suddenly reappears on the same road that mysteriously brought him to Grover's Corners. He turns toward the camera, says his farewell, climbs through the broken fence, and descends into the darkness.

* * *

Our Town, both play and film, introduces a new and innovative dimension to the traditional ghost story, the concept of a community of ghosts who remain bound together in death as they were in life. Although the setting is a realistic one (a small town in New England), the concept of a community of the dead who coexist comfortably with their living counterparts speaks to the notion of a single unbroken universe where living and dead are indistinguishable.

Wilder has deliberately stretched the boundaries of traditional theater and film in order to project a devastating comment on lives that are never fully lived or realized. Both play and film pointedly note that in this town, "our town," life and death are one and the same. No one ever leaves Grover's Corners and, more important, no one wants to. Passion, excitement, creativity, and agency have died, as well as beauty, hope, and redemption. Gone as well is the lone haunter, both Gothic and romantic. These ghosts have no place in the unimaginative stultifying atmosphere of Grover's Corners. They are left behind, buried in their own cornerstone of history, perhaps to be resurrected in some future time.

IV

THE CONTEMPORARY GHOST

CHAPTER EIGHT

Ghost

a film by JERRY ZUCKER
screenplay by BRUCE JOEL RUBIN

The ghost of the 1990s is a pale shadow of his predecessors. Stripped of his castle, coffin, or lonely house by the sea, today's apparition is homeless, forced to share the crowded, anxious space of the living. The modern ghost, the ghost of the streets, is no longer a solitary phenomenon, but part of a group, a community of ghosts, who, as a community, suffer the same anxieties of displacement, fear, and loneliness that plague their human counterparts. *Ghost* is a film that speaks to the times. Publicized as a love story, *Ghost* goes well beyond its commercial description to incorporate many of the social, cultural, and political issues at the forefront of our collective consciousness brought into startling apocalyptic focus by TV newscasters, talk shows, and horror films. The transition from mid century to *fin de siècle* has been difficult for the haunter.

In contrast to their Gothic and romantic predecessors, Ghost and *Truly, Madly, Deeply* are not adaptations of novels or plays. These modern versions of the ghost story represent an evolution of filmmaking that moves away from the classics, from the literary canon, to define itself as a separate genre. The ghost of the 1990s is thus no longer a "ghost" of his textual image. Like the prophetic song "Unchained Melody" in *Ghost*, this modern apparition is free from a literary precedent. Without a historical past or precedent, today's ghost dissipates into a mere reflection of the present, the time in which he or she lived and died.

The opening segment of the film *Ghost* is a phantasmal collage of disembodied, mechanical objects enclosed in a large undefined area not unlike a spaceship. The camera glides along this indeterminate, blurred, and shadowy realm colliding now and then with sharply defined objects presumably suspended in air: pieces of piping, long intertwined cables, ropes that seem suspended from space, a lamplike object covered in tattered white gauze, broken statues, and shattered columns. The camera drifts by a blurred, fencelike wall in which diamond-shaped openings glitter like thousands of unfocused eyes. These openings hazily gleam in a shadowy half-light. The unreality of this space, enhanced by the slowly moving camera eye, creates an aura of a living force rendered invisible—a palpable force, invisible but alive and watchful. The enclosed, dark world detailed in the opening scene is reminiscent of the old Gothic castle, the haunted house, with its secrets and hidden spectres. Juxtaposed against a soon-to-be visible chaotically vibrant contemporary society, this dark anachronistic space serves as a reminder of the Gothic when it was strong, secretive, and powerful.

Ghost brings the ghost film into the present. Haunting, in the modern sense, still retains the aura of possession, of a shared dimension, and of an unseen (but diminished) power that monitors, watches, and waits. The concept of an all-seeing presence is evident throughout the film, first by the illusionary "eyes" in the broken wall that appear in the introductory sequence, and then by various "surveillance" scenes. This concept of an all-seeing, unidentified, and manipulative presence is directly related to Michel Foucault's argument that the body (also unnamed and uncategorized) is the victim of diverse and sometimes nameless powers that exert unpredictable whirlpools of energy and influence. In *Discipline and Punish*, Foucault argues that

> The individual's body becomes an element that may be placed, moved, articulated on others. Its bravery or its strength are no longer principal variables that define it; but the place it occupies, the interval it covers, the regularity, the good order according to which it operates its movements [p. 164].

Because Foucault's theory is a construct in which the "body" defies specific characterization and embraces anonymity, the body itself is [de]subjectified and assumes certain ghostlike characteristics, the implications of which are that modern man and modern ghost are one and the same. Basic to Foucault's theory is the concept of the body's weakness; its manipulation by various forces as it moves through diverse realms of power. The film *Ghost*, which moves between two worlds, present and past, and which depicts forces, both real and not real, which coalesce to hurt, maim, humiliate, and manipulate, illustrates Foucault's theory.

This end-of-century ghost, therefore, is subjected to the same terror, fear, and humiliation that beset his or her human counterparts. Therefore, the singular powerful ghost or haunting that came into prominence with the Gothic novel and was later gently modified by the romantic ghost becomes in the 1990s a pale shadow of its predecessors. Weak, homeless, dominated by two cultures, that of his own community of ghosts and that of the outside world, and subject to the powers of the unknown as well, the 1990s ghost is divested of most if not all of its supernatural powers. In an inverse of the Gothic ghost story, today's ghost must seek help from the living (and the dead) in order to survive. This modern ghost does not haunt, it is haunted.

The present is thrust into this silent eerie world at the opening by the sound of banging and hammering: the camera pans to three figures breaking into the wall which conceals this shadowy dimension. Part of the wall falls away, and the three figures peer up into the space they have invaded. "Isn't it great?" Molly (Demi Moore) gasps. The three friends continue pummeling the wall until it falls forward into the camera eye, creating a momentary darkness. This shattering of space, this smashing down of walls, metaphorically destroys the barrier between worlds. Whatever existed within the faint twilight of the blurred and shadowy space is metaphorically resurrected by the broken wall.

The theme of crashing walls, of breaking through barriers, appears once more in the film when Oda Mae (Whoopi Goldberg) locks herself in a closet to escape Sam's (Patrick Swayze's) ghostly voice. When the voice does not stop, Oda Mae, in a desperate attempt to escape, throws herself against the closed door, it gives way and crashes to the floor. Suddenly, Oda Mae's family "gift" ("my mother had it, my mother's mother, they both had the gift, and they said I had it, but I never did, I never had it") comes alive. Oda Mae exemplifies the old Gothic convention of the ancestral flaw, the family secret that is well hidden and then brought to light by some unforeseen event. Oda Mae becomes the reluctant conduit between the living and the dead. She can hear and speak to the ghosts, and on occasion, if she chooses to, she can allow them to "use her body" to effect a mediumistic transference, but she cannot, does not, see them.

The camera eye is the intermediary between this cosmic world and the viewer. In a film in which ghosts have been diminished to merely aural ghosts, heard but never seen, the camera provides a glimpse into the atmosphere that encases the invisible entities. The camera maintains a privileged stance in providing [in]sight into this illusionary dimension. The voices of the dead are transmitted through a wonderfully fantastic psychic/medium, Oda Mae, who has the "gift" and becomes the all-powerful earthly means by which the ghostly voices can be heard. The aural ghost's vision doubles the role of the camera—a voyeur, longing to see and to be seen.

The voyeuristic silent ghost (his new status) is especially evident in a particular scene in Molly and Sam's home. An aura of watchful surveillance is suggested by an overhead opening in the ceiling that contains a record player that mysteriously operates without human assistance. The camera focuses on the record player as it selects and plays various songs. At one point, the camera and the opening in the ceiling appear to merge into one large, all-seeing eye that peers into the semidarkness below. The record that is being played is prophetically named "Unchained Melody." Ostensibly a love theme, its title also indirectly refers to the unbound, free-floating, displaced apparitions.

Sam is a man beset by anxieties. In an early scene, Molly asks the pensive Sam whether anything is bothering him. He responds: "I don't know, it's a lot of things. I just don't want the bubble to burst. It seems like whenever anything good in my life happens, I'm afraid I'm going to lose it." Molly, touched by Sam's fearful description of his happiness, tries to reassure him by telling him that she loves him, but she is interrupted by the blare of the television in which an "on site" newscaster is describing a plane crash with many fatalities. Sam reacts passionately to the voice inside the box: "Oh Jesus, another one! I should cancel my L.A. trip, these things always happen in threes. Amazing! Just like that, black-out!" The televised account of the plane disaster and Sam's seemingly irrational sense of impending doom is a foreshadowing of his own imminent violent death. In his book, *Nightmare on Main Street: Angels, Sadomasochism, and the Culture of Gothic*, Mark Edmundson explains Sam's anxiety in terms of the Gothic:

> One of the common functions of the Gothic is to turn anxiety, the vague but insistent fear of what will happen in the future, into suspense. The Gothic novel or film in effect gathers up the anxiety that is free-floating in the reader or viewer and binds it to a narrative [p. 12].

It is interesting that the televised broadcast of the plane disaster, immediately after Sam's premonitory declaration of doom, seems to reinforce his fears. Thus Sam's anxieties are amplified by a modern device, a TV camera, which is the medium that gives voice and substance to Sam's internalized anxiety. Edmundson defines the role of TV news in the 1990s:

> Perhaps the most influential apocalyptic-Gothic production in 1990s American culture is ... the evening news, the anchor man our well-groomed, tranquil guide to the terrors of the day. It's on the news that we learn to fear the serial killer, the molester, the abuser, the psychopath ... and all of the other Gothically rendered dangers [p. 30].

The 1990s ghost must of necessity contend with the terrors of the living world. And as we shall see, this ghost is not equal to the task.

Houses and Spaces

The space that Molly, Sam, and Carl have invaded is filled with ancient relics. Part of a building that is encased in a hull-like structure, the space speaks of a past time and place that begs not to be disturbed. As soon as the three friends enter this vast arena, Sam sees a sealed glass jar that contains one Indian head penny. He opens the jar and excitedly notes that it is an 1898 coin. He gives the coin to Molly as a lucky piece.

A spell has been broken and a spell has been created. A living place has been disturbed, and unknowing and unaware of the disturbance they have created, Molly and Sam have swept away the visible ancient relics except the jar and the coin. The coin that Sam is astonished at finding is, as Foucault describes, "a material memory," a piece of history whose relevance is summarily dismissed as a mere good-luck piece.

Since Sam is murdered because he has inadvertently discovered an intricate money-laundering scheme, the coin becomes a commentary on the dehumanization of the modern banking system, which no longer fosters the intimate collaborative interaction it once did, and which today has evolved into a vast, nameless, and terrifying power base.

In Sam and Carl's world of investment banking, the telephone and the computer, voice and image, are all that is required to circulate or distribute the ancient commodity of money from place to place, and from person to person. Monetary transactions assume the same ghostly indefinable characteristics as Foucault's shadowy body.

In contrast to the modernization of the banking system, the next scene interjects the ancient theme (and hope) of divine protection against evil by focusing on a religious icon. A huge plaster angel with folded arms and large wings is being hoisted up the side of the building. It is Molly's angel, something she wants in their home. The angel is reminiscent of the large religious forms and figureheads that were placed on the prows of ancient vessels as guardians of the faith or as a talisman against the darkness. The angel is brought into the building/ship/loft and is not seen again; it is simply there.

The angel metaphorically suggests an alliance with the good, with God, and a hopeful talisman against evil. Molly appears to have protected herself from evil forces, but Sam, a sad parody of a soon-to-be ghost, is paralyzed by uncertainty, fear, and violence, which appear to have taken

Molly's angel: A talisman against evil in *Ghost*. (Photofest)

control of his life. He is as oblivious and scornful of this strange and haunting object as he was of the old coin that had been preserved in the glass jar.

Carl, Sam's friend and coworker, is the villain of the piece. He has a hidden life; he is an investment banker like Sam, but unlike Sam, he is also involved in the dark undercurrents of a most modern crime, money-laundering. He has aligned himself with drug dealers, offshore banks, and hired killers. Because his life is a sham and a secret, he is given no identity or place other than his alliance with his two friends. He is seen when he visits Molly and Sam daily or at his desk in the bank. Carl is both an archaic and a modern villain. A stereotypical fiend, he masquerades as friend and family. In *Signs Taken for Wonders*, Franco Moretti describes this formulaic villain: "the criminal adheres to others only instrumentally: for him association is merely the expedient that allows him to attain his own interests" (p. 135). It is Carl's treachery that drives the narrative, but it is Sam's vulnerability that permits the crime (and his death) to occur.

Sam's dark view of his own future, his sense of impending doom, his dissociation from modern society and its dangers, brand him as a potential victim. His fears are motivated by his own insecurities; they have no basis in reality. But Carl moves easily and securely in society. Where Sam's fears are nameless and faceless, Carl knows his enemies. Whatever fears beset him, they are externalized, they belong to people—his enemies have names. Sam and Carl are corrupted doubles: good and evil, weak and strong, heaven and hell.

Oda Mae Brown, spiritual adviser and soon to be a true psychic/medium, conducts her sham séances in a gaudy storefront embellished with red, twinkling lights and spiritual music blaring from a record player inside the store. She and her two sisters have a thriving business that falsely provides grieving widows one last conversation or communion with their dear departed. The room in which Oda Mae conducts her séances is as fantastic as Oda Mae herself: a large table covered with a cloth emblazoned with spiritual patterns, a glass globe in the middle of the table, and a closet with a trick entrance through which Oda Mae mysteriously appears and disappears.

Oda Mae is a modern medium. Like her ancient predecessors, she has the "gift," although at the beginning of the film she is unaware of it, and she is a direct descendant of a matrilineal line of psychics. This family secret, the ability to communicate with the dead, places Oda Mae in an ancient mystical society of seers. What places her in the present is the confluence of several disconcerting factors: she has a criminal record (counterfeiting), her séances both real and fake are commercial enterprises, and she is outspoken and comical in her interactions with the bereaved: "I see him, he is wearing a black suit, could be blue." She is black and not overly happy dealing with a ghost who is white: "Are you white? I knew it! It's a white guy, I knew it!"

Oda Mae, a mixture of past and present, is Sam's dubious link with the living world. Oda Mae is the improbable heroine of the film. Unafraid of either the living or the dead, irreverent—"you don't think I'm giving this four million dollars to a bunch of nuns!"—sensitive, and empathic, she mocks and dominates Sam by her courage and commitment.

When Sam learns that his death was not a random street robbery/murder and discovers that his murderer is a threat to Molly, he follows the killer home. Frustrated by his inability to master the art of "ghosting," he wanders the streets until he reaches Oda Mae's store. The blaring music and her sign advertising her as a spiritual adviser draw him inside. Sam stands by silently as Oda Mae conducts her fake séance, and then he begins to chastise her for cheating. Much to her surprise (and Sam's), she can hear him. After much persuasion on Sam's part (he spends the night tormenting Oda Mae by singing), Oda Mae agrees to help him.

Sam's death and his temporary reincarnation as a ghost expose him to the horror and heartbreak of modern life. While living, Sam was depicted as young, attractive, well-to-do, and completely self-absorbed. Sam's knowledge of the world's woes were secondhand, fed to him by newspapers and television newscasts. Sam's reluctance to commit to a fully realized existence is further exemplified by his reluctance to marry Molly and his inability to use the word "love." When Molly says that she loves him, his response is "ditto." His death peels away the free-floating anxieties that have plagued him and resituates them in the city streets where he once lived.

Sam's ghostly travels through the city and his newly acquired sight and sensibilities are reminiscent of Charles Dickens's "A Christmas Carol," in which a self-absorbed, embittered old miser is given the gift of love (and sight) with the help of three ghosts who transport him back to his youth and then allow him a glimpse of his own death.

Community of Ghosts

Sam's encounters with the ghost world begin in the hospital, where his earthly body has just been covered and wheeled into a hallway. The first ghost that Sam meets is an elderly man who approaches the distraught Sam and speaks to him as though he knows him: "So, what happened to you? You're new, I can tell." As Sam watches in disbelief, the man thrusts his face through the sheet that covers Sam's body and cheerfully remarks, "Gunshot, that'll do it every time. Poor bastard." The man then seats himself next to Sam and gives him some kindly advice, "Hey, you might as well get used to it. You could be here for a long while. I'll tell you a secret, doors ain't as bad as you think, zip-zap, ain't nothing at all, you'll see, you'll catch on."

The two sit side by side watching a life-and-death struggle taking place in front of them. The elderly man comments that "he ain't gonna make it, I know, I've seen it a million times." As he speaks, Sam receives a glimpse of the vast dimensions and possibilities of his new existence. A large white light sprinkled with tiny glowing lights floats above the dying man. The man's soul disengages from his body and then merges with the light. Both float upward and disappear. The old man comments, "you see, here they come. Lucky bastard, could have been the other ones, you never know." As Sam turns to question the man, he finds himself alone.

Still fearful and insecure in his new role, Sam returns home. He sits and watches as the heartbroken Molly voices her misery and her loneliness. Sam tries to speak to her but Molly is deaf to him. The disconcerting concept of an all-seeing but ineffective apparition now applies to Sam. He has become part of the silent, voyeuristic, and impotent dimension that he and his friends so blithely disrupted only weeks before.

Sam is as ineffectual a ghost as he was a man. His attempt to follow Molly and Carl when they leave the apartment is a good example. The door slams behind Molly and Carl. Sam tries to turn the doorknob and open the door, but his hand, no longer a hand, slips through the knob. Half-remembering the hospital ghost's words, "doors ain't as bad as you think," Sam tentatively thrusts an arm through the door, then a shoulder. His feeble attempts are suddenly interrupted by a key turning in the lock and an all too familiar presence enters the apartment. Sam's killer has found Sam's home.

The terrors of the outside world, his own murderer, have invaded Sam's tenuous security. Paralyzed by fear, unable to utilize his new body effectively, Sam can only watch and agonize as the man rifles through the apartment. Molly returns unexpectedly and Sam fruitlessly shouts and dashes back and forth in an effort to warn her. Only when Molly begins to undress, and the murderer's gaze turns from fear of discovery to lust, does Sam devise a plan of action. Lacking the supernatural powers of his ghostly predecessors, Sam resorts to a cat, the paradigmatic all-seeing animal of Gothic lore, to terrify his tormentor. Sam frightens the cat, who leaps up and scratches the intruder's face. The man runs away, and for the moment Molly is saved.

Molly's close brush with disaster becomes Sam's call to action. He overcomes his fear of closed doors by thrusting himself through without hesitation; he dashes out into the street and follows his killer. The murderer has taken the subway and Sam follows him into the train.

There Sam encounters another ghost. Ghost appears to recognize ghost, and a wild-haired wild-looking man/ghost rushes through passengers and poles towards Sam. He shouts "get off my train!" and attacks the helpless Sam. This mad ghost has mastered the complexities of telekinesis and tries (with the help of special effects) to push Sam through the wall of the train, but Sam manages to escape this maniacal spectre and to continue his chase.

The pursuit ends in the murderer's room, where Sam overhears him on the telephone replaying his futile attempt to get the "information." Sam also hears him promise to return to the apartment to continue his search. Sam's inability to help Molly leads him to Oda Mae.

Sam's journey from his apartment into the subway and then to the killer's seedy room is a metaphoric descent into hell. Helpless in death as he was oblivious in life, Sam is propelled into the everyday occurrences of violence, madness, and mayhem that he once watched passively on TV.

Sam's first taste of reality comes with the knowledge that it was Carl who orchestrated his death. The good friend, Molly's present protector, is a thief and a murderer. Sam utilizes Oda Mae's psychic gifts to warn the stubbornly disbelieving Molly. In a scene in which Molly and Oda Mae meet for the first time, the plight of the modern ghost (Sam), his weakness and diminishment, are clearly portrayed. In her attempt to answer Molly's question about Sam's haunting, Oda Mae give a response that annoys Sam, and he angrily interrupts her:

> SAM: Would you stop rambling?
> ODA MAE: I'm just answering the question. He's got a attitude now.
> SAM: I don't have an attitude!
> ODA MAE: Yes, you do have an attitude!
> SAM: God dammit!
> ODA MAE: Don't you "God dammit" me! Don't you take the Lord's name in vain with me! I don't take that!
> SAM: Would you relax!
> ODA MAE: No! You relax! You're the dead guy!

Although this scene is clearly orchestrated to display Goldberg's formidable comedic talents, it also indicates how ineffective and subservient today's ghost has become.

When Sam first encountered the subway ghost, he was both frightened and amazed at the ghost's telekinetic prowess and his obvious madness. Sam seeks a second encounter with this maniacal phantom in order to learn the secret of his telekinetic powers. Determined to help Molly and Oda Mae, and to bring Carl to some sort of justice, Sam realizes that he needs a means of defense. Determined not to let the subway ghost get the better of him, Sam holds fast as the ghost orders him to "get off my train!" Sam's perseverance impresses the ghost and in a sudden change of heart, the ghost agrees to leave the train and instruct Sam.

Intent on mastering this power, Sam pays little attention to his raving instructor until he has learned how to project his anger into telekinetic movement. Later, Sam asks the ghost a question, and the ghost erupts into a violent burst of paranoia, kicking a cigarette machine and shattering the glass. He shouts wildly, "Who sent you? Who are you?" Rage and fear overrules his momentary docility, and the ghost jumps onto the tracks and into a passing train.

Oda Mae (Whoopi Goldberg) and the spiritual world in *Ghost*. (Photofest)

As the train disappears with its ghostly passenger, Sam realizes that he has encountered a ghostly image of the homeless, the mad, and the disenfranchised. As Sam stares at the swiftly disappearing train, his face reflects an infinite sadness for the plight of this mad apparition. Self-alienated from the community of ghosts, riding a train that goes nowhere, and desperately claiming space that he no longer has, the doomed ghost, a master of the purported "gift" of movement, is himself locked into an eternity of motion.

Much to Oda Mae's dismay, news of her gift has somehow reached the entire spirit world. When Sam returns to her store, he is shocked to find the room filled with ghosts and living alike. In an inverse of the living waiting to communicate with the dead, the dead wait patiently for their turn to communicate with the living. One overly anxious apparition, determined to speak to his wife, impatiently "jumps" into Oda Mae's body and proceeds to use this psychic transference to communicate with his incredulous living wife. Oda Mae furiously ejects the intruder, who falls weak and helpless to the floor moaning, "I can barely move!" The ghost is chastised by a fellow ghost: "Now you should know better than that. Jumpin' in the bodies wipes you out!"

This scene and the later scene in which Sam, this time with Oda

Mae's permission, possesses her body in order to touch and hold Molly one last time, overtly suggest the idea of exchanged gender roles and transferred sexuality. The first ghost who leaps uninvited into Oda Mae's body and then is forcibly and furiously thrust aside with the warning, "Don't you ever do that to me again!" suggests an aborted sexual encounter, which mocks the male ghost's powerlessness and, by implication, his metaphoric impotence.

The permitted possession scene in which Oda Mae allows Sam to use her body implies that it will be Oda Mae who will be caressing Molly. Indeed, the moment begins with Oda Mae's hands encircling Molly's hands and then, in a less controversial filmic compromise, it is Sam who continues the tentative love scene. The psychic transference depletes Sam's power just as it did the first unwelcome possessor, suggesting once more the impotence of the modern ghost.

In this film, and in *Truly, Madly, Deeply*, the vast community of displaced ghosts are male. They are sad remnants of the once-heroic Gothic and romantic ghosts who captured our imagination in mid–century. Oda Mae and Molly are the true heroes of the film, and they speak to the collapse of the stereotypic macho male image. The modern male ghost has lost the mesmerizing magnetic qualities that once made him so compelling. He is asexual, frightened, mad, and homeless. More child than man, certainly no longer possessed of an irresistible sexuality, this new ghost must, of necessity, turn to his more resourceful and powerful female counterpart for help. The first ghost that Sam encounters in the hospital (the hospital ghost), who tells Sam that being a ghost "ain't so bad, you'll get used to it," adds a small but significant piece of information. He tells Sam that he's waiting for his wife—"she's fighting it." This tiny bit of dialogue indicates just how far the male ghost has fallen.

Saying Goodbye

Sam's murderer (Rick Avila) pays the ultimate price for his crime. Petrified by Sam's demonstrations of his newly acquired telekinetic powers, he dashes into the street and is killed by an oncoming truck. Sam watches incredulously as the killer's spirit leaves his broken earth body and is immediately surrounded by the shadowy demons of hell. They surround the spirit and drag him screaming into purgatory. Carl suffers the same horrifying fate. Like his cohort in crime, he is literally frightened to death by Sam's mental maneuver and dragged away by the same ghoulish creatures.

Carl's death signals the end of Sam's brief sojourn on earth. As Oda Mae and Molly look on, a tunnel of light appears in the sky and reaches out to Sam. And as Sam's filmic image begins to blur and dissipate in anticipation of his ascent into the waiting heavenly sphere, Oda Mae and Molly are permitted to see Sam as he once was, and in his present state of grace. They both watch as Sam walks into the tunnel of light and then disappears.

* * *

Ghost is an excellent representation of the *fin de siècle* ghost. The almost cataclysmic decline of the fearsome Gothic apparition and his later, more romantic counterpart is as chaotic a fall as the time in which this ghost of a ghost finds himself. Weakened by his constant exposure to all society, bereft of the solitude of his ancient castle or seaside house, this weary spirit can do no more than wait for some heavenly intervention to release him from his earthly tortures. The distinction between living and dead (aside from the obvious) is as blurred and undefined as the ghostly image itself. Both are harassed, bothered, victimized, and confused.

Today, it is not merely the ghost who captures our imagination, but the unsettling image of man and ghost trapped in a godless, chaotic world. Like the community of ghosts in *Our Town*, whose state of death parallels their lives, today's ghosts helplessly flit and wander through and above the same towns, cities, and subways in which they once lived. Although Sam seems to have achieved a state of grace and redemption when he is permitted to enter the tunnel of light, he leaves behind a vast world of spirits who are still wandering and who remain lost.

Modern man and modern ghost are one and the same. The Gothic concept of doubling, of creating antithetical situations or people who clearly delineate the ancient opposing forces of good and evil, nature and man, order and disorder, disappear in the miasma of modern society. The old, splendid example of the haunter fades and merges into the angst and collective futility of the end-of-century world.

CHAPTER NINE

Truly, Madly, Deeply

a film by ANTHONY MINGHELLA

Like *Ghost*, *Truly, Madly, Deeply* opens with a dreamlike sequence in which a large multicolored sign reminiscent of an oversized bull's-eye dominates the screen. The bull's-eye, whose center is a large white globe—an eye—displays a sign "UNDERGROUND" diagonally stretched across its center. This sign, which splinters the "eye" into two distinct halves, metaphorically suggests a division, a divided perception that is carried throughout the film. Unlike the all-seeing "surveillance" eye in *Ghost*, which suggested a hidden manipulative power, this fractured sight suggests the absence of power, the loss of agency, the mind in turmoil. To Foucault:

> It is essential to observe that the function of "nature" and "human nature" are in opposition to one another ... nature, through the action of a real and disordered juxtaposition, causes difference to appear in the ordered continuity of beings; human nature causes the identical to appear in the disordered chain of representations, and does so by the action of a display of images ... which destroy the fabric of a chronological sequence [p. 109].

In this context, the camera, the once omniscient eye, provides a visual alternative, a silent commentary/subtext that acts to subvert the perception of reality.

The dreamlike sequence continues with the camera focused on a girl climbing up the subway stairs. She ascends from the darkness of the underground (subway) into the blackness of night. The camera eye follows her as she walks down another flight of stairs and crosses a dimly lit street. As she walks, her voice is heard in voice-over:

> Mostly when I'm walking, at night, or anyway by myself, he'll turn up; he'll talk about what I'm doing, give advice. He'll say, "don't be frightened; I told you, walk in the middle of the road at night," and I do. You know, he'll also

speak in Spanish to me, which is odd because he couldn't speak Spanish and I would be feeling low you know, very alone and hopeless and then, he's there, his presence, and it's okay, it's fine.

As she speaks, the scene suddenly shifts to daylight, and the girl is seated on a sofa in front of a large window. Her narrative continues with voice and image now firmly planted in present time. The girl (Nina) is speaking to a therapist. The therapist, seated far across the room, wonders how Nina feels when Jamie speaks to her; Nina responds that she feels "looked after, watched over, safe." When Nina mentions that Jamie speaks to her in Spanish, the therapist asks, "Is that significant?" Nina looks at the therapist, hesitates, and then quietly answers, "No."

The scene shifts to Nina's bathroom. The room is empty except for a large framed mirror that faces outward. A man's voice is heard off-frame speaking in Spanish, and Nina suddenly appears on screen facing her own reflection. The voice asks Nina, in Spanish, whether she has locked the back door, and she answers him in English. And then, like a dissonant musical chord, the therapist, in voice-over, adds her voice: "How long ago did Jamie die? Nina! Jamie, when was it he died?" Nina looks into the mirror, she stares at her own reflection, and then reaches up and shuts off the light. The screen fades into blackness and the question remains unanswered.

These short, staccato scenes analogous to short bursts of music begin the film. Unlike the opening sequences of *Ghost*, which are depicted as one continuous movement in which space and time seamlessly coalesce, these fragmented sequences, disjointed by sound, image, and time and dominated by the aura of discontinuous space, suggest Nina's displacement, her distorted perception of reality.

The following sequence introduces the voice that speaks to Nina. The scene begins with a cello and a cellist playing a Bach sonata. They are accompanied by an unseen piano and an unseen player (presumably Nina). The scene is juxtaposed with the opening film credits, which begin as the music starts. Photographed in grainy black and white, the camera encircles and embraces the cello and then swivels around the cello so that the instrument appears unanchored, in constant motion, rotating in space. Then the artist comes into view.

He first faces the viewer and then he is depicted with his back to the screen. All the while, arms, hands, and fingers are captured in detail as they lovingly caress and manipulate the bow of the instrument. The camera moves once more, rotating the cellist toward his unseen audience and then suddenly and swiftly freezes the image. This frozen image, now a photograph, is positioned on a wall.

Regis Durand suggests in his essay, "Event, Trace, and Intensity," that the movement from image to image, this doubling of images, alludes to "a presence and an absence." The cellist's movement, captured by the camera and then frozen into a photograph, indicates, as Durand explains, "a sort of internal rumbling ... a friction between the body-gaze and the reality that appears in a shutter" (p. 164).

As the cello music fades and player and cello disappear into the photograph, the piano loses its smooth, seamless voice and becomes thready and weak, and then Nina's voice is heard humming the music as she hesitantly and ineffectively picks at the piano. The film credits continue as the camera, having placed the photograph, moves slowly across the wall and pans across the room. It continues through the flat, hesitates as it passes a quiet, empty hallway with a flight of stairs and a large window at the top, and continues during the credits until it reaches the area where Nina is seated at the piano. The credits end as the camera reenters Nina's world.

This musical sequence, in which Jamie plays a Bach sonata and which also depicts Nina's inability to play without her ghostly partner, indicates the ambiguity of the relationship and the physical dislocation of the two protagonists. Because the sonata is not a recurring theme throughout the film, it connotes a transitory state in which the "players" will connect only briefly. The music, as Royal Brown suggests, "stands as an image in its own right. It joins other forms of fiction, other forms of image-making, to become an end in itself" (pp. 240, 249).

The ambiguity that surrounds the ghost in *Truly, Madly, Deeply* (is he or is he not?) is also made more evident by the lack of background, history, or visual flashback that would affirm that there had been an indisputable living relationship between Nina and Jamie. We have a cello, an unhappy young woman, and a therapist whose vocation it is to translate fantasy into reality. Her early question, "Nina! Jamie, when was it he died?" remains the film's ongoing mystery.

When Jamie returns to Nina, he returns, apparently, in the same capacity in which he lived—if he lived—as Nina's lover and housemate. His return is precipitated by a particularly difficult session with her therapist in which Nina hysterically weeps and bewails the misery and the void that Jamie's death have created:

> I'm completely numb. The kettle can be boiling away, or the telephone. I'm crying, crying ... I miss him, I miss him, I just miss him. It's anger, it's rage isn't it, it's rage. And I'm so angry with other people, people in love or out of love, or wasting love, women with children, growing children, fertile. Most of all, I'm so angry with him!

Nina's outburst externalizes her anguish, and her fears begin a series of events in which this litany of grievances comes alive and are reenacted throughout the film by various characters. And since Jamie's death overarches all Nina's woes, his appearance is also set in motion by her outburst. Each swift and subtle reenactment of these grievances represents a journey, a movement into different spheres of experience in which life and living are conceived and depicted as an amalgam of reality touched and tinted by the aura of magic.

Nina's journey begins with a scene immediately following her outburst. The segment introduces Maura, a pregnant Chilean woman whom Nina is tutoring in English. Maura's appearance underscores Nina's misery at not having children—"fertile," Nina cried. The two women companionably walk together across a field admiring the beauty of nature and translating this beauty into simple words, tree, sky, and clouds. The scene is swift but informative; it ends with the camera focused on two trees symbolically positioned at either end of the screen, one heavy with leaves, the other barren and apparently fruitless.

The two women are initially photographed in the foreground of the frame; the camera unmistakably comments on their contrasting physical conditions. As the scene ends, however, the women are positioned in the center of the frame, flanked on either side by the two trees and photographed in the far background of the screen. The camera captures and freezes the women within the limitless boundaries of the three words that they had been translating—trees, sky, and clouds—thus connecting their presence with the ever-changing possibilities of nature.

The next scene introduces Nina's sister Claire, who embodies Nina's anger at people with children and people out of love. Claire is married; she has one child, Nina's beloved nephew Harry, and another child on the way. When Nina asks Claire how her husband (Nick) is, Claire responds by telling Nina of Nick's fantastical plan to climb Mount Everest. Concerned, Nina asks when Nick is leaving, whether he will be home when the baby is born. Claire responds that the baby will be three months old before Nick leaves, and she adds, with embarrassment, that Nick's presence really isn't all that important, that he isn't particularly good with children, that he is actually rather helpless around them. The camera focuses on Claire's face as she speaks. It captures the uncertainty and unhappiness that flit across her face and that lie beneath her words.

Claire's loss of love has desensitized her to love in general. She mentions to Nina that Harry is taking cello lessons and that at some point in time, he will be required to have his own instrument. Claire wonders whether she can borrow or buy Jamie's cello because "you don't play it." Nina responds by asking Claire whether she knows how much the cello is worth. Claire misunderstands Nina's statement by assuming that Nina has placed a monetary value on it, and she offers to pay her for the instrument. Nina's response is anger, "I can't believe you're so insensitive! It's all I've got of him; 'tis him, 'tis him. It's like asking me to give you his body." Claire, still distanced from Nina's anguish, feebly offers an apology but it falls on deaf ears.

The "wasting of love" is embodied in two people: Titus, Nina's eccentric Polish carpenter, and Sandy, Nina's employer, the lovable owner of the haphazard translation agency where Nina works. Sandy is divorced and he has a son whom he loves dearly. The boy's mother is Spanish and the boy writes to his father in Spanish. Nina translates all correspondence between father and son. Although Sandy truly loves the boy, he refuses to learn the language and he depends on Nina to act as intermediary, to translate the boy's almost constant correspondence. This division between Sandy and his son can be measured by distance, the lack of a common language, and Sandy's incapacity to overcome these surmountable barriers and embrace the boy.

His love for his son is obvious, for when Nina translates the boy's description of an illness, or an uneasy encounter (he writes of nude bathing with another boy), Sandy reacts with passion and frustration. But he makes no effort to see his child, telephone, or write back. The relationship has become attenuated by time and inattention. The "waste" lies in missed and ignored opportunities and Sandy's inability to establish a living link between himself and his son. Nina, as a translator, acts as a medium between two absences. Her role as intermediary momentarily joins the fractured relationship, the fractured "eye" depicted in the opening scene.

Titus constantly professes his love for Nina. He knocks at her door at all hours of the day and night. He is homesick for Poland, for Polish food (especially bread), and he loves to cook his native borscht for Nina. He is a completely eccentric, lovable, and loopy individual. Because Nina allows him to come and go more or less as he pleases, he has designed a fantasy world in which he believes that Nina secretly loves him. He decides (without informing Nina of his plans) to take Nina on a week-long trip to Paris. When Titus shows up at Nina's door, plane tickets in hand, Nina is obliged to shatter Titus's dream of a week of "lovemaking," and send him home. But Titus's capacity for love and lovemaking goes beyond Nina. He is the father of Maura's child (this piece of information is concealed until Maura gives birth), and the beautiful, exotic Maura, who loves Titus dearly, is cheated and betrayed by Titus's mental philandering.

Then the elusive Jamie makes his appearance. He returns to Nina immediately after the revelatory session with her therapist. That evening, Nina sits at the piano and miserably tries to play. The music just doesn't seem to come and suddenly, from a distance, Nina hears the cello, and the music, which had first eluded her, ends in a poignant phantom duet. As Nina plays, the cello suddenly becomes visible and then, when the music ends, Jamie emerges from the darkness, and in a particularly moving scene, Jamie and Nina are reunited.

Jamie has come back, he says, because "death was like living behind a glass wall" in which he could see that "everyone got on with missing me." The "everyone" is nonspecific, but one must assume that it includes the inconsolable Nina. The glass wall that Jamie mentions also metaphorically suggests the all-seeing camera eye that has captured Nina's anguish and with godlike power has created Jamie's image.

Their ghostly cohabitation takes on the semblance of a true relationship in which the two appear to continue their lives as if death hadn't intervened. The difference now is that Jamie is constantly cold. In order for them to kiss, Jamie considerately blows on his lips to warm them. The flat must be heated to extremes to accommodate Jamie's lifelessness. At the beginning, the very first week after Jamie's return, Nina, overjoyed at his reappearance, doesn't appear to mind the overheated apartment, the multitude of blankets and coats that must cover their bed as they sleep.

For one glorious week, Nina doesn't leave her flat. She and Jamie supposedly make love, they play glorious, wonderful music (cello and piano), and Nina is overjoyed and overwhelmed at Jamie's appearance. And then one morning, Jamie awakens Nina and reminds her that she hasn't been to work in a while, that she should, she must, make an appearance. Reluctantly, Nina leaves Jamie and returns to her office. Nina's return to the outside world begins another chain of seemingly unrelated incidents that ultimately affect her ghostly relationship with Jamie.

When Nina emerges from "the underground," as Sandy comments when she enters the office, she is astonished to find Maura cleaning the office. Nina chastises Sandy for allowing Maura, who is now days away from delivering her baby, to do such taxing work. Titus is also there doing some carpentry work in the office, and he walks by Nina with an embarrassed and dejected look. Maura and Titus are now tenuously connected by Nina's reemergence into the world. And just as Nina has resituated

Titus from her environment into Maura's, it is Maura who inadvertently introduces Nina to Jamie's future replacement.

On this day in which Nina emerges from her blissful reunion with Jamie, she and Maura go for a walk and then stop for coffee. Before they enter the restaurant, Nina asks Maura whether she believes in ghosts. Maura translates the word *ghosts* as spirits and yes, she tells Nina, there are spirits all around, they are everywhere. The strange, almost hallucinatory episode in the restaurant lends credence to Maura's words. This scene is a disturbing blend of social realism and injustice that is defused by a touch of magic.

First Maura is enthusiastically and warmly greeted by her friend Roberto, and then Roberto, a doctor forced to wait tables, proceeds to monitor Maura's blood pressure. Maura explains that since she and her fellow compatriots have moved to England, they have been subjected to social and professional discrimination. In Chile, Maura was a documentary filmmaker (whose most notable film had to do with the spirit world); she now works as a waitress or cleaning woman. Roberto's professional lack of status is just as disturbing.

As Roberto puts the pressure cuff on Maura's arm, the owner of the restaurant bursts into the dining room and accuses the pair of being lazy, of being thieves, of stealing food and money from him. The horror of the moment is defused when a young man seated across the room startles the combatants by performing a hastily improvised magic trick—he shouts that he has nothing up his sleeve, nothing on his plate, all he has is a novel, a Russian novel—"it must always be a Russian novel"—and he flings the book into the air, upon which it becomes a bird that flies into the group and ends the altercation.

Nina and Maura see the peacemaker as they leave the restaurant and laughingly recount the experience. The very appealing, very earnest young man is standing by his car, and he offers the two women a lift back into town. Nina hesitantly refuses. In this scene, novel and film, two forms of illusion, empowered to create illusion, are jointly summoned to mitigate the injustice and the horror of reality.

Community of Ghosts

In discussing the community of ghosts as they are depicted in *Truly, Madly, Deeply*, a comparison with *Ghost* is inevitable. In *Ghost*, men, both living and dead, are weak and ineffectual. The dead are part of a large free-floating community of ghosts all of whom exhibit the same idiosyncratic asocial behavior endemic in modern society. *Truly, Madly, Deeply* removes the ghost and his companions from the realm and the anxiety of modern living. In this film, the ghost becomes a wish fulfillment, a desire driven into a sense of reality.

Like Sam in *Ghost*, Jamie has a job to do before he can return to heaven. (In this context, Jamie is frequently seen looking out the window and knowingly gazing into the sky.) Unlike Sam, whose task it was to discover his murderer, effect heavenly retribution, and protect Molly, Jamie must find the means by which Nina will abandon her dream and resituate her great capacity for love onto another living being. Jamie begins Nina's transition by first insisting that the flat be excessively heated to alleviate his constant feeling of cold; then by insisting that Nina return to work; and finally by introducing "the boys"—his heavenly cohorts—into the equation. Where Nina has/had no life and few friends, Jamie makes it abundantly clear that he does.

Houses and Spaces

Nina's flat is the locus of this heavenly invasion, but before Jamie's arrival, Nina's flat was already unhappily occupied with workmen and infested with rats. Nina's interaction with these men (Titus and Sandy included) and the rats was/is an uneasy mixture of fantasy and reality. The workmen—an assortment of carpenters, plumbers, exterminators, her employer, and other nameless workers—interact with Nina in a playful, intimate manner. To them, she is beautiful and wonderful, and they collectively manage to tell her so many times during the day. Nina agrees, "I am the most beautiful woman in London."

Nina is in fact a rather plain woman, one whose nose runs copiously (and unattractively) when she cries (which is often), and who cares little about her appearance. And yet Nina is the center, the heartbeat, of this little living world of men. More caretakers than workers, more family than lovers, this small group of men encircle Nina in a comforting, protective atmosphere. The remarks concerning Nina's beauty are more spiritual than sexual, and the men care for Nina in a motherly fashion: they cook for her, they even wash and dry her dishes. And like mother hens, they stand together, washcloths in hand, and collectively mourn Nina's unhappiness. This odd role reversal is reminiscent of "Snow White and the Seven Dwarfs" or "The Sleeping Beauty" in which a virginal princess is lovingly watched over and cared for by a group of asexual motherly dwarfs until a handsome prince/man manages to break through the metaphoric barriers that encircle the princess and awaken her.

The rats make their appearance in a most disconcerting fashion. When Nina is playing the piano, a rat appears on the top of the piano, finds a crumb or two, and busily munches as Nina watches in horror. When she is asleep, her eyes open to see a rat walking quietly across her bed. Man and beast seem to have occupied Nina's home, as George the exterminator shouts over the din of the other workers, "Nina, this is very important. We've got a very serious problem here. We're not only talking about rodents, we're talking about infestation, we may even be talking about nesting!" Jamie's appearance momentarily puts an end to the nesting. Nina stops the workmen from coming by telling them that she has guests, and the rats inexplicably disappear. For a short idyllic time, Nina has the flat and Jamie all to herself.

The "nesting" aspect, along with an ominous sense of annoyance at Jamie's presence, begins right after the scene in which Nina meets the young magician. Nina is asleep/resting in the bathtub, her face covered in white cream. Jamie pops up from nowhere and frightens Nina awake. Annoyed, Nina tells Jamie, "Don't do that! It's a bad time, go away! I can't even lock the door on you anymore! Leave me alone for a bit." As Jamie leaves the bathroom, he gives Nina some disconcerting news:

> JAMIE: Listen, sweetheart, some of the guys wanted to come back and watch a couple of videos.
> NINA: What guys?
> JAMIE: Friends, just friends.
> NINA: Dead friends?
> JAMIE: I suppose so, yes.
> NINA: You're telling me that there are dead people in my living room watching videos?

When Nina enters the living room, she is introduced to Jamie's friends. They are a small, endearing group of dead movie buffs who are particularly enamored of classic films. The slight altercation that began in the bathroom extends to the living room when one ghost disappointedly mentions that one film labeled *Manhattan* was not *Manhattan* at all. Nina apologetically answers that she always has trouble using the video machine, and that when she was taping *Hannah and Her Sisters*, she must have inadvertently taped over *Manhattan*.

The group are gently appalled at Nina's mishandling of Woody Allen, and Jamie adds his own displeasure at her clumsiness: "She did that with *Strangers on a Train*." The scene ends on an Allenesque note with the ghosts and the viewer watching a film within a film (Allen used this reflexive technique in *Purple Rose of Cairo*). The film they/we are watching is especially telling; it is David Lean's *Brief Encounter*, the story of a short-lived but deeply emotional love story. The last scene of the film is of particular interest. The last few words are repeated fervently and verbatim by the ghostly audience: "whatever your dream was, it wasn't a happy one, was it? You've been a long way away, thank you for coming back to me." The movie ends as the smitten ghosts wipe their tears and applaud the film. *Brief Encounter*, by title and especially in the scene highlighted in the film, speak directly to Nina's past obsession and her current dilemma. So begin Nina's ghostly invasion and her discontent.

Nina next sees the magician when she is running to catch a bus. The two bump into one another as the man and a group of disabled children are leaving the bus. The young man makes an attempt to ask Nina for a date. But before he has finished his sentence, Nina interrupts with "yes!" Because of Jamie, Nina hesitates before giving him her home phone number, so in a happy compromise, and for lack of pen, pencil, and time, the so-far nameless magician writes his phone number on Nina's hand.

Nina has tentatively and metaphorically taken the future by the hand. But there is still Jamie and his ever-expanding group of ghostly friends. In a scene that is a replay of the "unanswered question" sequence, Nina returns to her therapist for guidance. What would happen, Nina wonders, if she returned home and found Jamie there? "Then what?" she asks. Sometimes, Nina says, she can imagine that Jamie is back; "Isn't that ridiculous?" she says. The therapist asks, "What is ridiculous? What are you saying that is ridiculous?" Nina responds, "Everything, everything, I don't know!" and as she speaks, she is back in her living room, where Jamie and a group of ghostly musicians are giving a concert.

The word *ridiculous* echoes above Nina's head as she unhappily watches, but does not listen to, the sublime music that fills the room. The concert continues as the room and the question fade into darkness. The film begins with music, a sonata in which Jamie plays without an orchestra but with an unknown accompanist, presumably Nina. This duet, cello and piano, has an implied intimacy in which the players live in the same moment and share the same experience. By expanding the duet to a full orchestra, the intimacy is shattered. Jamie's concert connotes Nina's displacement and their impending separation.

Nina is late for her first date with the magician. Since this scene follows the heavenly concert, the assumption must be made that Nina has called him, that she has tentatively started her move away from Jamie. Nina apologizes for being late and, in response, a bunch of roses mysteriously appears from beneath the magician's coat. In a change of heart, Nina insists that she cannot stay and she refuses the offer of a lift into town. The disappointed magician, whose name is Mark, tells Nina that he and his group of children have been busy drawing trees. As the enchanted Nina listens, he offers another reading of the metaphoric image of the tree that inadvertently address Nina's problem: "You draw a tree and then on the roots you put in the names of people who were important in forming you, stabilizing you, or taking care of you, Mum, Dad, sister. And then you put on the names of the people who are with you now." Mark has written Nina's name on one of the leaves of his imaginary tree.

The tree image recurs throughout the film to indicate Nina's separation from reality, her dissociation from a fruitful and fulfilling life. By utilizing the tree image to describe the past (people who were important in forming you) and then moving the tree/leaf image to suggest a future (he has written Nina's name on a leaf), Mark offers Nina a way back into the world.

Nina then tells Mark that he can walk her to the underground. Mark seizes this opportunity to suggest yet another way of getting to know one another—each is to hop to the underground on one foot, and as they hop, they are to recite their entire history. Mark begins: he gives his full name, he is an art therapist, his parents are alive, his father was an amateur magician and Mark was his assistant, he has a child but the child's mother left him for a theology student; he is therefore an atheist. Nina joyfully enters the game. She gives her full name, her family background, the fact that she is seeing a therapist and then suddenly, the sound of a cello floats through the air. Nina stops, turns, and sees Jamie, seated in front of a café, playing the cello. As she walks toward Jamie, the figure changes and becomes someone else, a stranger.

Later that night, Nina returns home. As she approaches the house, she throws the roses that Mark has given her into the dust bin. As she enters, Jamie is playing the cello. He asks her whether she has something to tell him. She responds by telling him that she has the uncomfortable sense that he is with her all day, that the idea of a constant continuing presence disturbs her. Jamie quietly denies that he is with her all the time.

Then Nina asks where the video and the television are. Jamie responds that he has moved them into the bedroom because it is too cold for his friends (and him) in the living room, and besides, he likes to play the cello undisturbed. When Nina protests, Jamie responds that she might try talking to his friends, that conversation might alleviate her discomfort. Nina angrily answers, "They're dead people! The rats have gone and now I'm infested with ghosts!" Jamie sadly and quietly says, "If you want me to go, just tell me." The guilt-ridden Nina answers that she doesn't want him to go, she just doesn't know what she wants.

Jamie's last few hours with Nina begin with a late-night telephone call. In order to answer the ringing phone, Nina must climb over a floor filled with sleeping ghosts covered in sheepskin blankets. The phone call informs Nina that Maura is in the hospital about to give birth and Nina is wanted. Nina rushes to the hospital and finds Maura about to be taken to the delivery room. The frightened Maura, overjoyed at Nina's arrival, begs Nina to stay with her until the baby is born. And finally confessing that Titus is the baby's father, she asks Nina to call him. The birth scene is most notable because it depicts Nina's total involvement, her joy and happiness at Maura's delivery of a beautiful little girl. The scene poignantly ends with Maura giving Nina the baby to hold, and Nina, mesmerized by the child, murmurs, "a new life, a new life."

When Nina arrives home after her long night at the hospital, she finds the flat in total disarray; all the furniture has been rearranged, books are piled all over the floors, and Nina's favorite rug has been rolled up and is about to be thrown away. All Jamie's friends are involved in this massive undertaking, and Nina responds in a fury, "Everytime I come home, I feel like I'm being burgled! It's my flat, Jamie, it is my flat!" Because Jamie's friends are witness to this scene, Nina furiously orders them to leave, to get out! Alone, each sitting at opposite ends of the room but facing one another, Nina explains, "You see, I held that baby. It's life, it's a life I want." And then, in a disconnected but fervently spoken line, Nina adds, "I longed for you, I so much longed for you." A saddened Jamie responds by asking Nina whether she would translate a poem (Pablo Neruda's "The Dead Woman") for him:

> ...forgive me.
> If you are not living,
> if you, beloved, my love,
> . . . .
> have died,
> all the leaves will fall on my breast,
> it will rain upon my soul night and day,
> . . . .
> my feet will want to march toward where you sleep,
> but
> I shall go on living....

Neruda's poem utilizes the tree image to combine death, loss, and life. Neruda uses the pronouns "you" and "I" to construct a hauntingly beautiful image of life communing with death so that life may continue. The poem's title, "The Dead Woman," specifically speaks to Nina, and it is her release and Jamie's farewell. In this scene, Jamie and Nina are seated at either end of the room. Their physical separation, their apartness, makes the poem all the more meaningful and poignant.

Nina leaves the flat and Jamie's friends reappear and kindly and gently close about him. They ask him, "Well?" And Jamie sadly and mournfully replies, "I think so, yes."

Nina walks and thinks. She sits for a long time looking at the sky, and then she finds herself at Mark's school. He and "his children" happily greet her, and then the two are seen about to get into Mark's car. Nina hesitates, she begins to cry, and then she tells Mark that she had once loved someone very very much and that he had died. They agree to go to Mark's flat, to go home as Mark suggests, and talk. On the way, Nina make a quick, decisive move. She spots a pharmacy, orders Mark to stop, and runs out and buys a toothbrush. The scene ends with the camera moving through Mark's flat, through the kitchen with the remnants of dinner still on the table, and through to the bedroom where Mark and Nina are asleep.

It is daylight and Nina enters her now-vacant apartment. She calls for Jamie, but no one answers. And then she sees the roses that she had once discarded, beautifully arranged in a vase on the piano. It is Jamie's farewell and his acknowledgment of Nina's new life. As Nina polishes Jamie's cello and prepares to put it away, she notices that the rat has returned. She puts the cello in its case, calls Mark, and tells him to come and get her. Cello music is heard in the background as Nina quietly turns out the lights and leaves. And as the door closes behind her, the music grows louder, and Jamie and the ghosts reappear shrouded in darkness. They move forward, shadows all, until they reach the window. They watch as Nina and Mark embrace. Jamie smiles as his friends thoughtfully, sympathetically, pat him on the shoulder, and they stand watching and waving farewell as Nina and Mark walk away.

* * *

Truly, Madly, Deeply is an unusual story told in an unusual manner. It is related to *Ghost* in that in both films portray a young woman who grieves for a dead lover, a strong camera presence, and a community of ghosts. *Ghost*, however, has a strong central narrative that is presented in classic linear style. The apparition is first depicted in his living state

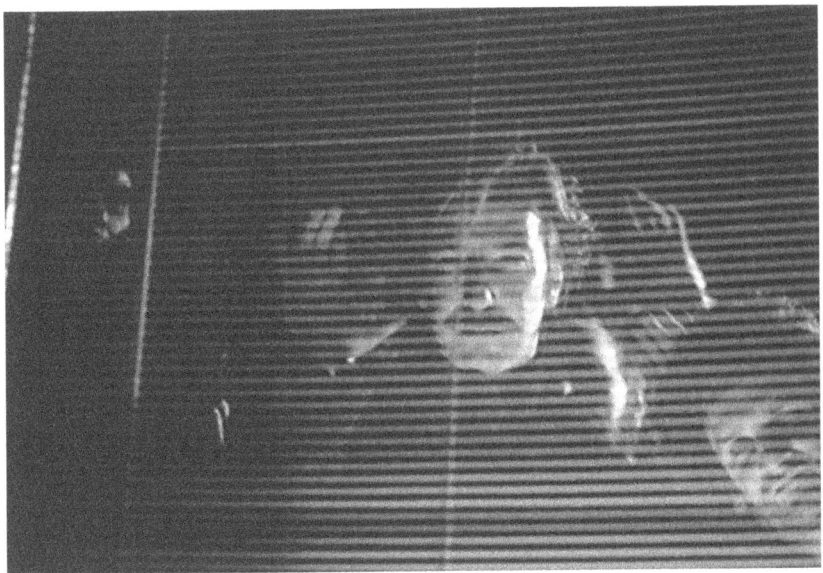

Truly, Madly, Deeply: Jamie (Alan Rickman) bids a ghostly farewell. (Photofest)

complete with lover, home, friends, and job. After his death, and as a ghost, he traverses the city and attaches himself to a medium who in turn helps him communicate with his grief-stricken lover. The film's ending, in Hollywood fashion, resolves all outstanding issues: the killer is destroyed in a typical bloody confrontation, and the three protagonists are united in a final touching farewell. That Sam lived is never in question, since the first few scenes clearly establish his existence.

In contrast, in *Truly, Madly, Deeply* the ghost seems never to have lived at all. There is no history, no indication that Jamie and Nina ever shared a life together. Nina's sister adds to the dilemma by suggesting that Nina stay with her while the apartment is being renovated because "it's not like Jamie lived here." Who and what Jamie is or is not is the film's continuing mystery. The camera (not Nina) tells us that Jamie is a cellist because he is introduced in a scene that features a cellist. However, it is the cello and not the artist who dominates the scene.

Throughout the film, the camera directs our vision and, in this context, it assumes the role of the Gothic double. It is given a voice and a particular point of view; it is the nonhuman purveyor of an uncertain but alternate truth. The opening sequence that depicts a bull's-eye with a large white globe (eye) diagonally fractured in half metaphorically signals the camera's contradictory interpretation. While Nina's point of view is a constant and drives the film, the camera, like an ancient Greek chorus, provides its own visual commentary.

The film is a finely drawn picaresque journey that defies either a beginning or an ending and that places the fantastic, the fanciful, the grotesque, and the magical in the living world and not in the beyond. But it is the strange inclusion of a male-dominated ghostly community that places both this film and *Ghost* in contemporary time. The weakened ghost, the ghost of a ghost, is unmistakably present in both films. But how and why? As a potent indicator of the impermanence of today's world, both films disdain marriage—death always intervenes. Men are paralyzed by anxiety while women, like Nina, Molly, Maura, and Oda Mae—though momentarily shaken, momentarily derailed—are able to push ahead and get their lives back in order. The ghost, however, is as unstable in death as he was in life. In *Ghost* the ghostly community is composed of modern apparitions who carry their modern-day angst into the beyond.

Truly, Madly, Deeply puts another spin on the ghostly community by presenting its members as a true community bound together by common interests. We have cinephiles, musicians, chess players, and the like. These ghosts contain the memory, the history, the essence of the past. Jamie, by virtue of his weary appearance, his tired walk, and his slow speech, is an old spirit, one who has done this job many times before. His friends who ask him "Well?" are also part of a tired troop of spirits whom the living constantly disrupt and displace because of their constant "missing." Homeless, always on the move, these old recycled spirits "nest" for a short while, resolve their given tasks by becoming a houseful of unwelcome guests, and use their earth time to catch up on the films they have missed. These are the new ghosts as they are depicted today. No longer a solitary apparition locked away in a lonely house, the modern ghosts are time and space travelers who, as Maura says, "are all around us."

Jamie's community of ghosts is a complete reversal of the Gothic apparition born of the romantic idealization of death and solitude. The Gothic ghosts of Heathcliff and even Cap'n Gregg derive from the death fantasies of 19th-century literature. As we end the 1990s, we see how far away from this Gothic death wish the ghost has come. Haunting now indicates the dangers of isolation and solitude, of closing oneself in psychologically and physically, *Truly, Madly, Deeply* argues that our lives are full of ghosts, as memories; as music, as poetry, and that novel and film have the ability to create illusion, to recreate these ghosts. Like a fairy tale, film can transform a plain woman into someone beautiful, an ordinary man into a magician, the dead into life. Jamie exists because the camera created him.

In our current "visual" culture, the ghost has evolved from novel to film because people value the exterior look over content. It is the ghostly presence we crave. But the novel remains: the literary ghost, who lurks in the background, a ghost waiting to be resurrected.

Bibliography

Affron, Charles. *Cinema and Sentiment*. Chicago: University of Chicago Press, 1982.
Allday, Elizabeth. *Stefan Zweig: A Critical Biography*. Chicago: J. Philip O'Hara, 1972.
American Federation of Arts and the Pennsylvania Academy of the Fine Arts. *Facing the Past: Nineteenth-Century Portraits from the Collection of the Pennsylvania Academy of the Fine Arts*. New York and Philadelphia: 1992.
Andrews, J. Dudley. *The Major Film Theories*. New York: Oxford University Press, 1976.
Auerbach, Nina. *Private Theatricals: The Lives of the Victorians*. Cambridge, Mass: Harvard University Press. 1990.
Bakhtin, Mikhail. *Rabelais and His World*. Translated from the Russian by Helene Iswolsky. Cambridge, Mass. M.I.T. Press, 1968.
Barrie, J.M. *Peter Pan: A Fantasy in Five Acts*. London: Samuel French, 1928.
Barthes, Roland. *Elements of Semiology*. Translated from the French by Annette Lavers and Colin Smith. New York: Noonday Press, 1973.
Basinger, Jeanine. *A Woman's View: How Hollywood Spoke to Women, 1930–1960*. New York: Alfred A. Knopf, 1993.
Bauman, Zygmunt. *Intimations of Postmodernity*. London: Routledge, 1992.
Beja, Morris. *Film and Literature*. New York: Longman, 1979.
Bellour, Raymond. "The Phantom's Due." Translated from the French by Lynne Kirby. *Discourse* 16, 2 (Winter 1993-94): 164–73.
Benjamin, Walter. "The Work of Art in the Age of Mechanical Reproductions," in *The Critical Tradition*, ed. David Richter. New York: St. Martin's Press, 1989, pp. 571–88.
Braudy, Leo. *The World in a Frame: What We See in Films*. Chicago. University of Chicago Press, 1976.
Briggs, Julia. *Night Visitors: The Rise and Fall of the English Ghost Story*. London: Faber and Faber, 1977.
Brontë, Emily. *Wuthering Heights*. New York: Caxton House, 1930.
Brown, Royal S. *Overtones and Undertones: Reading Film Music*. Berkeley: University of California Press, 1994.
Cook, David A. *A History of Narrative Film*. New York: W.W. Norton & Company, 1981.

Cox, Michael, ed. *The Oxford Book of Twentieth-Century Ghosts*. Oxford: Oxford University Press, 1996.
Daiches, David. *A Critical History of English Literature*, vol. 4. 2d ed. London: Secker & Warburg, 1969.
Dalle Vacche, Angela. *Cinema and Painting: How Art Is Used in Film*. Austin: University of Texas Press, 1996.
Dick, R.A. *The Ghost and Mrs. Muir*. London: Ziff-Davis, 1945.
Dostoevsky, Fyodor. *Notes from Underground*. Translated from the Russian by Richard Pevear and Larissa Volokhonsky. New York: Vintage Books, 1994.
Durand, Regis. "Event, Trace, Intensity." Translated from the French by Lynne Kirby. *Discourse* 16, 2 (Winter 1993-94): 119–20.
Edmundson, Mark. *Nightmare on Main Street: Angels, Sadomasochism, and the Culture of Gothic*. Cambridge, Mass.: Harvard University Press, 1997.
Eisner, Lotte. *Fritz Lang*. New York: Da Capo Press, 1986.
Felstiner, John. *Translating Neruda: The Way to Macchu Picchu*. Stanford, Calif.: Stanford University Press, 1980.
Finucane, R.C. *Appearances of the Dead: A Cultural History of Ghosts*. London: Junction Books, 1982.
Foucault, Michel. *Discipline and Punish: The Birth of the Prison*. Translated from the French by Alan Sheridan. New York: Vintage Books, 1979.
———. *The History of Sexuality. Vol. 1, An Introduction*. Translated from the French by Robert Hurley. New York: Vintage Books, 1979.
———. *The Order of Things: An Archaeology of the Human Sciences*. (A translation of *Les Mots et les choses*.) New York: Vintage Books, 1994.
———. "What Is an Author?" In *Language, Counter-memory, Practice*, edited and translated from the French by Donald F. Bouchard. Ithaca, N.Y.: Cornell University Press, 1977.
Freud, Sigmund. *General Psychological Theory: Papers on Metapsychology*: New York: Macmillan, 1963.
Galperin, William H. *The Return of the Visible in British Romanticism*. Baltimore: Johns Hopkins University Press, 1993.
Geduld, Harry M. *Authors on Film*. Bloomington: Indiana University Press, 1972.
Giannetti, Louis. *Understanding Movies*. 3d ed. Englewood Cliffs, N.J.: Prentice-Hall, 1982.
Gilbert, Sandra M., and Susan Gubar. *The Madwoman in the Attic: The Woman Writer and the Nineteenth-Century Literary Imagination*. New Haven, Conn.: Yale University Press, 1979.
Gissing, George. *The Odd Women*. New York: W.W. Norton, 1977.
Grafe, Frieda. *The Ghost and Mrs. Muir*. London: British Film Classics, 1995.
Haining, Peter, ed. *The Complete Ghost Stories of Charles Dickens*. New York: Franklin Watts, 1983.
Hollinger, Robert. *Postmodernism and the Social Sciences*. Thousand Oaks, Calif.: Sage, 1994.
James, Henry. *The Turn of the Screw*. New York. W.W. Norton, 1966.
Koch, Howard. "Script to Screen with Max Ophuls." *Film Comment* 6, 4 (Winter 1970-71: 41–43.
Lang, Andrew. *The Book of Dreams and Ghosts*. New York: AMS Press, 1970.

Lukács, Georg. *The Theory of the Novel: A Historico-philosophical Essay on the Forms of Great Epic Literature.* Cambridge, Mass.: MIT Press, 1971.
Lustig, T.J. *Henry James and the Ghostly.* Cambridge: Cambridge University Press, 1994.
Macardle, Dorothy. *The Uninvited.* Garden City, N.Y.: Sun Dial Press, 1944.
Meyerhold, Vsevolod Emilievich. *Meyerhold on Theatre.* Translated from the Russian by Edward Braun. New York: Hill and Wang, 1969.
Molnár, Ferenc. *Liliom: A Legend in Seven Scenes and a Prologue.* New York: Samuel French, 1921.
Moretti, Franco. *Signs Taken for Wonders.* Translated by Susan Fischer, David Forgacs, and David Miller. London: Verso, 1983.
Morford, Mark P.O., and Robert J. Lenardon. *Classical Mythology.* Longman, 1985.
Nathan, Robert. *Portrait of Jennie.* New York: Knopf, 1939.
Perez, Gilberto. *The Material Ghost: Films and Their Medium.* Baltimore: Johns Hopkins University Press, 1998.
Propp, Vladimir. *Theory and History of Folklore,* vol. 5. Minneapolis: University of Minneapolis Press, 1984.
Punter, David. *The Literature of Terror: A History of Gothic Fictions from 1765 to the Present Day.* London: Longman Group, 1980.
Salter, W.H. *Ghosts and Apparitions.* London: G. Bell & Sons, 1938.
Shelley, Mary. *Frankenstein.* New York: Signet Classics, 1965.
Simon, Linda. *Thornton Wilder: His World.* New York: Doubleday, 1979.
Steiner, George. *After Babel: Aspects of Language and Translation,* 2d ed. New York: Oxford University Press, 1992.
Stewart, Garrett. *Death Sentences: Styles of Dying in British Fiction.* Cambridge, Mass.: Harvard University Press, 1984.
Taylor, Joshua C. *Learning to Look: A Handbook for the Visual Arts,* 2d ed. Chicago: University of Chicago Press, 1981.
Turner, David. *Moral Values and the Human Zoo: The Novellen of Stefan Zweig.* Hull University Press, 1988.
Tyrrell, G.H.M. *Apparitions.* New York: Collier, 1963.
Waxman, Virginia Wright, with Karen Hollinger, eds. *Letter from an Unknown Woman.* New Brunswick, N.J.: Rutgers University Press, 1986.
Wilde, Oscar. *The Picture of Dorian Gray.* New York: Airmont Books, 1964.
Wilder, Thornton. *Our Town: A Play in Three Acts.* New York: Harper & Row, 1938.
Wilt, Judith. *Ghosts of the Gothic: Austen, Eliot, & Lawrence.* Princeton, N.J.: Princeton University Press, 1980.
Wolstenholme, Susan. *Gothic (Re)Visions: Writing Women as Readers.* Albany: State University of New York Press, 1993.
Zweig, Stefan. "Letter from an Unknown Woman," in *The Burning Secret and Other Stories.* Translated from the German by Jill Sutcliff. New York: E.P. Dutton, 1989, pp. 216–50.

Index

Alice in Wonderland 53
Allday, Elizabeth 71, 72
Allen, Lewis: *The Uninvited* (1944) 98–104
Allen, Woody 168–69; *Hannah and Her Sisters* (1985) 168; *Manhattan* (1979) 168; *Purple Rose of Cairo* (1985) 169
Anderson, Judith 101
Andrews, J. Dudley 23
Appearances of the Dead 57
Atkinson, Brooks 130
Avila, Rick 158

Bach, J. S. 4, 161, 162
Bakhtin, Mikhail 98, 104, 108–9, 112
Barrymore, Ethel 57
Basinger, Jeanine 32
Bazin, André 23
The Bishop's Wife (1947) 2, 50
Bloomsbury 88
Bogart, Humphrey 99
Borzage, Frank: *Liliom* (1930) 3, 118–119
Boyer, Charles 120, 121
Brief Encounter (Lean, 1946) 169
Briggs, Julia 40
Brontë, Emily 3, 9–15, 50, 71, 73, 91; see also *Wuthering Heights*
Brown, Royal S. 162

Carnival *see* Bakhtin 108, 109, 112; *Liliom* 108, 109, 110n, 112, 113, 114, 118
Carousel: *Liliom* 109, 110, 111, 113, 114, 117n, 119, 120; *Carousel* (King, 1956) 113, 124n; (Rodgers and Hammerstein, 1945) 3, 113
Carroll, Lewis 53
Casablanca (Curtiz, 1942) 99
Casper (1995) 2
Chandlee, Harry 136
Chaplin, Charles 121–123
A Christmas Carol 28, 154
Cinema and Painting: How Art Is Used in Film 47, 63, 64
Cinderella 32, 33
Cook, David A. 1, 118, 119
Cotten, Joseph 57, 59, 62
Cox, Michael 2
Craven, Frank 126, 136
Crawford, Joan 1
A Critical History of English Literature 44, 53

Daiches, David 44, 53
Dalle Vacche, Angela 47, 63, 64
The Dead Woman 171–172 *see also* Neruda, Pablo
Dick, R. A. (Leslie, Josephine Aimée Campbell) 33, 38, 41, 42; *The Ghost and Mrs. Muir* 31–49
Dickens, Charles 28, 154
Dieterle, William; *Portrait of Jennie* (1948) 3, 50, 56–67, 83, 86, 99, 104, 107
Dostoevsky, Fydor 70–72, 76
Durand, Regis 162

181

Edmundson, Mark 150
Eisner, Lotte 119, 121, 122
Euripides 57
Everest, Barbara 103

Finucane, R. C. 57
Fitzgerald, Lord Edward 89
Fitzgerald, Pamela 89
Fontaine, Joan 76, 101
Foucault, Michel 73, 151, 160; *Discipline and Punish* 148, 164; *What Is an Author* 69, 73, 86
Frankenstein 9, 12
Freud, Sigmund 72

Ghost 4, 5, 147–159, 166, 167, 172, 173, 174 see also Zucker, Jerry (director, film); Rubin, Bruce Joel (screenplay)
The Ghost and Mrs. Muir 1, 31–49, 75, 82, 86, 88, 99, 102; *see also* Dick, R. A.; Mankiewicz, Joseph
Ghostbusters (1984) 101n
Ghosts of the Gothic: Austen, Eliot, & Lawrence 13
Gish, Lillian 57
Glazer, Bernard 107, 108, 115
Goldberg, Whoopi 149, 155, 156, 157, 158, 159
Gothic (Re)Visions 13

Hannah and Her Sisters (Allen, 1986) 168
Hansel and Gretel 24
Harrison, Rex 42
Henry James and the Ghostly 75
Herrmann, Bernard 5, 42
A History of Narrative Film 1, 118, 119
Hitchcock, Alfred: *Rebecca* 99, 101, 102; *Strangers on a Train* 168
Hussey, Ruth 99

Jones, Jennifer 57, 60
Jourdan, Louis 76

Keats, John 43, 44
Koch, Howard 76, 78, 85

Lang, Fritz 3, 118–125
Lean, David 169

Lenardon, Robert J. 81
Lesser, Sol 136, 141
Letter from an Unknown Woman 1, 68–86, 99, 107, 119, 122; *see also* Ophuls, Max; Zweig, Stefan
Liliom 3, 107–125, 127, 135, 136; *see also* Lang, Fritz; Molnár, Ferenc
Literature of Terror: A History of Gothic Fiction 9, 52
Lukacs, Georg 4, 68, 69, 86
Lustig, T. J. 75

Macardle, Dorothy 87–104
The Major Film Theories 23
Manhattan 168
Mankiewicz, Joseph 3, 42–49, 82, 86, 87, 102, 104
Mediums: *Ghost* 149, 153, 156, 157, 158, 173; *Portrait of Jennie* 57, 60–63, 66; *The Uninvited* 104
Meyerhold, Vsevolod 114, 115, 126
Meyerhold on Theater 114, 115, 126
Michael (1990) 2
Milland, Ray 99
Minghella, Anthony 160–175
Molnár, Ferenc 107–118
Moore, Demi 149
Moral Values and the Human Zoo: Novellen of Stefan Zweig 75, 81
Moretti, Franco 152
Morford, Mark, P. O. 81
Murnau, F. W. 64

Nathan, Robert 3, 50, 54, 56, 59, 70, 73; *The Bishop's Wife* 2, 50; *Portrait of Jennie* 50–56, 70, 73
Neruda, Pablo see also *The Dead Woman*
Newman, Alfred 5
Niebuhr, Gustave 2
Night Visitors: Rise and Fall of the English Ghost Story 40
Nightmare on Main Street: Angels, Sadomasochism, & the Culture of Gothic 150
Notes from Underground 70–72, 76

Oberon, Merle 25, 26
Ode to a Nightingale see Keats, John 43, 44
Olivier, Laurence 25, 26, 101
Ophuls, Max 3, 75, 76–86, 88, 99, 107, 109, 119, 122

Orphic Myth 80, 81
Our Town 126–144; *see also* Wood, Sam; Wilder, Thornton
Overtones and Undertones 162
Oxford Book of Twentieth-Century Ghost Stories 2
Ozeray, Madeline 120

Pevear, Richard 71
The Picture of Dorian Gray 52, 70
Portrait of Jennie 1, 50–67, 70, 73, 83, 86, 99, 107; *see also* Dieterle, William; Nathan, Robert
Portraits: *Ghost and Mrs. Muir* 37–39, 46–48; *Portrait of Jennie* 54–55, 62–63, 66; *The Uninvited* 101
The Preacher's Wife (1996) 2
Punch-and-Judy Show 112, 114n, 120
Punter, David 9, 52
Purple Rose of Cairo (Allen, 1985) 169

Rabelais and His World 98, 104, 108, 109, 112
Rebecca (Hitchcock, 1940) 99, 101, 102
Rickman, Alan 173
Rodgers and Hammerstein 3, 113
Rubin, Bruce Joel 147–159; *see also Ghost*

Sanders, George 44
Seances: *Ghost* 153; *Portrait of Jennie* 57; *The Uninvited* 96–97, 104
Shelley, Mary 9, 12
Simon, Linda 126, 130
Signs Taken for Wonders 152
Skinner, Cornelia Otis 101
Snow White and the Seven Dwarfs 167
Spiritualism 40, 57; *see also* Mediums; Seances

Stefan Zweig: A Critical Biography 71, 72
Stella by Starlight 99
Strangers on a Train (Hitchcock, 1951) 168
Swayze, Patrick 149

The Theory of the Novel 4, 68, 59, 86
Thornton Wilder: His World 126, 130
Tierney, Gene 1
Truly, Madly, Deeply (Minghella, 1991 2, 4, 5, 160–175
Turner, David 75, 81

"Unchained Melody" 150
The Uninvited 87–104; *see also* Allen, Lewis; Macardle, Dorothy

Wilde, Oscar 52, 70
Wilder, Thornton 3; *Our Town* 126–144; *Woman of Andros* 126
Wilson, George 81
Wilt, Judith 13
Wolstenholme, Susan 13
A Woman's View: How Hollywood Spoke to Women, 1930–1960 32
Wood, Phillip 141
Wood, Sam 136–144
Wuthering Heights 9–28, 50, 60, 71, 73, 74, 86, 91, 99, 102 *see also* Brontë, Emily; Wyler, William
Wyler, William 3, 15–28, 48, 86, 81, 99, 102

Young, Victor 99

Zucker, Jerry 147–159
Zweig, Stefan 71, 72, 76, 77, 79, 83, 84; *Letter from an Unknown Woman* 68–76

www.ingramcontent.com/pod-product-compliance
Ingram Content Group UK Ltd.
Pitfield, Milton Keynes, MK11 3LW, UK
UKHW042014140426
5217IPUK00015B/1168